the thief

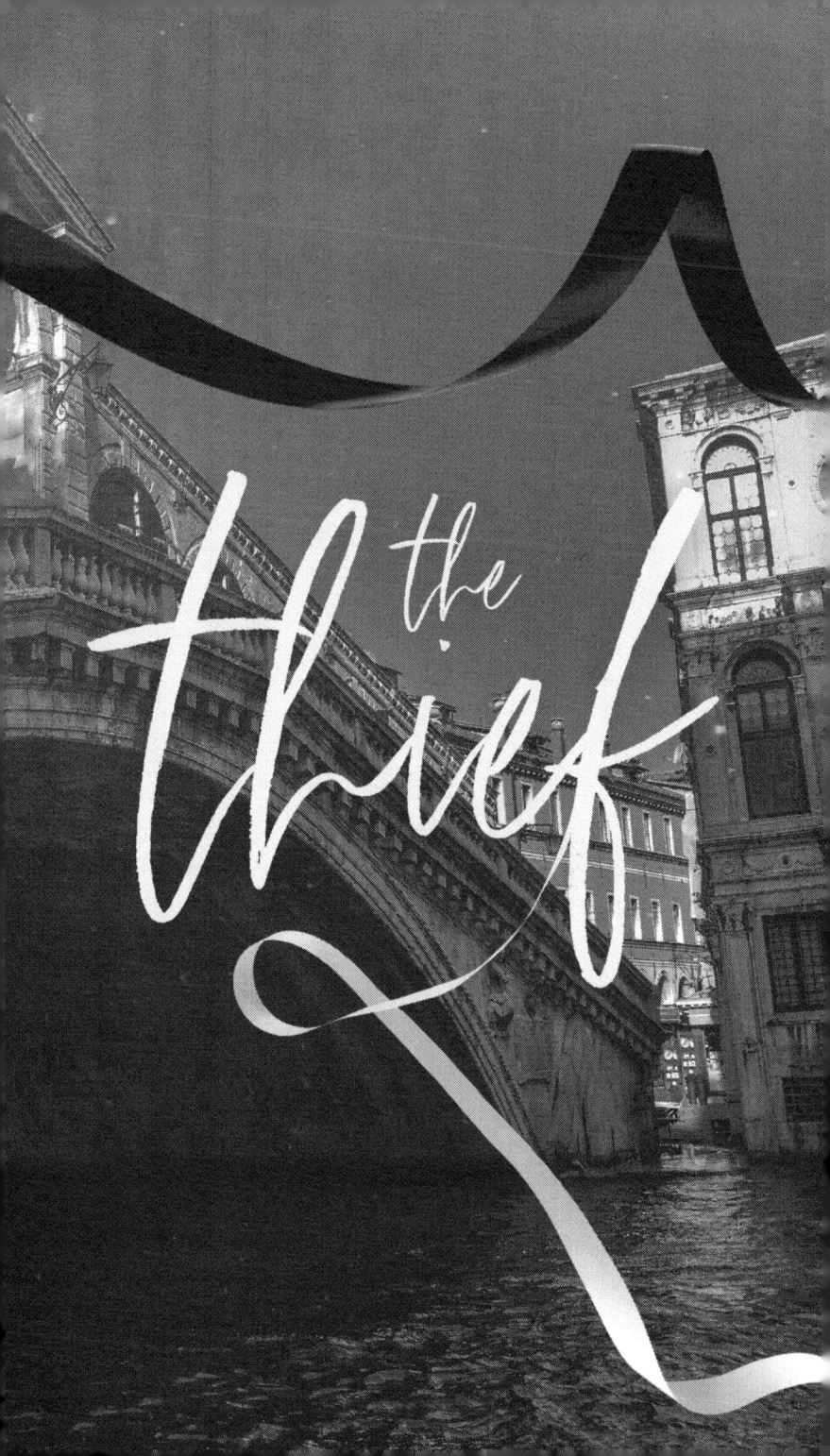

the thief

Text copyright © 2023 Tara Crescent

All Rights Reserved
No part of this book may be reproduced in any form or by any electronic or mechanical means including information storage and retrieval systems, without permission in writing from the author. The only exception is by a reviewer, who may quote short excerpts in a review.

This book is a work of fiction. Names, characters, places, and incidents either are products of the author's imagination or are used fictitiously. Any resemblance to actual persons, living or dead, events, or locales is entirely coincidental.

Editing by Molly Whitman at Novel Mechanic,
www.novelmechanic.com

Cover Design by Natasha Snow Designs,
https://natashasnow.com

Interior Design by BZN Studio Designs,
https://covers.bzndesignstudios.com/

Interior Layout by Polgarus Studio,
https://www.polgarusstudio.com/

Many, many thanks to Becca, who sprinkled her fairy plotmother magic all over this book.

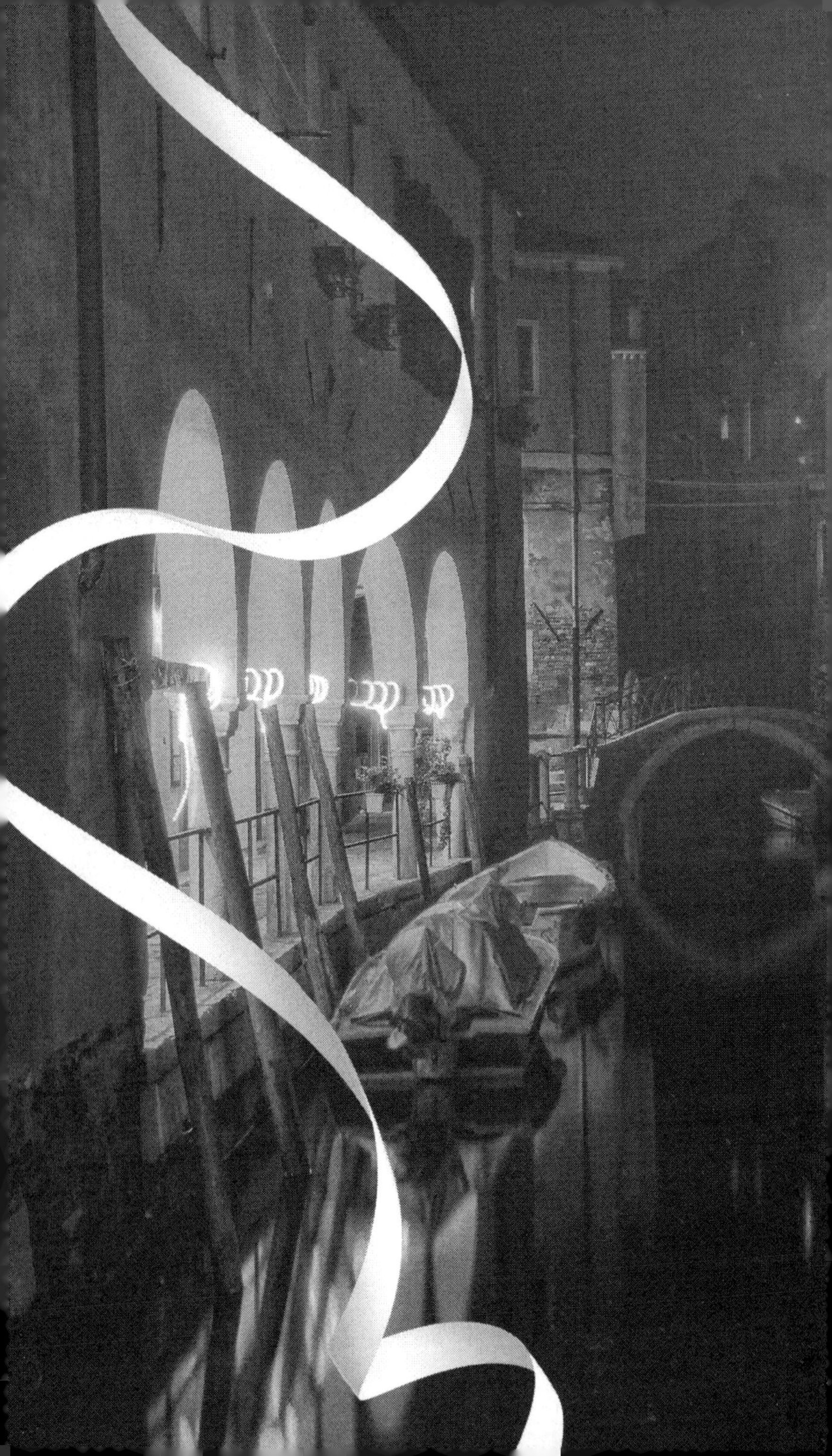

PROLOGUE
LUCIA

I am very drunk, and everything is hazy.

It's a dark night—cloudy, moonless, and foggy. I've been wandering for hours, not paying attention to where I'm going, and I've ended up in a neighborhood I don't recognize. Venice is a safe city, but this section of town is far from the tourist core. The boats aren't pleasure yachts; they're working fishing vessels. Warehouses dot the docks, and there are more rats than people this late at night.

A week ago, I was working on my senior thesis

in Chicago. I didn't know my mother was dying of cancer because my parents had kept her illness a secret from me. Which meant I didn't know she'd gone into hospice either.

I never got the chance to say goodbye.

I lift the bottle of vodka I'm clutching like a lifeline to my mouth and take a healthy swig.

Three days ago, I got a call that destroyed me. My mother had succumbed to the cancer ravaging her body. My father, unable to contemplate life without his wife, put a bullet in his brain. One day, I was wondering if I could convince my art history professor to grant me an extension for my final paper. The next, I was flying back home to bury my parents.

A hint of movement jerks me to the present. Something rustles to my right. Before I have time to react, three bodies coalesce from the fog and surround me. One of them holds a knife to my throat. "Don't move, and don't shout, signorina," he growls. "I don't want to hurt you. Give me your purse."

The Thief

I'm being robbed.

Numbly, I hold out my bright green bag. I bought it on Calle Larga XXII Marzo from a *vu compra* who'd set up shop opposite the Dolce and Gabbana store. Mama and I did a bunch of tourist things before I left for college: we visited St. Mark's Basilica, listened to musicians at the *piazza*, rode a gondola, and ate at a restaurant a stone's throw from the Ponte di Rialto. The vendor insisted that the bag was actually Prada, not a fake, and my mother laughed at him. "We're not tourists," she said and haggled with him for the next fifteen minutes.

I should have realized she was sick. She'd lost weight, and for the last couple of months, she wouldn't FaceTime me. "My cell phone broke," she said. "I have to go buy a new one."

I should have suspected that something was badly wrong.

One of the men snatches the imitation Prada bag from my hand while another shines a flashlight in my face. "Your necklace too."

Things are moving too fast for me to process, but those words penetrate my drunken stupor. The necklace I'm wearing, a filigreed ruby pendant dangling on a gold chain, belonged to my mother. My father gave it to her as a wedding present, and she never took it off. She's gone now, and this is all I have left of her. It's my most cherished possession.

"No."

"Don't be stupid, signorina," the man with the knife snaps. "It's not worth your life. Take off the goddamn chain and hand it to me before you get hurt."

"Someone's coming," Flashlight Guy says, his voice nervous. "We're not authorized… We need to get out of here." He makes a lunge for my necklace. The chain digs into my neck, and I yelp in pain.

A tall, lean man glides out of the shadows, his face obscured by the brim of his hat. "Stop," he says, his cold voice slicing the moisture-laden air like a whip.

The Thief

One word. Just one word, but the reaction is electrifying. The man holding my purse takes one look and bolts. "Fuck," the guy who made a grab for my chain swears. The knife clatters to the ground, and the thief who held it holds up his hands in a gesture of surrender. "I'm sorry," he says, his voice trembling. "I didn't mean to... I didn't know—"

"You didn't know I was here. But I'm always watching. You should remember that." My rescuer's voice is ice. "Leave."

The remaining two criminals flee.

The man turns in my direction. He studies me for what seems like an age, his gaze lingering on the side of my neck. "You're hurt."

"I am?" I reach up, and my skin stings where the necklace cut me. "Yeah, I guess." The pendant is safe, though, and that's all that counts. "It'll heal."

He moves closer, his breath warming my face, and he touches the cut with a feather-light touch.

"Who did this to you? Which one of them?"

A shiver runs down my back. Once again, everything is moving with bewildering speed, events rushing past me like leaves in a windstorm. The vodka has scrambled my thoughts, and this man isn't helping. His voice and touch aren't supposed to permeate my numbness, but they are, and I don't know how to react.

"The guy holding the flashlight."

"Marco." My hero's voice promises death. His eyes settle on me again, and his tone softens. "You're cold, signorina." He pulls off his jacket and drapes it around my shoulders, and warmth descends over me like a blanket. "This isn't a good part of town to be in alone. Alone and drunk."

My gratitude evaporates in a rush. He's judging me? What the hell does he know about my life? "You shouldn't offer unsolicited advice either, but here we are." Okay, that's quite rude. Mama would be shocked. "But thank you for your help," I add grudgingly, turning to leave.

"You're welcome," he replies, falling in step with me.

"What are you doing?"

"Escorting you home," he says, as if it were obvious. "Like I said, this is a dangerous neighborhood, and I would hate for you to get hurt again."

Home is filled with memories I'm trying to obliterate with a bottle of vodka. "I don't want to go home," I mutter sullenly. "And I don't care if I get hurt."

There's a long pause. "But *I* care, signorina."

Why? "We're at an impasse, then." I take another deep drink of my vodka, and then, out of some strange impulse, I offer the bottle to him.

I expect him to turn it down. I'm even prepared for him to do something dramatic, like fling it into the canal. But shockingly, he does neither. He pries it gently from my fingers. His lips wrap around the mouth of the bottle, the way mine did a second earlier, and he drinks. Then he hands it back to me, his fingers brushing mine.

Heat blossoms in my chest.

We walk in the darkness, taking turns drinking from the emptying bottle, neither breaking the silence. "I buried my parents today," I finally blurt out.

He glances in my direction. "I'm sorry."

"I'm not sad." It's not exactly a lie. *Sad* is too simple an emotion to describe how my world has been shattered. "I'm angry. I'm *furious*. My mother was sick, but she hid it from me. And when she died, my father blew his brains out."

He doesn't say anything.

"It wasn't just my parents who lied," I continue. "They all did. My best friend didn't tell me either. Did they think they were protecting me?" I take another healthy swig. "Because I don't feel protected." My voice comes out defiant, shrill, and bitter. "I feel abandoned. I *hate* them for that."

He remains silent, but this time, the silence prickles at me. "What are you thinking?" I demand. "Are you going to give me the same advice the priest did? Are you going to tell me to forgive them?"

"I would never presume to tell you how to feel."

I stumble over a coil of rope. I'm about to fall, but his arms are around me before I do. His touch feels. . . solid. Reassuring. *Shockingly male.* "So, what then?" I persist. He's a tall body in the darkness, a warm presence at my side. I still can't see his face, and maybe that's what loosens my tongue. Or maybe it's the vodka. "You don't have any advice for me?" I keep stabbing at the open, bleeding wound. "If you were me, if your parents abandoned you like mine, what would you do?"

"I didn't know my parents," he says without inflection. "I was left at a church as a baby."

Oh. *Oh.* "I'm so sorry."

"I don't need your sympathy, *tesoro*." The easy, relaxed set of his shoulders is replaced by stiffness. This is clearly not a welcome topic, and it's obvious he'd much rather talk about my problems than his own.

"Give me advice, then," I breathe. "Tell me what

to do. Tell me how to move forward from this."

He still has his arm around me, and I've made no effort to pull away. It's nice to be held. His touch is a portal into a fantasy world where I'm not suddenly alone. A world in which there's someone who cares for me. Someone who will catch me before I fall.

"Did your parents love you?"

I nod wordlessly. That's why their betrayal hurts so much.

"We don't make our best decisions under pressure," he says quietly. "When we are hurt, when we are in pain, we don't think. We hide, we lash out. I can't pretend to understand your parents' decision. Maybe they thought they were protecting you. Or maybe they didn't want your last memories of them to be filled with pain."

I make a scoffing sound, but he's not done.

"As for moving forward," he says softly. "You just do. You remember that you were loved, and you put one foot in front of the other. Until one day, you think about them without pain. The anger and grief will fade, *cara mia*, and you'll be left with the good memories."

We've been walking steadily toward civilization. The Ca'Pesaro looms before me, casting ornate shadows into the canal. I drain the rest of my vodka and fling the bottle into the water.

He tracks the angry movement. "Where are you staying?"

I cannot go to my parents' apartment. I just cannot. I can't be in the place where they died. I can't run into the neighbors, and I cannot cope with their sympathy and concern. "I don't know." I reach for my phone and realize it's in the bag the thieves took. "My purse is gone." I take a deep breath and fight the urge to burst into tears. "I have no money."

He puts his hand on the small of my back, a comforting gesture that tells me I'm not alone. "Come with me, signorina. Let's get you settled for the night. We'll find your purse in the morning."

My rescuer takes me to a hotel. The lobby is brightly lit, and I turn to him to finally see what he looks like, but all that vodka has caused me to see double and triple of everything. I get the sense of a firm jaw and full lips, but that's it.

"A room," he says to the clerk behind the counter.

The man jumps to attention. "Si, Signor," he says. There was respect in his voice but also a trace of fear? Or am I imagining it? I can't tell.

A key is produced. The well-dressed stranger steers me to the ancient elevator. Can I really call him a stranger if I've spent the better part of the last hour pouring out my troubles to him? I slump against him, my bones turning to liquid. "You smell nice," I tell him. It seems important that he knows that. "Like the ocean." I sniff him again. "And something else. Pine, maybe? I like it."

He doesn't reply, but his grip on me tightens slightly. I like that too.

We reach the room, and he follows me in, heading to the bathroom. I collapse on the bed, feeling his absence like a loss. I hear water running, and he returns with a glass, motioning me to sit up. "Drink this," he orders. "It'll help with your hangover."

"I don't get hangovers."

He laughs shortly. "Oh, you will, *cara mia*." It's the second time he's called me that. He cups my cheek with his hand and looks deep into my eyes. "Go to sleep," he says, his voice gentle. "Things will look slightly less bleak in the morning."

He turns away from me. I stare blankly after him. Only when he's almost at the door do I realize he's leaving. "Stop!" I don't want him to go. "I don't want to be alone tonight." I grip the bedspread with my fingers and take a deep, shaky breath. "Please?"

He hesitates for a long moment, then he relents. "Okay." He turns off the lights, and the room plunges into comforting darkness. A minute later, the mattress sags with his weight as he gets into bed with me.

My eyes close. Sleep tugs me under, but I fight it. I want one more thing tonight. "I don't know your name."

"Antonio."

"Antonio." I try it on my tongue. "I'm Lucia."

"A lovely name for a lovely woman." The words feel trite, but the weight in his voice makes me believe him. "You're safe here. Sleep well, Lucia."

When I wake up the next morning, I'm alone. There's no sign that anyone was ever with me. In fact, if I wasn't in a strange hotel room, I'd be convinced I imagined the whole thing.

I get out of bed and wince. Antonio was right. My head feels like it's going to explode. This is what I get for drinking an entire bottle of vodka in one evening.

I go to the bathroom and splash some water on my face. The skin around my neck is abraded and raw where the thief tried to yank my chain off. I finger the pendant absently, a complicated cocktail of emotions churning through me. Antonio's words from last night ring in my head. *The anger and grief will fade, and you'll be left with the good memories.*

There's a knock at the door. I open it to a staff member wheeling in a cart of food. "Breakfast, signorina."

I'm starving, but I have no money to pay for the food. I'm about to tell him I didn't order anything when he adds, "Also, this was left for you at the front desk."

The *this* in his hands is my bag. The green, imitation Prada bag my mother bought for me before I left for college. And it's untouched. My passport, money, and phone are all in there.

My gallant rescuer strikes again.

Tucked in a front pocket is a thick, cream-colored card.

A phone number is printed on the front, and

there's a handwritten note on the back. *Call me.*

I stare at it for a very long time.

Last night, Antonio took care of me. Stayed with me, listened to me. He made sure I was safe. When everything around me was crumbling, when I desperately needed someone to lean on, he was there.

But safety is a myth. Your world can shatter in the blink of an eye. People betray you. They hide illness from you and die. They shoot their brains out and leave you bereft.

The last three days have taught me I can't afford to lean on anyone.

I take a deep breath and tuck the card back into the purse. "Can you call me a cab in an hour?" I ask the man.

"Of course, signorina. Where to?"

"The airport." There's nothing left for me in Venice. Not anymore.

LUCIA

Chapter One
Ten years later...

When you're a museum curator moonlighting as an art thief, having a hacker for a best friend is a pretty good deal. Especially when it's time to plan your next heist.

It's Friday evening. I pour myself a glass of cheap red wine, settle in front of my laptop, and call Valentina. I feel the familiar stirring of excitement as I wait for her to connect. My first art heist was a mad impulse, but recently, I've been targeting rich and powerful people who knowingly acquire stolen art. People who think their wealth provides them immunity. It gives me great satisfaction to steal from them and return the paintings to their original owners.

And I can't wait to kick off this year's project.

The last time Valentina and I talked, I presented her with a list of seven potential targets, compiled by scouting through news reports, auction listings, and talking to my parents' old fence, Alvisa Zanotti. Signora Zanotti might be retired, but she keeps her finger on the pulse of the art world and stays updated on the ins and outs of black-market art. Valentina promised to look into the seven and narrow it down for me.

Italy is six hours ahead of Boston, so it's midnight in Venice. When Valentina logs on, she looks exhausted. "Long day?" I ask sympathetically.

Valentina and I have been best friends since

kindergarten. Growing up, we spent practically every waking hour together. Valentina often took refuge at our house because her parents fought constantly. Some of my fondest memories are of the two of us spending long afternoons doing homework at our battered kitchen table, my mother supplying an endless stream of snacks.

"You could say that." She fills her wine glass right to the brim. "Some of the other children have been bullying Angelica, so I pulled her out of school."

After the death of my parents, I didn't talk to Valentina for two years. I blamed her—unfairly—for the secrets my parents kept. But Valentina didn't give up. No matter how often I ignored her, she kept reaching out. Our friendship finally resumed when she sent me a picture of a newborn. "This is Angelica," she wrote. "My daughter. Will you be her godmother?"

Anger stirs in me now. "Why were they bullying her?"

Valentina shrugs wearily. "Because she doesn't have a father."

"Ah." She's never once talked about the guy. I asked about him once, and she shut me down. Since then, we've reached a tacit understanding that neither of us will talk about the past. She doesn't mention my parents, and I don't ask why Angelica's father doesn't play a role in his daughter's life.

"I'm sorry," I tell her, wishing I had something more helpful to say. Something I could do, something more useful than offering support from afar. "That sucks."

"Yeah." She drinks deeply from her glass. "I haven't had time to look at your list."

"Forget the list." Valentina looks like she's at the end of her tether. I can't blame her. It's been one thing after another the entire year. Angelica broke her ankle in January. Then Valentina was sick all summer, and to cap off a truly shitty year, her father died in August. The two of them weren't close, but even so, I know it's taken a toll on my friend. As for

Angelica, she's been having nightmares ever since her grandfather died.

And now this. My poor friend.

"How's Angelica doing?" I lean forward. "How are *you* doing?"

"I'm fine," she lies. "I'm putting her in a different school. A more international, diverse one." She stares morosely into her glass. "I miss you. Sometimes, I wish you were closer—" She cuts off whatever she's about to say next. "How's the job hunt going?"

"Miserable." My employment troubles are nothing new. I'm trained as a curator, but museum funding is highly volatile, and permanent positions are few and far between. I've spent my adult life hopping from one short-term contract to another and lived in eight cities in the last ten years. My last contract ended a couple of weeks ago. I've sent out some feelers, but it's getting close to the end of the year, so hiring is slow.

But that's not what's bothering me now. It's

Valentina's despondent expression. Her uncharacteristic melancholy.

She's never once complained about the physical distance between us. Never once expressed discontent that I hadn't met Angelica in person.

Both her parents are now dead. They weren't much, but they're gone now, and she's spending her first Christmas without them.

I remember my first Christmas alone. The crippling loneliness and aching sense of loss. I would never wish that on my worst enemy. How can I do that to my best friend?

On impulse, I look at job listings in Europe. Then I go perfectly still.

Because there's a job opening in Venice. A four-month contract at the Palazzo Ducale to digitize their catalog.

Speaks fluent Italian? *Check.*

In-depth knowledge of Italian art? *Check.*

The pay is... well, I won't starve. And most importantly, I'll be there for Valentina.

Can you do it? Can you go back to Venice, the city you fled ten years ago?

My heart starts to race. I take a deep breath and order myself to calm down. It's only four months. I'm not going to stay forever.

Out of sight of the camera, I open my purse and fish out the business card I've held onto for a decade. It's faded. Dog-eared. I run my thumb over the handwritten note.

Call me.

I wonder if the number still works.

I'm tempted to call. *So tempted.*

It's been ten years, Lucia. He's probably married with a handful of children by now.

I tuck the card away.

Valentina says, "Lucia?"

"Sorry. I got distracted by something on my phone." I'm more than qualified for the Palazzo Ducale role. I should be a shoo-in for the job. I won't tell Valentina until I know for sure, but after ten years away, it looks like I'm finally returning home.

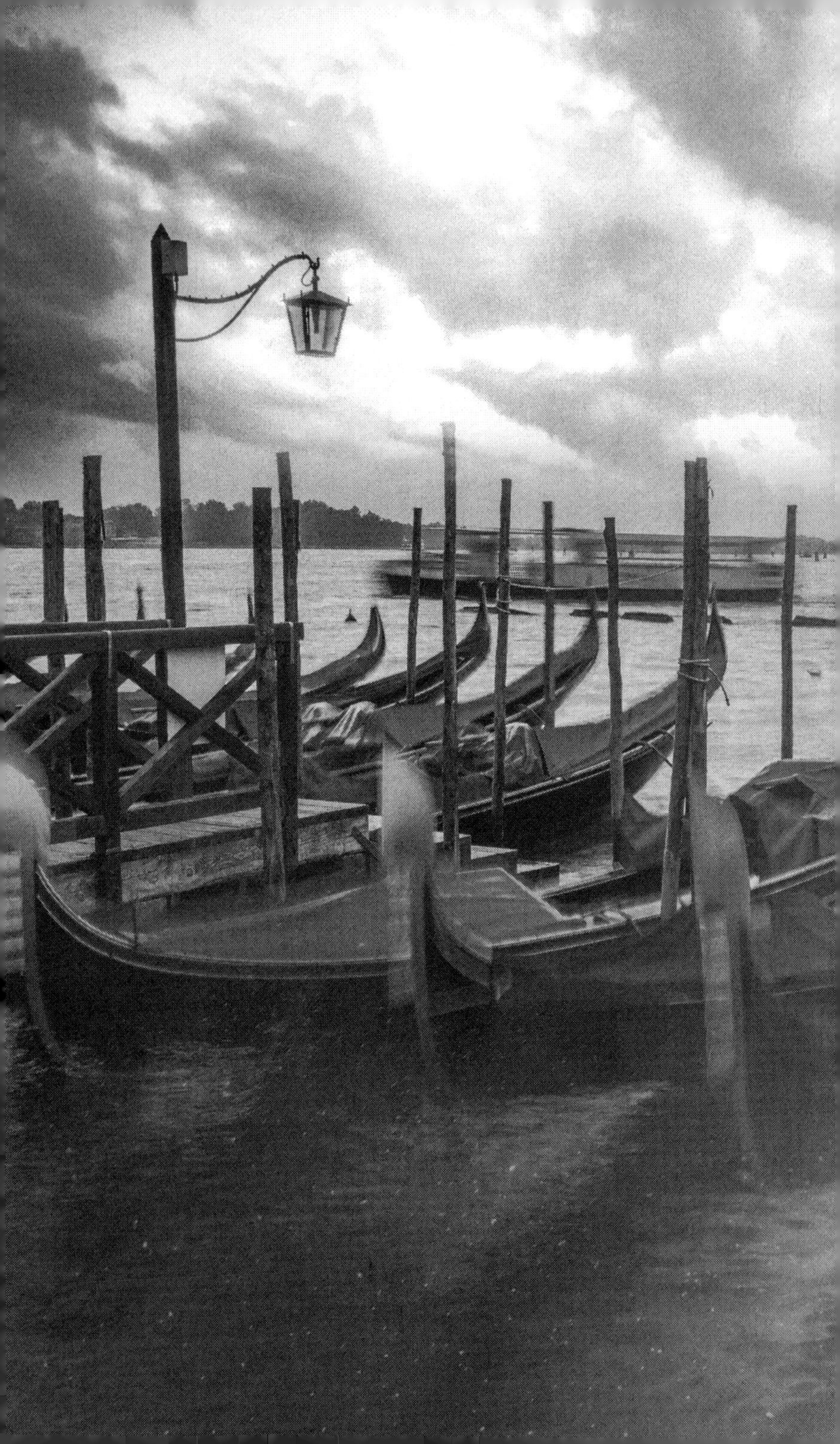

ANTONIO

Chapter Two

Venice is my city. I head up her mafia, run her casinos, and rule her underworld. I know every dark alley and every narrow canal. All her secrets are mine. I started life with nothing, and I've fought my way to the top. Everything I've ever wanted is within my grasp.

And still, lately, I've been so fucking *bored* with it all.

I walk into our weekly meeting a good twenty minutes late. My second-in-command, Dante, glances pointedly at his watch as I enter. He's the only one who dares. My other lieutenants—Joao, Tomas, and Leonardo—ignore my tardiness and greet me respectfully.

"Sorry I'm late," I say crisply. "Let's get started."

Joao delivers an update on our smuggling operations. Leo goes next, and then it's Tomas, our numbers guy. As usual, his presentation is detailed and thorough. I normally find his briefings fascinating, but today, I have to work hard at faking interest.

"We're flush with cash," Tomas finally finishes. "Business has never been better. I have identified some investment opportunities. Padrino, I recommend—"

"Send me an email with the options," I say, cutting him off before he gets into the weeds. "Is there anything else?"

Dante, who's been silent all meeting, nods. "We have a problem," he says grimly. "The bratva has been spotted in Bergamo."

I sit up. Bergamo is only a couple of hours away. Too close for comfort. "Who?"

"A couple of foot soldiers of the Gafur OPG. Should I reach out to the Verratti?"

Salvatore Verratti runs Bergamo, and I can't see him forming alliances with the Russians. As far as I know, the family's finances are in good shape, and even if they weren't, Federico, Salvatore's father and the former head of the crime family, loathes foreigners.

And yet my instincts urge me to proceed cautiously. "Not yet," I reply. "Not until I have a better sense of what's going on."

"You don't trust Salvatore?"

I give Dante a dry look. "I don't trust *anyone,* as you should know by now. Get Valentina to intercept their communications." Valentina Linari is my most talented hacker. If she can't keep the Russians under surveillance, no one can. "If the bratva makes contact with the Verratti family, I want to know immediately."

"Yes, *padrino*." My lieutenants look alert, almost excited by the prospect of a turf war. Not me. I just feel a headache coming on.

I look around the room. "Anything else?"

"One more thing." Dante opens the folder in front of him. Extracting a note, he pushes it in my direction. "You got a letter from Arthur Kirkland."

The name is vaguely familiar. I search my memory. "The art collector?"

"Yes."

That explains the letter. Arthur Kirkland is eighty and doesn't believe in computers. I scan the sheet of paper with a frown. "He's warning me about an art thief. Do you know what this is about?"

Dante has an answer, of course. He always does. My second-in-command is loyal, ruthless, and, above all, unfailingly competent. "Arthur Kirkland collects Italian art. Some of his collection has been acquired through dubious means."

"Most of his collection," I correct, remembering

more of the details now. "The Third Reich looted Italy in 1943, and Kirkland's uncle, a Nazi sympathizer, mysteriously ended up with priceless paintings when the war ended." I glance at the letter again. "This mystery thief stole one of his pieces last year."

"I think I like this thief," Joao says. Dante glances at him, and he lifts his hands in an expressive gesture. "What? You expect me to feel bad for a Nazi looter?"

Can't say I disagree with Joao's sentiment. "Kincaid says his security people have put together a profile of the thief."

"Yes, there was a dossier enclosed with the letter." Dante reads from his file. "The thief's specialty is sixteenth-century Italian religious art. Ten major works have been stolen, all from that period. And all from private collectors. Interestingly, the targeted paintings were also all previously stolen." He pauses for effect. "And they've all been returned to their rightful owners."

That *is* interesting. "A thief who fancies himself a modern-day Robin Hood?"

"Herself," Dante corrects. "At least, that's what Kirkland's investigative team concluded."

"A woman?" A current of anticipation hums through me. "How did they determine that?"

Dante pushes forward a tablet. "One of the cameras from Kirkland's compound took this before it shorted out."

I play the video. The thief is wearing a faded sweatshirt, its hood obstructing her face. But it's definitely a woman. The baggy sweatshirt can't hide her curves.

There's something about the way she moves that tugs at my memory.

"Kirkland wants her caught, padrino," Dante finishes. "It feels personal. He's written to everyone who might be her next target."

"Has he now?" I have an extensive collection of Venetian art that was mostly bought in public auctions, but not all.

Not my Madonna.

Painted by Titian himself and valuable beyond measure, the *Madonna at Repose* was my first big job. I stole it from the Palazzo Ducale when I was sixteen. I should have fenced it immediately but couldn't bring myself to part with it. It currently hangs in my bedroom.

I play the five-second clip again. There's nothing here—nothing to identify the thief—and yet something continues to tickle the back of my mind. The way she moves feels familiar somehow.

Tomas is reading the file. "Weird," he says. "She targets people all over the world but always strikes between November and January. Every single time."

"Well, it *is* Christmas," Leo points out. "People are distracted during the holidays."

"You know what else is strange?" Tomas continues. "Look at her targets. Vecchio, il Giovane, Lorenzo Lotto... These are all Venetian painters. But she's never struck in Italy."

I look at him curiously. "I didn't realize you were interested in art."

Tomas flushes. "I like to paint, padrino. It's a hobby of mine."

Dante takes the file from Tomas and scans it with a frown. "You're right," he says. "That is strange. There's plenty of stolen art in Italy, but it's almost as if she's avoiding coming here. You want Valentina to look into this?"

The puzzle pieces finally connect. I pull up my tablet and run a search to confirm my hunch.

Teresa Petrucci, died the seventh of December.

Paolo Petrucci, died the seventh of December.

And now I know why the woman seems familiar.

Teresa and Paolo were art thieves. And Lucia Petrucci, their only child, wandered the wharfs the night after she buried her parents, clutching a bottle of vodka and nursing raw grief in her heart.

Lucia, who graduated from the University of Chicago with a master's degree in art history.

The Thief

The timing matches up. The thief stole their first painting ten years ago on Christmas Day. That would have been only two weeks after Lucia's parents died.

She's been stealing a painting every year since her parents died. A way of remembering them, perhaps?

Beautiful, *reckless* Lucia. Where is she now? I run another search, and the Internet provides me answers. After stints worldwide and ten years away, she's finally coming home. She starts as an assistant curator at the Palazzo Ducale next week.

Ten years, and I still remember the bottle green of her eyes. Ten years, and I still remember the hitch in her voice as she asked me to stay with her. *Don't go,* she whispered, her lips quivering. *I don't want to be alone tonight.*

She didn't call me the next day, and when I stopped at the hotel after dealing with the trio who accosted her, she wasn't there. She'd left for the airport. Flown out of Venice and out of my life.

Now she's back.

And she's an art thief.

I can't wait to see her again.

Venice is my city. I head up her mafia. I rule her underworld. Nobody steals in my city without my permission.

"I know who she is." Sharp hunger fills me, a hunger I haven't felt in years. "Don't involve Valentina; she has plenty of other things to do. I'll take care of this thief personally."

Dante studies me thoughtfully, but whatever he's thinking, he keeps to himself. "Yes, padrino."

LUCIA

Chapter Three

I'm right—I *am* a shoo-in for the museum job. I arrive in Venice on a Sunday afternoon in early October, and on Monday, I show up at the *palazzo* for my first day of work.

My boss, Nicolo Garzolo, gives me the behind-the-scenes tour, introduces me to my coworkers, and takes me to lunch. After that, he drops me off at my office with an air of relief and leaves me alone to familiarize myself with my work. This isn't a snub; I was hired to manage and digitize the collections, and my boss is deeply suspicious of computers.

I'm both jet-lagged and a little sleepy after my meal, so instead of sitting down to review the digital records, I wander through the storage rooms where the museum keeps the paintings and sculptures that aren't on display.

That's where I find a Titian that doesn't seem to exist in our catalog, tucked away in a dusty corner.

The canvas is small, only eight inches by twelve. But I can't take my eyes off it. My hands shake as I lift it off the rack. The painter has depicted the Madonna sitting in a chair, dressed in everyday clothes, with her child on her lap. Most depictions of the Madonna show her in a solemn mood, but not this one. Here, she's laughing and playing with baby Jesus.

This doesn't make any sense. Tiziano Vecelli, or Titian, was one of the most famous Venetian painters of the sixteenth century. For the Palazzo

Ducale to lose track of a Titian—imagine if the *Mona Lisa* was found in a storage room in the Louvre. It's that shocking.

I take the painting into the light. At first, I don't realize it's a copy. Then I study it again, and my spine tingles. The colors are faded in a very uniform manner, and the cracks in the canvas—a sign of its age—are wrong. The cracks in Italian paintings from this period should be thin and skinny.

But they're not. Instead, these are swirly, randomly distributed cracks.

The painting is a fake.

I feel a familiar prickle in my spine, the first stirrings of anticipation. There's a mystery here, and I'm determined to solve it.

Someone stole the museum's Titian and replaced it with a copy.

I'm going to find out who took it, and I'm going to steal it back from them.

Target identified.

The game is on.

After work, I return to my parents' apartment on Calle de la Testa. I guess my apartment now, as they left it to me when they died. For ten years, I've rented it to a succession of tourists. The agency that managed the rentals decorated the place with a collection of Ikea furniture, but they emptied it out when I terminated their contract.

When Valentina found out I was coming home, she offered to buy me stuff. I turned her down. "It's a four-month gig. I don't need much."

So now, the only furniture in the apartment is a blowup mattress and a folding chair. It didn't seem worthwhile to buy anything else.

My refrigerator is also empty, but I open it out of habit. The only thing there is the solitary pear I bought at the airport yesterday, so I eat it as I open my laptop.

It's time for research.

The painting wasn't in the electronic catalog, but I found a paper tag with a reference number on the back of the frame. The reference number means the painting isn't rogue—it was part of the collection once upon a time. The museum might be lagging behind on digitizing its catalog, but everyone who works at the Palazzo Ducale is an expert in their field. They wouldn't have tagged a fake.

Which leads me to my first question: *When was the Titian stolen?*

After an hour and a half of painstaking research, I have my answer. The *Madonna at Repose* was last displayed fifteen years ago. It wouldn't have been exhibited if the curator had any doubt about its authenticity, meaning the Titian was stolen sometime between then and now.

Not exactly the most helpful answer in the world, but it's better than nothing.

Valentina texts me as I'm brainstorming ways to proceed.

> We still on for dinner tonight?

> Yes! Where?

She sends me an address not too far from me.

> See you in fifteen.

It's good to see Valentina in person. Really good. After some hugging and some tears, we settle down with a glass of wine and some *cicchetti*. "Where's Angelica?" I ask. "I thought you'd bring her."

"I was planning on it, but her new best friend invited her for a sleepover." Her lips twitch. "Mabel has a puppy and a kitten."

"I know my limits," I say, laughing. "I can't compete with that." I lean forward, powerfully glad to see her. "Tell me everything."

I speak to Valentina every week, but seeing her in person is very different from talking online. We spend the entire evening catching up, chatting about my parents and hers, our nonexistent dating lives, and everything else.

Finally, when we're done eating, I broach the subject of the painting. "I found a fake Titian at the Palazzo Ducale today," I tell her. I pull up the photo of the *Madonna* on my phone and pass it to her. "Buried in a storage room, tucked away in a forgotten corner."

She goes still. "Interesting."

She doesn't look as excited as I thought she'd be. "That's one way of putting it, yes. Can you find out who painted the fake? That might be a way to track down who stole the original."

"No." Valentina sets the phone down in front of me and leans back in her seat, folding her arms, her face serious. "Lucia, I love you. You're my best friend, and I don't want anything to happen to you. Do not steal in Venice."

"What?" I gape at her. Valentina's warning is shocking. My best friend has never discouraged me from risky behavior—half the time as teenagers, she was the instigator. "Why not?"

"Because Antonio Moretti owns the city. Nobody commits crimes here without his permission."

"The mafia, really?" I start to laugh. "Come on, Valentina. I plan to reunite a stolen painting with the museum that owns it. First, that's not a crime. Second, since when does the mafia deal with art? I thought they were more interested in drugs, weapons, and illegal gambling."

"You're forgetting cyber currency," Valentina remarks. "Lucia, you're not taking me seriously. You should." She doesn't look afraid. She looks *torn*. "For once in your life, please listen to me. Let this one go."

Of course, I don't let it go. I go about my week, the Titian never far from my mind. Something keeps nagging at me, and it's only as I'm walking back home Thursday that I realize what Valentina unintentionally let drop.

When I showed her the painting, she said, *Do not steal in Venice, Lucia.*

Which can only mean one thing. The stolen Titian is still here, and *Valentina knows who took it.*

And when it comes to art thefts in Venice, nobody knows more than Alvisa Zanotti.

I go see Signora Zanotti Friday evening. She lived in a crumbling palazzo, steps from la Piazza. I offer her the flowers and wine I brought, and once the pleasantries are done, I ask her about the *Madonna at Repose*. "It's a Titian," I say, showing her a photo of the fake. "Stolen at some point in the last fifteen years. I think it's still in Venice. Any idea who might have it?"

Her response is immediate. "A Titian? No, nothing on the marketplace—I would have heard about it. A private job, maybe?"

"Someone hired a thief to steal a Titian. Who?"

Her voice turns somber. "Someone so wealthy and powerful there hasn't been a whisper of gossip about it."

"You're not going to tell me to forget this painting, are you? Valentina already tried." I smile at Signora Zanotti to rob the words of their sting. "You know I'm not capable of doing that."

She's quiet for a long time. "I was afraid you'd say that." She sighs heavily. "The man you're looking for is a lawyer who works for the mafia. Daniel Rossi. He lives near the Chiesa di San Francesco della Vigna." She shakes her head. "Don't get caught."

The palazzo where Daniel Rossi lives is surprisingly secure. There's a guard in the lobby who stays awake through his shift, the roof has cameras, and the windows are connected to a sophisticated alarm system.

The Thief

If Valentina were in a cooperative mood, she could have done something about the security, but she made her opinion pretty clear. She wants no part of this job, and I can't hack into the system without her help—I'm not nearly as skilled as she is.

There is an easier but riskier way. It could simply be an inside job.

And so I start working night shifts at Rossi's cleaning company. I let the supervisors know I'm looking to pick up any available daytime shifts. I strike gold on a Saturday afternoon, twelve days after I started. The lawyer's usual cleaner calls in sick, and I'm asked to cover for her.

Yes!

After that, it's easy. I slip on gloves so I'm not leaving prints and keep my head down so the cameras inside Rossi's apartment can't catch my face.

The painting is hanging in the lawyer's office. He's leaving it out in the open where anyone can see it? My lips tighten in disapproval over Rossi's remarkably careless attitude toward this priceless work of art. Or maybe he's assuming that everyone's forgotten about this Titian. After all, it's been fifteen years since it was last displayed.

There are no cameras in sight. I approach the *Madonna*, tilting the frame and peering behind to see if any wires will set off an alarm. There are. I take care of them, and then I'm free and clear.

Twenty minutes later, I've swapped the real painting for the fake, and I'm out of Rossi's apartment. I walk down the Calle del Tedum, wondering how long it will be before the lawyer notices his stolen art is gone. I'm almost at the Ponte del Fontego when a boat pulls up at the canal on my left.

A man with dark hair, piercing blue eyes, and a stubble-darkened jaw gets out. His face is narrow, and his cheekbones are sharp enough to cut. He's tall, lean, and corded with muscle, and his charcoal gray suit only accentuates his physique.

The Thief

He's gorgeous, predatory, and intensely, overwhelmingly *sexual.*

For a second, I ogle openly. Then my brain stutters to a halt.

Standing in front of me is the most powerful man in Venice.

The man Valentina warned me not to cross.

Antonio Moretti.

My heart starts to race.

"Lucia Petrucci," he says, his voice silken. "You know the rules. You were warned." Something stirs in his eyes, something dark and dangerous. "And yet, here you are, with an illicitly obtained Titian in your bag." He holds out his hand to me. "Get in the boat."

It's twilight, and there's no one around. There's nowhere to run. Nowhere to hide.

This was a set-up. Moretti knew I was going to steal this painting. Who betrayed me? Was it Alvisa Zanotti? Or was it Valentina?

I try to keep my fear at bay and fail abjectly.

Taking his hand and doing my best to ignore the shiver that runs through me, I climb into the speedboat.

ANTONIO

Chapter Four

Lucia doesn't recognize me? I guess I shouldn't be surprised. After all, we met just once ten years ago on a dark and foggy night, and she'd been very, *very* drunk.

Her green eyes are more vivid than I remember. Her face is thinner, the only real sign it's been a decade since I last saw her. Her shoulders are tight, her chin held high, but she can't disguise the shiver that runs through her.

Her defiance is only skin-deep.

She's afraid of me.

I remove my coat and drape it over her shoulders. Her eyes widen at my gesture. I half-expect her to throw the coat back at me, but she's smarter than that. She hugs the thick woolen garment around her shoulders. "Where are we going?"

I don't reply.

We emerge from the narrower canal onto El Canalasso. Even in December, other boats are around, and I can practically hear Lucia's thoughts. She's debating whether she can shout for help, wondering if they would hear.

They would hear, yes. But they won't act. Lucia has much to learn about Venice. There are very few people that would dare cross me.

"Don't do it," I warn her. "I know where you work and where you live. It would be a very bad idea to scream."

"I wasn't planning on it," she lies. "Alvisa Zanotti

told me about Daniel Rossi. She tipped you off, didn't she? What did you do to get her to talk? Did you threaten her?"

"I don't need to issue threats."

She swallows, fear flashing in her eyes. "Did you hurt her? Oh my God, what did you do?"

I should let her sweat. She's stealing from me. In my city, without my permission. She's wise to fear my retribution.

"I'm not going to hurt an old lady. She owed me a favor."

"That's why she sold me out?" Lucia looks betrayed. Signora Zanotti was her parents' fence, and she's helped her pick the paintings to steal for the last ten years. She's known Alvisa her whole life, practically making her family.

And once again, her family betrayed her.

Lucia's expression—haunted, sad—brings back memories of the night we met.

Guilt pinches my chest. "She made me promise I wouldn't hurt you."

"And do you keep your promises?" She glances at me, her expression wary. "Never mind. I don't want to know the answer. Where are you taking me?"

"Giudecca."

"Why? Is it easier to make a body disappear there?"

My lips twitch. Giudecca, the island immediately south of Venice, has a checkered past but is now home to Italy's most interesting contemporary art scene. It's also one of the few places in Venice where the locals outnumber tourists. "I live there."

"You're taking me to your home?" Her expression turns confused. "Why?"

I wish I knew. I should have sent Dante or Leo to warn her not to steal in my city. But I didn't do that. *Instead,* I've spent all my spare time over the last two weeks discovering everything I can about Lucia. Against my better judgment, I set a trap for her, baiting it with a painting I knew she'd find irresistible.

None of this makes any sense.

And now I'm taking her to my home.

Dante is waiting at my private dock. No doubt my second-in-command doesn't approve of my obsession with Lucia. The Russians could be a threat, and Dante probably feels I should consolidate my power and prepare for war.

I pull the boat alongside the dock and throw the line overboard. Dante ties it in place. I can see the exact moment he notices Lucia is wearing my coat because a smirk grows on his face. I give him my best quelling look as I get out. "See that we aren't interrupted."

I turn around and extend my hand to Lucia. She ignores it and climbs out on her own, and Dante's grin widens. "Of course, padrino."

As soon as we reach my living room, Lucia pivots toward me. "You planted the Titian in Daniel Rossi's apartment," she accuses. "You made sure I was hired at the cleaning company. Why set me up?"

"I wanted to meet Venice's newest art thief." I open a bottle of Barolo. "Would you like a drink?"

She ignores the offered glass, her mouth twisting into a wry grimace. "I thought it felt too easy." Another thought strikes her. "Why did you want to meet me? To warn me to stay away from the painting? You didn't need to—I doubt I would have found it without Signora Zanotti's help."

She's in my house, thinks she's in danger, and she's still fishing for information. This woman is *magnificent*. Part of me worries for her, and the other part wants to get down on my knees and propose marriage.

Where did that thought come from?

"Enough questions," I say harshly. "First things first. You have my painting. I want it back."

"It's not yours," she snaps. "It belongs to the Palazzo Ducale. Who stole it for you?"

Another question. There's a fine line between

fearless and reckless, and Lucia seems determined to zigzag all over it.

I take a sip of the full-bodied red. "The *Madonna at Repose* is in the bag you're clutching to your chest. I'd prefer not to, but I can take it from you by force if it comes to that."

She sinks onto the couch. Her hands tremble as she opens her bag and lifts the painting out, swaddled protectively in fabric.

I'm scaring her. I feel like an asshole as I unwrap the precious canvas. "You haven't damaged it," I murmur, staring at the picture of the mother playing with her child. The first time I laid eyes on it, I felt a deep sense of recognition, of belonging. I thought the feeling would fade with time, but even though it's been fifteen years since I stole it, it hasn't. "That's good."

"I'm a curator. I know how to handle artwork."

The words are pert, but her voice is subdued. I wrap the painting back up, set it aside, and then sit across from her. "To answer your earlier question, I didn't hire a thief to steal the painting. I did it myself."

Surprise flashes across her face. "Really?"

"Really." I push the wine toward her. This time, she takes the glass from me with a nod of thanks. "It was my first major job," I continue. "I should have fenced it immediately, but I couldn't bear to get rid of it." Why did I tell her that? "It's been hanging in my bedroom ever since."

"You stole it from the palazzo? When?"

"When I was sixteen. The museum hosted a reception for a visiting donor. I dressed as a waiter and sneaked into the gathering."

She leans forward, giving me a tantalizing glimpse of her cleavage. Desire punches me in the gut and takes my breath away. Fuck me, I want her.

"And Signora Zanotti knew you stole it. I should have guessed when she warned me away." She tucks a strand of hair behind her ear, an unconscious gesture that I find deeply sexy. "You still haven't told me why you wanted to meet me."

I have to hand it to her; she's persistent. "Ten paintings in ten years, each returned to its lawful owner. You haven't exactly been subtle, Lucia. You might think you're flying under the radar, but people have been paying attention. Arthur Kincaid's investigative team managed to capture a clip of you."

I hand her my phone. She watches the short video with a frown. "I don't understand."

"The moment I saw it, I recognized you. You don't remember me, do you?"

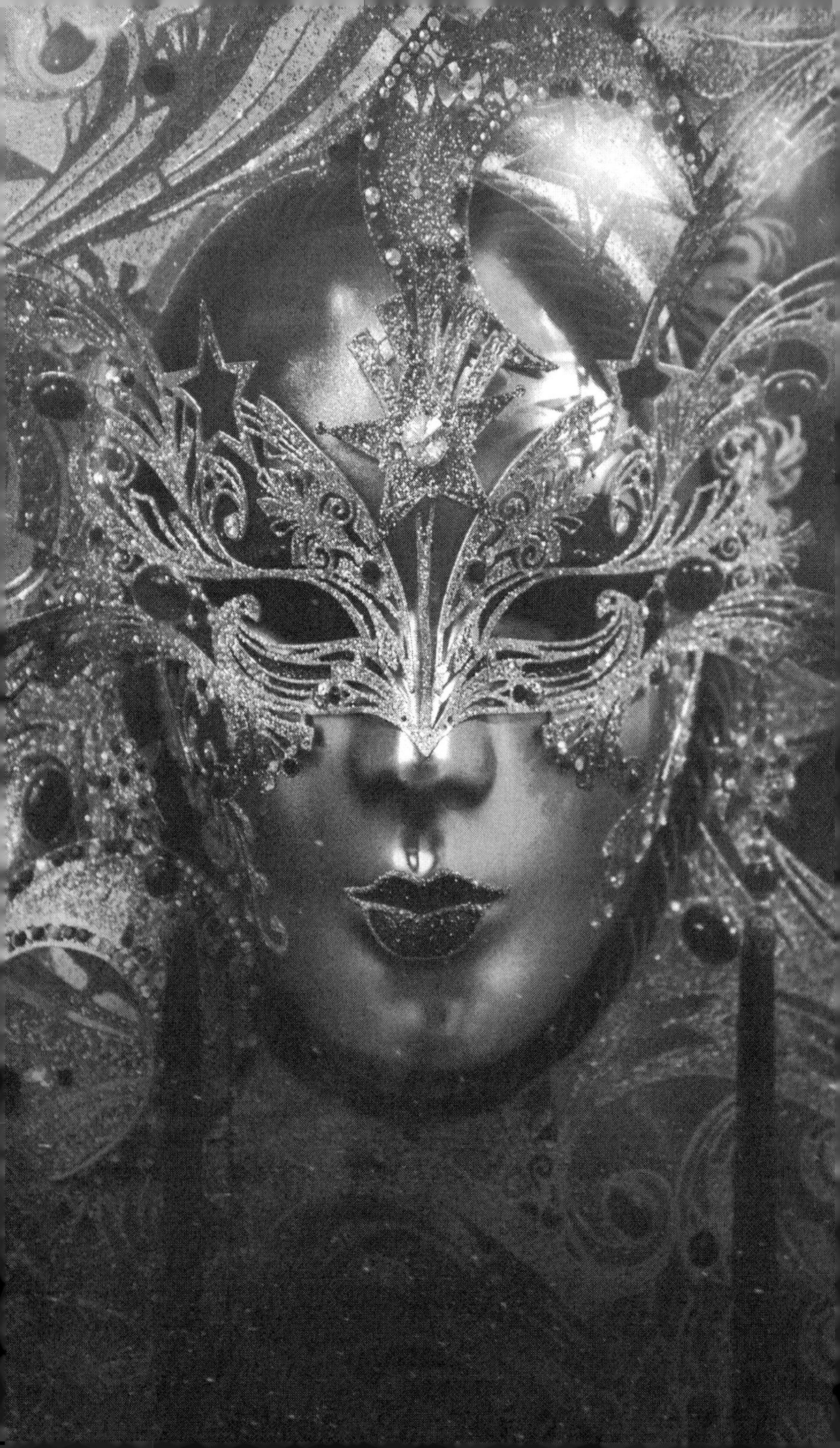

LUCIA

Chapter Five

In a flash, I know. It's *him*.

Antonio Moretti, the powerful king of Venice and the ruthless head of its mafia, is my mystery rescuer.

I stare at him, my thoughts churning. Maybe I should have figured it out earlier, but Antonio is one of the most common Italian names. And I'd been too drunk that night to see his face properly.

"Ten years ago," I whisper. "That was you."

"Yes."

"Oh." Fear leaches from my body. I don't know

Antonio, but I cannot believe the man who walked with me on the worst night of my life because he didn't want to leave me alone would hurt me now. Even if he just kidnapped me. "Thank you for your help that night," I say softly. "I probably would have fallen into the canal if it weren't for you." Then I think about the men who tried to rob me. "Or worse. You didn't have to stay with me either, but you did, and I'm truly grateful."

He looks almost shocked by my words. Is he not used to being thanked? "It was the least I could do." He leans forward to refill the wine I've drained without realizing. "You never called me."

Our fingers graze. A tingle jolts through me, and it strikes me anew that Antonio Moretti is a very good-looking man. Even through the grief, Past-Me knew it when she asked him to stay in her hotel room.

"I was a wreck. I was in no place to talk to anyone." I put my hand over his. "More than once, I wanted to reach out."

The Thief

And I'm stroking his fingers.

What am I doing?

I snatch my palm away, and an ironic smile creases his face. "Scared, cara mia?"

Cara mia. My darling. He called me that ten years ago. I only recall bits and pieces of that night, the images almost dream-like, but I remember this. I remember the caress in his voice, the way it deepens ever so slightly.

"Should I be?" I lift my fingers to my neck, my thumb stroking the long-faded scar from that night. I remember his hand touching my skin. I remember him asking me who did this to me.

"Everyone in Venice is afraid of me." His voice is harsh, but his eyes burn. "Alvisa Zanotti is, and so is Valentina. She warned you about me, didn't she? She told you not to steal in Venice."

Ice trickles down my spine, and I set my wine glass down with trembling hands. "How do you know Valentina?"

I don't think he's going to answer, but he does.

"She works for me." He takes in my tension, and a frown creases his forehead. "Relax. Valentina is a valued member of my organization; I won't make her choose between us. Her loyalty to you runs deeper. She doesn't know anything about this."

Valentina works for him? I did not know that. Then again, I didn't know Kincaid had a video clip of me, either.

But none of that seems to matter right now. Not with Antonio Moretti sitting on the couch next to me, a glass of wine cradled in his large hands, staring at me with heat in his eyes.

He's going to kiss me.

The air between us charges with anticipation.

I feel myself move toward him, almost imperceptibly. For ten years, I've looked at the card he left, traced my fingers over his writing, and wondered what-if? And now he's here, and I don't have to wonder anymore. "I wanted to sleep with you," I whisper. "That night."

"I know," he responds, a smile in his voice. "You

The Thief

weren't very subtle about it."

"Why didn't you take me up on it?"

"I like my women conscious, for one thing," he says dryly. "You passed out as soon as you hit the bed. But even if you weren't drunk, I wouldn't have. You weren't in the right place."

"And now?" We're both tap-dancing around it, but neither of us is oblivious to the chemistry between us.

"And now you're back home."

Home. That word is the hard jolt of reality I need. Because I might be in Venice, but I'm not home. Home was ripped away from me when my parents died.

I'm in Venice for one reason and one reason only. To be here for Valentina and Angelica. My time here is an interlude. When my contract ends in four months, I'm leaving.

The fact that I'm not staying won't matter to Antonio. The planned expiration date will probably be a point in my favor. I'm sure he's game for a no-strings-attached affair.

And normally, I would be too.

But Antonio isn't just a sexy and dangerous man. Over the last ten years, I've built him up to be a heroic, mythic figure. Daydreamed about him falling in love with me, buying me roses in the market, and bringing me breakfast in bed.

When I was a thousand miles away from Venice, when he was a distant figure from my past, the fantasies I constructed—about him, about us—were safe.

They're not now.

I can't sleep with him; I don't trust myself not to get involved. And life has taught me to protect my heart.

I pull back from him. "Unfortunately," I say, tucking my hair behind my ear. "I'm not into bad boys."

"A pity," he says. He drains the rest of his wine and rises to his feet. "It's good to see you again, Lucia. I enjoyed our conversation, and I'm glad

The Thief

you're back home. But now that you're in Venice, you should know the rules."

A mask falls over him. The Antonio I thought I knew disappears. "The Titian belongs to me, and it's going to stay in my possession," the king of Venice says. "I will turn a blind eye to your crimes as long as they occur elsewhere. Just not in my city."

I see red. "And if I don't fall over myself to obey you, you'll do what?" I snap. "Send your men to beat me up? Let's get one thing straight, Antonio. I'm not a member of your organization. I don't work for you. You don't get to tell me what to do."

He holds my gaze. Looks me up and down in a slow caress. I'm dressed in the ugliest uniform in the world, and he looks at me like I'm wearing the most beautiful lingerie. "I'm attracted to you," he says. "Unless I'm mistaken, you're attracted to me as well. But you're not going to do anything about it because, as you say, you're not into bad boys."

A light sparks in his eyes. "To answer your

question, Lucia, I won't send my men to beat you up. But if you try to steal my Madonna again, I will assume you're sending me a message."

"And what is that?"

"That you want me to fuck you." He gives me a pleasant smile. "Choose your next move wisely, cara mia."

LUCIA

Chapter Six

All the way home, I'm fuming from Antonio's ultimatum. But underneath my anger, a reluctant admiration simmers. There's no doubt about it. If we're fighting a battle for the Titian, he won the first round with laughable ease.

Damn him.

Bad boys do nothing for me; I wasn't lying about that. But Antonio Moretti isn't a boy. He's a *man.* A complicated, *morally gray* man.

He's one of the richest people in Italy. He has the finest private art collection in Europe. He owns a half-dozen vineyards in Veneto, Piedmont, and Tuscany, an ownership stake in a Formula One racing team, and so much more. He also supposedly speaks a half-dozen languages and constantly escorts beautiful women to events. He's powerful and capable of violence and ruthlessness.

And yet...

And yet, ten years ago, on a night when I desperately needed a shoulder to lean on, Antonio was there. I was a complete stranger, but he came to my rescue. I was so drunk I couldn't see straight, and instead of judging me, he took care of me. He listened. He was kind.

Choose your next move wisely, cara mia.

The smug jerk won this round, yes. But he's not going to win the war. I won't let that happen.

No matter how sexy I find him.

As for his ultimatum?

The Thief

I won't be manipulated by him. I refuse. He doesn't get to unilaterally set the terms of engagement.

I fish the faded business card out of my purse when I get to my apartment and text him.

> I'm going to steal that painting. And whatever you might think, that's not a sign that I'm interested in you.

He responds almost immediately.

> You kept my card. I'm flattered.

Heat creeps up my cheeks. I didn't mean to mention that. Now my actions have made a lie of my words.

> I'm not joking about the painting.

> I didn't think you were. Good luck, Lucia. May the best thief win.

Gah. I fling the phone on my counter. I have no

idea why I spent so long fantasizing about this guy. Antonio Moretti is the worst.

To nobody's surprise, I dream of Antonio that night.

I'm in his house again, standing in the center of his living room, my heart hammering in my chest. A shiver runs through my body. I tell myself that it's terror I feel, not arousal. "You're going to have to take me by force," I accuse.

He settles himself on the couch, legs stretched out, and surveys me with knowing eyes. "But we both know I don't need to force you, Lucia." He says my name like a caress, and my insides flutter at his tone. It's been a long time since a man has spoken to me this way. With heat and with the promise of passion. "You want this as much as I do."

I *hate* that he's right. "What are you going to do to me?"

He tilts his head to the side and studies me, a smile dancing around his lips. "What would you like me to do, cara mia?"

Everything.

I clamp my mouth shut and refuse to answer. Antonio laughs under his breath and crooks two fingers at me. I move toward him before even thinking about refusing. He closes his hand around my wrist and tugs me closer.

"I'm going to punish you." The words are a threat, but his eyes promise I'll enjoy every minute. "I'm going to bend you over my knees and spank you hard for thinking you can steal from me." He pulls me onto his lap. "But only if you ask nicely."

My breath catches. His nearness short-circuits my brain. "Yes," I say, my voice a mere whisper. "Please. . ."

He strips me naked, positions me over his lap, and presses a hand on the small of my back. "Beautiful," he says quietly. "So very beautiful, tesoro."

Then he spanks me.

At first, there is pain, sweet and delicious, and then it is replaced by a rush of pleasure. He strokes me between the spanks, and every nerve ending in my body responds to his touch. The slap of his palm against my reddening ass fuels my arousal. I wriggle on his lap, grinding my pussy shamelessly against his thighs, desperate for any bit of friction against my aching clit.

My muscles tighten and tense. The heat builds. . .

And that's how I wake up. Poised on the knife's edge of release, shaking with need, drenched with sweat, Antonio's name on my lips.

I can scream until I'm blue in the face that I'm not interested in him, but my subconscious just made a liar out of me.

I want Antonio Moretti.

Damn it. Damn it all to hell.

The Thief

Someone's banging at my door. I crack an eyelid and grope for my phone. It's seven in the morning. What the hell? That's far too early for a Sunday, damn it. Even the church bells are silent.

I slide out of bed, put a robe on, and go out to investigate.

Valentina and her daughter Angelica are at my front door. The moment my best friend sees me, she sags against the doorframe in relief. "You're okay."

"Umm, yes?" I raise an eyebrow at my goddaughter, wondering if she knows what's going on, and she shrugs her shoulders. "Come on in."

She marches in, Angelica at her heels. She looks around my living room, and I expect her to point out I still don't have any furniture. Instead, she pulls an iPad out of her bag and hands it to her daughter. "Watch something, baby," she says. "I need to talk to Aunt Lucia alone."

I'm mystified. I let Valentina drag me into my bedroom and shut the door. "Are you okay?" she demands, whirling toward me. "Truly okay?"

"Yes. Will you tell me what's going on?"

"You," she splutters. "Antonio Moretti. At his house. Any of this ringing any bells?" Her eyes narrow. "You looked into the Titian, didn't you?"

"I did."

She throws up her hands in the air. "Lucia, do you ever listen to anything I say?" She takes a deep breath. "Did he hurt you?"

"What? No."

She looks me up and down as if to satisfy herself that I'm telling the truth. "Tell me what happened."

"Fine." I sink onto my air mattress and pat my side. "Join me. Angelica's got the only chair in the house."

She aims a disapproving glare at my poor imitation of a bed. "When are you going to get yourself proper furniture? You've been here three weeks."

"And there it is," I say with a grin. "You must have really been worried if you waited this long to nag."

The Thief

Her expression promises death if I don't fill her in, so I add hastily, "Okay, okay. Here's what happened. Signora Zanotti told me the painting was in Daniel Rossi's possession."

"A trap," she says flatly.

"Yes, well, I didn't know that. So I infiltrated his cleaning crew—"

"Without telling me."

"Are you going to let me finish?" I ask pointedly. "I infiltrated his cleaning crew, got into his apartment, and stole the painting. Unfortunately, Antonio intercepted me on my way out."

"And?"

"And nothing. He brought me to his house, took the painting back, and warned me not to steal from him."

"That's it?"

"More or less."

She stares at me. "You were wearing his coat when you arrived at his house."

As usual, my best friend is alarmingly well-informed. "It was cold. Antonio was just being polite."

She raises an eyebrow. "Antonio? You're on a first-name basis with him? Lucia, Antonio Moretti is not polite to the people who steal from him. He *destroys* them. You arrive wearing his coat. He tells his lieutenants he isn't to be disturbed. The two of you spend an hour together?" Her voice rises. "What the hell is going on?"

Argh. Valentina is like a bloodhound. I might as well tell her everything because I want to interrogate her about Antonio. From experience, I know that the only way to get information from Valentina is to offer her gossip of equal or greater value.

"We've met before. Once, ten years ago. The day I buried my parents."

I tell her the whole story, and she listens in perfect silence. "Wow," she says when I'm done. "Well, that explains a lot." She leans forward. "So, he gave you his card, and you threw it away, but judging by your expression, you've always remembered him fondly."

"It's worse than that." I fish the dog-eared business card out of my purse. "I kept it."

"Aww. My heart. I can't take it."

"Are you being sarcastic?"

"Only a little." She grins at me. "Come on, you have to admit that's an embarrassingly sappy gesture. Are you attracted to him? You are, aren't you?"

That's an understatement if there ever was one. "He told me that if I were to make another attempt at the painting, he would construe it as an invitation into my bed."

Valentina bursts out laughing. I shoot her a death glare, but it doesn't diminish her mirth. "Oh, come on," she says through her giggles. "That's pretty funny."

Fine, it's a little funny. "Come on, I'll make you coffee. And while I'm doing that, you can tell me how long you've been working for him and why you never told me about it?"

Her smile fades. "It's a long story."

"I have all day."

Over coffee in the kitchen—Angelica happily watches cartoons on the iPad and doesn't pay us any attention—Valentina fills me in. "I've worked for him for the last six years." She stares into her mug. "Do you remember anything about the old mafia?"

I shake my head. "My parents shielded me from that stuff." A familiar pang hits my heart. "They hid all the unpleasant things in life from me."

"Domenico Cartozzi, the former head of the Family, was terrifying. One moment, he'd be laughing, joking with you, and the next minute, he'd explode. He was unpredictable and had a vicious temper, with a mean streak a mile wide. I fell in love with one of his capos when I was twenty-one." She fiddles with her napkin. "You haven't asked me who Angelica's father is."

"I asked you once, and you didn't want to talk

about it." An icy suspicion fills me. "Is it Antonio?"

She jerks her head up. "What? Dio, no. I barely knew Antonio in those days, and in any case, he's not my type. When Roberto first asked me out, I was flattered by the attention. Then I realized what a piece of shit he was. I walked out the first time he hit me, but Domenico decided I should give him a second chance, and everyone knew you couldn't say no to the Padrino."

Valentina is my age, so all this stuff was going down shortly after my parents died. When I pulled away and wasn't there for her.

Not for the first time, I wish I'd been a better friend.

"Then I got pregnant. I knew I would never make it out if I stayed with Roberto. If it wasn't for Antonio..." She takes a deep breath. "When he took over, he asked for my help. I owe him a debt of gratitude I can never repay, so of course I said yes."

"You're sure you're not interested in him?

Because if you are. . ." If she is, I'll step aside. If there's anyone who deserves to be happy, it's Valentina.

She rolls her eyes. "Lucia, I've never been interested in Antonio Moretti. Besides, I've learned my lesson. Hell will freeze over before I fall for someone in the mafia. If you going to make a play for him—"

"I'm not going to make a play for him." I might have had the hottest sex dream of my life, and my entire body might have been left quivering with unfulfilled sexual need, but no. Not Antonio Moretti. He's just too damn smug. "He's not my type either. I don't date bad boys."

Except on the loneliest day of your life, he made sure you weren't alone.

What would Antonio be like in bed? Would he be a kind, considerate lover or a forceful, demanding one? Would he give me the spanking I secretly crave? Tie me down and thrust into me, forcing orgasm after orgasm on me?

Enough. I'm in Venice for three more months, and the two people I've returned for are in my apartment. Valentina and Angelica are my priority.

Antonio Moretti is not important. He's sexy, yes, but ultimately, he's nothing but a distraction. And I don't have time for that.

"You're sure about that?" At my vehement nod, she continues, "Good. In that case, you can drop your obsession with the Titian. Let's identify a new target."

Choose your next move wisely, cara mia.

"Okay," I reply reluctantly. "Let's do that."

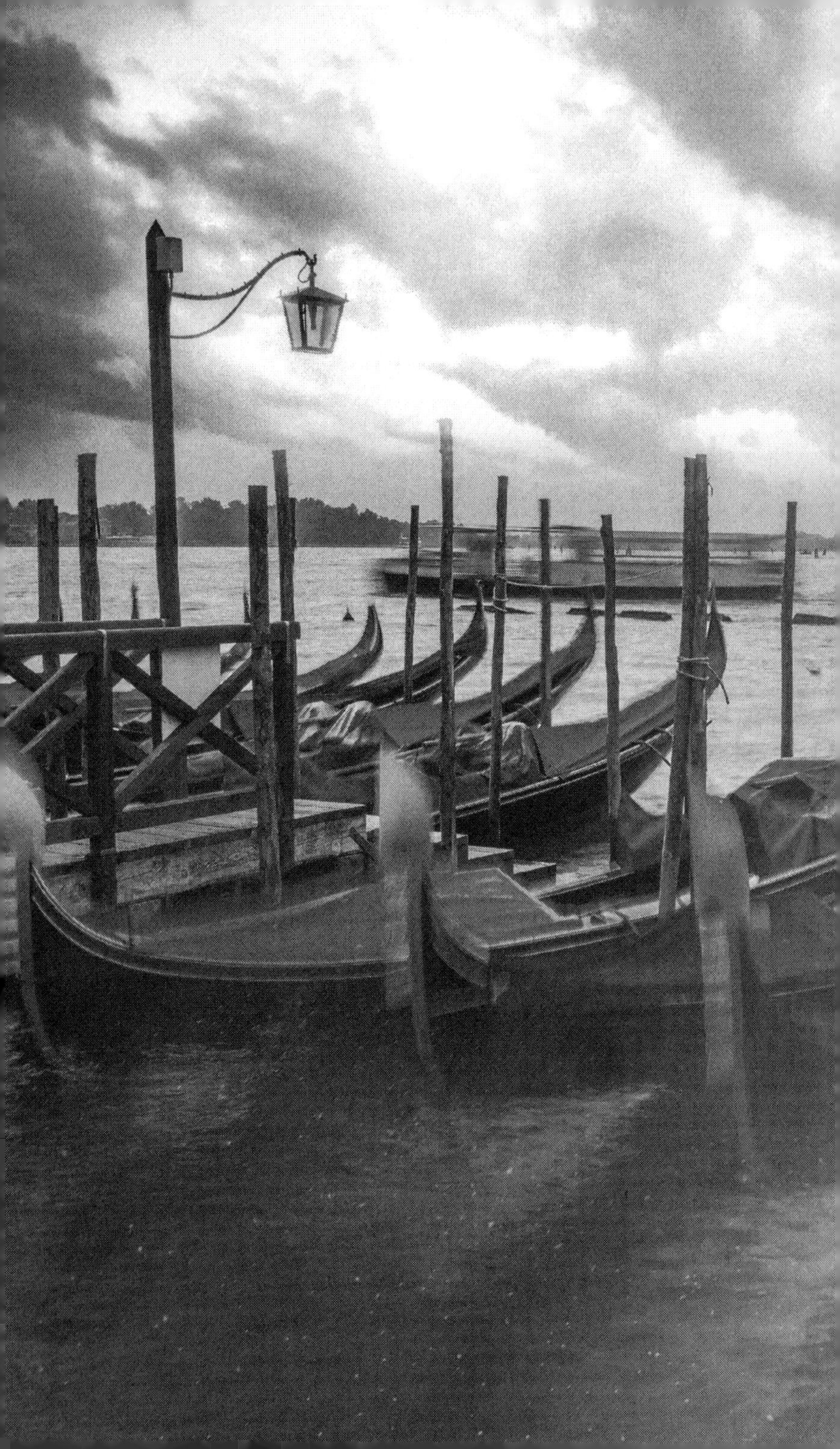

ANTONIO

Chapter Seven

Salvatore Verratti is avoiding me, and the Gafur OPS is in Bergamo. I can't afford to be distracted.

And yet, my thoughts keep returning to Lucia. I asked her out, and she said no. If she had left it there, I might have stayed away.

But she didn't.

She texted me. She kept the card I gave her ten years ago. And she announced her intention to make another attempt at the painting.

Challenge accepted, little thief. The game is on.

Valentina doesn't have much luck intercepting their communications, but I soon find out why the Gafur OPS was in Italy. Ilya Kozlov, son of the *pakhan*, requests an audience with me on a Tuesday afternoon.

The Russians want to smuggle weapons through Venice to the rest of the continent.

"We can get the guns to Croatia through Poland and Hungary," Kozlov says once we finish with the preliminaries. "Then we ship them across the Adriatic to Venice. From there, an overland route to France and then across the channel to the UK." He smiles at me persuasively. "Of course, we would never dream of coming through Venice without your permission."

"It's always best to have a local partner," I say blandly. "Venice can be such a dangerous city. Take last year's explosion in the harbor, the one that caused that yacht to sink. What was its name, Dante?"

"The *Kalinin*," my lieutenant replies with a straight face.

Kozlov flinches at the reminder. That move was orchestrated by Meych, one of the smaller OPGs operating in Moscow. The group bribed a handful of port officials, loaded the *Kalinin* with five tons of cocaine, and tried to bring it into my city.

Without my permission.

I sank it, and Meych didn't survive the financial loss. Looks like the Russians got the message.

Ilya rearranges his face into a neutral mask. "Such an unfortunate incident. My father agrees that we would like to avoid similar unpleasantness. And, of course, we'll make it worth your while. The margins in this line are very good."

He's ready to talk money. Time to put this to a halt. I hold up my hand. "Let me stop you before you get into the details. I'm not interested."

Dante's shoulders relax imperceptibly.

"What?" Ilya splutters. "Why?"

There are a thousand good reasons to avoid this line of business. The Russians aren't reliable partners, and letting them get a foothold in my city is pure folly. Also, Gafur OPS is currently engaged in a power struggle with a competing organization, and I don't want to get dragged into their muck.

Finally, an epidemic of smuggled weapons hitting the streets gives ambitious politicians a perfect incentive to declare a 'war on crime,' which will disrupt my current business and endanger my people.

But mostly, I just don't like guns.

And I don't owe Ilya Kozlov an explanation. "Like I said, I'm not interested," I say, getting to my feet. "Dante, will you escort our friend out?"

Ilya's face turns red. He's young still and not good at masking his emotions. "We have buyers lined up and a transport network in place. You're making a big mistake, Moretti."

Buyers *and* a transportation network? We're going to have our work cut out investigating this mess. "That's your opinion, not mine," I respond coolly. "Have a safe journey home."

Dante comes back in an hour. "What do you think?" I ask him.

"That it's a terrible idea to smuggle guns into France and England." He shakes his head. "What the hell is Salvatore Verratti thinking, making a deal with the Russians?"

"You think he did?"

"Kozlov said they had the transportation network in place. If you want to flood the streets of Paris, what better route than through Bergamo and Milan?"

He's right, damn it. I have no great love for Verratti, but I didn't think he was a fool. Time to reassess my opinion. "Look into this, Dante. Find out what the Russians have on Verratti."

"Yes, padrino."

He lingers in front of my window, looking like

he wants to say something. "Is there something else?" I prompt.

"Lucia Petrucci."

I direct a frosty glare at my second-in-command. I'm in no mood to hear a warning from Dante about how I should stay focused on Gafur. "Yes?"

"I figured it out," he says. "In all the time I've known you, I've seen you lose your temper once. Ten years ago, you ordered Marco out of town after he tried to rob a woman at the docks. It wasn't until last night that I realized that woman was Lucia Petrucci."

Damn it. This is the problem with hiring the smartest people in the room. Eventually, they figure out your secrets.

"Kicking Marco out of Venice was complicated," Dante adds, in what must surely be the understatement of the year. "He was Domenico's nephew. Back then, if you told me you did it for a woman, I would have called you the biggest fool in the world."

He looks up from his pacing. "But things are different now. You've worked hard to make this city safe, to make sure we're secure. Lucia Petrucci is obviously important to you. Maybe it's time to finally take care of yourself, Antonio."

As it happens, I'm one of the Palazzo Ducale's biggest donors. Every year, I write them a massive check, and every year, the museum director, Signora Sabatino, writes to me with effusive thanks.

Once Dante leaves, I pull up the director's latest letter and scan the contents. She thanks me for my generous gift, gives me an update on the important conservation work the museum is doing, and, most importantly, invites me to visit anytime. "The chief curator would be delighted to give you a private tour of our Venetian collection."

I'm not interested in a tour by the chief curator. But a private tour with the newly hired assistant curator in charge of conservation and collections management? That, I would *love*.

With a grin, I head toward La Piazza.

Signora Sabatino is thrown by my unexpected arrival but does her best to take it in stride. She fawns over me and then personally escorts me to the chief curator's office. "Signor Garzolo will be a much better guide than I am," she admits with a small laugh. "My knowledge of early Venetian art is regrettably quite limited."

Just then, I spot Lucia. She's walking in my direction, in intent conversation with an older man walking with a limp.

Signora Sabatino beams and holds out a hand to stop them. "Ah, Nicolo, there you are. I was on my way to your office. Signor Moretti, may I introduce you to Dottore Nicolo Garzolo?" She appears to be searching her memory for Lucia's name before adding, "And our newest assistant curator, Lucia Petrucci."

Lucia's head snaps up. When she sees me, her shoulders stiffen, and her eyes flash with anger.

Hello to you, too, my little thief.

"Dottore Garzolo," the director continues, "This is Signor Antonio Moretti. He's one of our most generous benefactors." She gives the other man a meaningful look. "He would like to view the Venetian artwork on display."

The curator appears bemused. "I'll be happy to show you around, Signor Moretti."

"Your leg appears to be bothering you, Dottore. I wouldn't want to make it worse." I'm all warm concern as I turn to Lucia. "Perhaps Signorina Petrucci would be kind enough to give me a tour instead."

Lucia looks like she wants to strangle me, but her voice is pure sweetness when she speaks. "I would be delighted."

Signora Sabatino and Nicolo Garzolo pull Lucia aside, presumably to tell her what an important donor I am. As soon as we are alone, Lucia whirls toward me. "What are you doing here?" she demands. "Do you think this is funny?"

"Tsk, tsk. Didn't your bosses tell you to be nice to me?"

"I'm supposed to do anything to make you happy." She rolls her eyes. "How much money do you give the palazzo, anyway?"

"Last year, I believe it was fifteen million euros."

Her mouth falls open. "But that's almost twenty percent of our operating budget." She blinks before recovering her wits. "Then again, you did steal one of our paintings. Is the large donation a way to soothe your guilt?"

"I have no time for guilt. What are you showing me today?"

"I thought we'd start with a forged Titian," she says, utterly deadpan. "I discovered it in a storage room a few weeks ago."

The Thief

I laugh out loud. "We could do that," I agree. "But I'd also like to see the Illuminated Manuscripts exhibit if the galleries are open for viewing."

She looks surprised that I know about the upcoming exhibit. "I've been told the entire museum is at your disposal. Are you hoping to steal a sixteenth-century Bible, Antonio?"

"Not today." Sunbeams bisect the passageway, shining through graceful arches with views of the piazza below. "You've been working here for what, three weeks now? How do you like your job?"

"It's fine."

She doesn't sound terribly enthusiastic. I look at her sharply. "Is someone giving you a hard time at work?"

"No, no. Like I said, the job's fine. Being back in Venice, though. . ." Her voice trails off into a sigh. "Most days, I'm okay. And then I'll turn a corner and stumble upon the park my mother used to take me when I was a child. . . Or walk on the street where my dad taught me to cycle."

I want to offer words of comfort, but they freeze on my tongue. Anything I could say would sound trite.

My silence doesn't seem to bother her. "You told me you didn't know your parents. When I'm having an especially bad day, I wonder if it would have been better that way. If I didn't have memories of them. . ."

Time hasn't yet managed to erase the darkness in her eyes. I usually avoid talking about my parents, but today, it's better than the alternative. "You were loved, and I was abandoned in Il Redentore as a baby," I say quietly. "You don't want my life, cara mia."

The Chiesa del Santissimo Redentore—Il Redentore as it's called—is in Guidecca, a five-minute walk from my house. Lucia knows the church's location because her expression softens. "Is that why you live on Guidecca?" she asks gently. "Because it's where you were found?"

"It's a quiet neighborhood," I prevaricate.

"Thankfully, not too many tourists bother with it."

I'm being evasive, but she lets it go. "I shouldn't have compared my life with yours," she says instead, her voice apologetic. "It was thoughtless of me. I'm sorry."

I accept her apology with a nod. Complex, beautiful, and fascinating. There's a reason I've never been able to forget Lucia Petrucci.

"And here we are." She gestures to a set of stairs on the right. "The Illuminated Manuscripts."

Lucia is an excellent guide. She warns me as we enter the exhibit that this isn't her area of expertise, but it becomes obvious that she's selling herself short. She can link the paintings in the manuscripts with the history of art patronage in Venice, making a dry topic come alive with her enthusiasm. We spend more than an hour in the gallery, and I barely register the passage of time.

"Have lunch with me?" I ask when we're done.

She gives me a strange look. "I already told you I'm not going to sleep with you."

"Is that the only reason I'd want to eat with you?"

She shrugs. "I'm not exactly your type."

Her words stop me in my tracks. "What do you mean by that?"

"Last month, you were photographed attending a party with Tatiana Cordova," she responds. "I'm neither a supermodel nor a world-famous actress. We don't belong in the same world."

She looked me up. Is she jealous? I bite back my smile of triumph. "You're wrong. You're an art lover and a thief. Trust me, Lucia. You're *exactly* my type." I hold out my hand to her. "Have lunch with me."

"Are you asking me or telling me?"

I lift my shoulders in a shrug. "Whatever you want it to be." I'm the museum's biggest donor, and the director is eager to keep it that way. We both know Lucia isn't in a position to decline my lunch invitation. What can I say? I can be an asshole sometimes.

She glares at me. "Very well," she says through stiff lips. "Let's eat lunch. But that's all it is. I don't care if you give the museum fifteen million euros or fifteen billion—I'm not sleeping with you."

"The lady doth protest too much," I say blandly. "Where would you like to eat?"

She ponders me for a minute, and then laughter sparks in her eyes. "Your house," she says gleefully. "I didn't get a good feel for your security on Saturday. This time, I'll pay better attention."

"You realize you're giving me mixed messages?" I rest my hand on the small of her back and steer her toward the exit. "On the one hand, you keep telling me you're not going to sleep with me, and on the other..."

She tosses her head but doesn't pull away from my touch. "You don't make the rules, Antonio."

"Actually, cara mia, you'll find that in Venice, I do."

We walk out to the piazza, and I lead her to the nearest dock where Stefano, one of my men, is waiting with my boat. As I help her in, I'm struck by a hard truth. I don't typically take the women I want to fuck to my house, and yet, this is the second time I'm taking Lucia home.

LUCIA

Chapter Eight

I'm about to have lunch with Antonio Moretti, and it feels surreal.

There are a thousand reasons I shouldn't do this. We're from two different worlds, and already, after just one encounter, I'm too involved. I googled him and became jealous when he was photographed with other women. I have sex dreams about him night after night. The king of Venice is not good for my peace of mind.

But he showed up at my workplace and invited me to lunch. He told me that I was *exactly* his type. And maybe, *just maybe,* for the space of one meal, I can put my reservations on hold and let myself believe him.

We dock in front of Antonio's house, and he helps me out. Opening his front door, he gestures me inside. I step into his foyer and look around curiously.

I was too afraid to notice anything when I was here three days ago. Today though, I let my gaze wander over the space, soaking in the details: black-and-white tiled floor, salmon-pink walls dotted with a collection of wooden masks, lush tropical plants, and a carved antique bench crowded with turquoise, indigo, and forest-green cushions. The room is eclectic, colorful, and fascinating.

Antonio rests his hand on the small of my back. "Would you prefer a tour now or after lunch?"

My stomach rumbles, reminding me I skipped breakfast this morning. "After lunch, please."

The large eat-in kitchen is just as visually interesting as the foyer. Weak winter sun shines through a massive glass window overlooking an inner courtyard. It's too cold to eat out there today, but I imagine it's beautiful in summer. I gawk unashamedly at the copper appliances, green plants, and the Talavera tiles forming the backsplash. A vase overflowing with lilac, lavender, and honeysuckle sits on the table, and I inhale the delicate aroma of the flowers with pleasure.

Antonio quirks an eyebrow at me.

"They smell like spring," I explain. "It's my favorite season. I had you pegged as a minimalist," I add bemusedly. "But you're not, are you?" I admire a collection of blue-and-white pottery. "Where did you find these?"

I expect him to tell me his interior designer sourced them, but he surprises me by saying, "Portugal." His lips twist into a rueful smile. "I grew up with nothing, and I'm afraid it's turned me into a bit of a pack rat."

"Your house doesn't look cluttered. It's very. . . cohesive."

He chuckles. "That's not what my friends say."

Antonio Moretti has friends? I barely have time to register that before he asks me a question. "What about you?"

"Right now, I'm *extremely* minimalist. I don't have any furniture."

"Why not? Your parents left you their apartment, yes?"

Antonio undoubtedly has a file on me, but it's good to know that there are some gaps in his knowledge. "They did. But I couldn't bear to look at their stuff after they died." That's putting it mildly. "I had it placed in storage, where it still sits." Before he can say anything, I add, "I also like color. And plants and patterns and fabric." I can feel him looking at me. "Good furniture is expensive, and I move too often to invest in it. But I don't like the cheap, disposable stuff, so I'm stuck in limbo."

"Hmm." I can't tell what he's thinking. Not

surprisingly, he's good at keeping a poker face. "Would you like something to drink?"

"Just water, please. Sparkling, if you have it." *If you have it.* What a ridiculous thing to say. Antonio Moretti has everything.

"Of course," he responds. "The antique market at the Piazzola sul Brenta has some good pieces. They set up every Sunday. Would you like to go?"

Is he asking me out? I must look as confused as I feel because he adds, seemingly out of nowhere, "I'm not dating Tatiana."

"What?"

"Tatiana Cordova," he says. "You mentioned her, so I thought I'd clarify that I'm neither dating nor sleeping with her. Or anybody else." He holds me with his gaze. "The only person I'm interested in is you."

My mouth falls open. I don't know what to say. Nobody I've been with, not a single guy I've dated, has made it so explicitly clear that they want to be with me.

Antonio opens his refrigerator door as if nothing has happened. "Let's see what's in here," he says lightly. "There's a roasted chicken, and I can make a green salad. If that doesn't work, I can cook you something else."

I feel dangerously off balance. "You know how to cook?"

He chuckles. "You sound so skeptical, Lucia," he teases. "I think I'm a little offended. Yes, I know how to cook, although my housekeeper Agnese does most of it these days. However, she's visiting her sister in Florence for the week." He grins. "Go ahead, test me. What can I make for you?"

That smile is irresistible. My body tightens with need. "Unfortunately, I have to be back at work."

"Then, chicken and a salad it is." He pulls lettuce, tomatoes, and a cucumber out of his refrigerator and begins the prep.

"Can I help?"

"You can set the table. The plates are in the cabinet above the sink."

The Thief

We talk about art as we eat. As I found out when I showed him around the Palazzo Ducale, Antonio knows quite a bit about Italian art. Most of the rich people I've met buy paintings because they're good financial investments or a place to hide ill-gotten profits. But Antonio is a connoisseur, and it shows.

The conversation flows effortlessly and moves from art and travel to an antique market in Venice and one in Mestre. "Dessert?" he asks when we're finished eating.

I glance at my phone and realize with shock that over two hours have elapsed. "I can't," I say regretfully. "I really should be getting back." *I don't want to leave.* "Can I have my tour now?"

He glances sideways at me. "Still planning on stealing my painting?"

His words echo through my mind. *If you steal my painting, I'm going to assume you want me to fuck you.*

I bite my lower lip as fresh heat surges through

me. "Do you really think I'm going to warn you before I make another attempt at the Titian? Why would I do that? So that you can alert your security team?"

He shakes his head, laughter dancing in his eyes. "I wouldn't warn them, Lucia. That wouldn't be in keeping with the spirit of this game."

I'm feeling very brave suddenly. "It's almost as if you want me to steal it."

"It does seem that way, doesn't it? Think about it." A smile touches his lips as he gets to his feet and holds his hand out to me. "Come. Let me show you around."

Antonio's house is a bohemian symphony of color and texture. Collections are everywhere. Bronze masks from Benin, ceramics from Mexico, black-and-white rattan baskets—everything co-exists in a riotous harmony. The furniture is sturdy, the rugs are antique, and the overall impression is warm and welcoming. This is my dream house, I think at one point during the tour.

Then he opens the door to his bedroom, and I stop thinking.

His bed is unmade, his duvet rumpled. My imagination throws up an image of him sleeping, naked, and a shiver runs through me.

"Want to see the Titian?" he asks, gesturing me in.

Walk into my parlor, said the spider to the fly. I swallow the lump in my throat and enter Antonio's bedroom. It takes all my willpower to focus on the small, invaluable painting. "A Titian in your bedroom," I murmur. "A bit excessive, don't you think?"

"Does art only belong in a museum?"

"This one does," I point out, though there's no real bite in my voice. It might be because of the white wine I drank during lunch, or maybe it's the company. It's hard to get riled up on behalf of the Palazzo Ducale when I'm inches away from

Antonio's massive bed. Both the headboard and the footboard are slatted, and I imagine myself naked and tied up, spread open for Antonio's gaze. His to touch, his to possess. . .

Stop it, Lucia.

I press my legs together as unobtrusively as I can.

"So you say." There's a dark, seductive glint in his eyes. "Are you going to do anything about it?"

Stop pretending you don't want to sleep with him, the devil inside me whispers. The bed is *right there.*

With difficulty, I ignore that voice. "Thank you for lunch." I lean forward to brush my lips against his cheek, a polite kiss between acquaintances. The smell of him fills my nostrils. Spice and smoke and man. I breathe it—him—in, and he turns his head towards me. His lips are only an inch from mine, and I'm more tempted than I've ever been, tempted beyond measure. . .

I lean in and kiss him.

The Thief

For an instant, Antonio freezes, and I wonder if I've miscalculated. Then a wicked light flashes in his eyes, and he *moves*. With a growl, he pushes me against the stucco wall. His tongue slides into my mouth, hot and insistent. His fingers stroke my necklace, then my neck, and I gasp softly, the long-dormant memories surging to life. Ten years ago, he stroked me the same way. When I hissed with pain, he growled, hot and furious, and asked who hurt me. He promised me they wouldn't go unpunished.

Those memories only serve to inflame my lust. I wrap my arms around Antonio's neck and pull him closer. He fists my hair and sucks my lower lip between his teeth. Desire punches me in the gut, and my brain only has room for one thought.

More. I want more.

He wedges a knee between my thighs, and I part them as best as I can. Antonio makes a noise of impatience and yanks my skirt up to my waist before lifting my leg and wrapping it around his hip.

Oh wow. In this position, I can feel his erection pressing against me. My heart hammers in my chest. The feel of him, hot and thick... I'm a creature made of want. I'm wound so tight I'm going to explode.

He unbuttons my shirt and spreads it open. "So beautiful." His voice is soft, reverent. His eyes, though? His eyes are hot with need.

"It's an ugly bra."

"I wasn't talking about the bra."

I squirm on his knee as he palms my aching breasts, squeezing them hard. He pulls the bra cups aside and rolls my nipples between his fingers, making me arch in response.

"Please..." My nipples are tight, swollen buds. I need his mouth on them. I need—

He bends his dark head. His tongue circles my engorged nub, and I squirm again, impatient for more. He sucks them into his mouth, one after the other, and I whimper out loud. He takes a tender nipple between his teeth while his fingers pinch the other harder than before. Delicious pain winds down my body, and I gasp out loud.

That sound breaks the spell.

It's the middle of a workday. By now, everyone in the museum would have learned that I gave Antonio Moretti a private tour of the galleries. They know I left to have lunch with him. My colleagues aren't stupid. And now I'll be late getting back. If I don't show up for the rest of the day, everyone will talk. Not just in Venice. All over the world. The art world is small and extremely gossipy.

And nobody will take me seriously again. I'll be the woman who let the most notorious man in Venice seduce her. My skills and knowledge, everything I bring to the job, will be for naught.

I need to get out of here before I do something I'll regret. "I have to go," I gasp.

Antonio pulls back. His face is expressionless as he says, "I got carried away. My apologies."

Honesty compels me to speak. "I liked it." I

smooth down my skirt and hastily finger-comb my hair. "But it's the middle of a workday, and I need to get back."

"Ah." He crooks two fingers at me, just like he did in my dream. I move to him before I realize what I'm doing, and he buttons my top. "Who am I to keep you from the Palazzo Ducale?"

"Finally realizing your importance in the scheme of things, I see."

He laughs softly. "I'll see you soon, Lucia."

I almost tell him I'd like that, and then alarm bells start to ring. What am I doing? I'm getting sucked in. I'm letting myself fall for this guy.

Love only leads to heartbreak.

"No," I say harshly. "I'm not going to sleep with you. Don't call me. Don't drop by the museum unannounced and ask me to show you around. This thing, whatever it is, needs to stop."

LUCIA

Chapter Nine

I told Antonio to leave me alone. Did I expect him to call me anyway?

Yes, I did.

But he doesn't. Wednesday and Thursday go by with no word from him. On the first day, I'm hopeful. But on the second, I feel like a fool.

You asked him to stay away. He's respecting your boundaries. And you're annoyed by that? You are such a hypocrite.

Okay, I'll admit it. On some level, I thought he'd pursue me harder. He is a predator, and I'm prey, and I was enjoying the hunt. I wanted him to chase me.

Gah. I am such an idiot.

By the time Friday rolls around, I'm in a huge snit. When Giana Caputi, our department assistant, knocks on my office door, it takes everything I have not to snarl at her.

Then I notice the vase she's holding.

Flowers burst exuberantly from a blue-and-white ceramic vase in a riotous celebration of spring, filling my tiny office with their delicate aroma. The lilacs are white, the hyacinths pink. The honeysuckle is yellow, and the lavender adds pops of deep purple.

"These came for you while you were at lunch," she says, her eyes sparkling with curiosity. "But there wasn't a card."

A card isn't required; I know exactly who they're from. A smile spreads on my face as I

The Thief

inhale the scent of the blossoms. "Thank you, Giana."

"You also got this." She hands me a pale pink rectangular box tied with a silk ribbon. The logo is a string of pearls spilling from a seashell, and the words La Perla Nera are stamped on the bottom.

"La Perla Nera is a lingerie store," Giana tells me, her voice hushed. "A very expensive one. They see customers by appointment only." She's not brave enough to ask me who sent me the gift, though I can tell from her expression she dearly wants to.

"Thank you, Giana," I say again, taking the package from her. The department admin is the biggest gossip in the museum. By the end of the day, everyone will be speculating on who's sending me expensive underwear and flowers.

Giana lingers for another ten minutes, making small talk and hoping I'll reveal the identity of my mystery gift-giver, but I refuse to engage. Eventually, she departs in a huff. I shut the door behind her, lock it for good measure, and open the box.

Oh, wow.

I'm speechless as I carefully remove each piece from the tissue-wrapped packaging. There are four garments—a pair of panties, a bra, a camisole, and a robe—all made from lightweight, bottle-green silk trimmed with black lace.

The bra is a piece of art. The cups are green silk with a lace overlay, and the straps and elastic bands are covered with the same fabric. The panties are just as luxurious, crafted from the same exquisite silk with sheer lace across the hips. The camisole has lace cups and slits up both sides, and the robe is a masterpiece. Delicate lace outlines the neckline, cuffs, and hem. The silk fabric glimmers in the light, its glossy sheen coaxing me to stroke it.

I run my fingers over the robe, marveling at its softness. Each item has been crafted with staggering attention to detail. I've never been given a gift like this before. Never owned something so beautiful.

The Thief

And yet...

This isn't the kind of underwear a woman would wear on a daily basis.

No, this is lingerie a woman would wear for one reason and one reason only.

To drive a man mad with lust.

I told Antonio Moretti I wasn't going to sleep with him, but he's ignoring my words.

Isn't that what you wanted?

If I wore the lingerie, would he tug the panties off me with his teeth? Or would he rip the silk off my body with growly impatience?

A shiver of pure desire runs through me.

The flowers are beautiful, and I love them. But sending me lingerie as if my surrender was a foregone conclusion?

Hell, no.

I'm not going to let Antonio get away with this.

I take a ferry to Giudecca and march up to Antonio's house. Two guards intercept me before I can reach the front door. "This is a private residence, signorina," one of them says, his voice polite but firm.

"I know that," I snap. "I'm here to see Antonio Moretti."

The other man smirks. "And would Signor Moretti want to see you?"

"Oh, I'm quite sure he does." I'm hanging on to my temper by a hair. "Tell him Lucia Petrucci is here."

The instant they hear my name, their demeanor changes. The two men practically jump to attention. "Immediately, Signorina Petrucci," the first guard says, throwing the front door open. "Please, go in."

Umm, okay. The guards' reactions are *unexpected*.

What the hell am I getting myself into?

ANTONIO

Chapter Ten

"It's been an eventful week," I tell my lieutenants on Friday. Dante, Joao, Tomas, and Leo are here in person, and Valentina, who rarely attends these meetings, is logged in remotely at my request. "Ilya Kozlov is back in Vladivostok. He got back Wednesday."

"So that's it?" Joao asks. "He's going to accept your decision?"

"I doubt it. The Gafur OPS did not get to where

it is by taking no for an answer. This is merely the calm before the storm. Dante, alert our people in Padua, Verona, and Brescia. I want them on the lookout for the Russians."

"Brescia is practically on Verratti's doorstep," Dante says.

"And that's why I'm sending you," I reply. In the organization, Dante's nickname is the Broker. Nobody is better at making things happen than he is.

"Yes, padrino."

Matters are escalating. My attention should be focused on preparing for this upcoming war, but more often than not, I find myself wanting to talk to Lucia. My hands keep reaching for my phone, and I am constantly on the verge of dialing her number.

Like a lovesick fool.

I turn to my financial wizard. "Tomas, eliminate risk from our portfolios. We're about to be under attack, and it could come from anywhere."

My lieutenant looks less than thrilled. "We'll take some losses."

"Crippling losses?"

"No, but—"

"Do it, then. I'll leave the details to you. If war is coming, we'll need to be on as secure a financial footing as possible." I turn to my security expert. "Leo, alert the troops. I want everyone ready for open hostilities."

A disquieting thought strikes me. I visited Lucia at the Palazzo Ducale. We ate lunch together. If Gafur has eyes on me—and I have no reason to think they wouldn't—I've potentially identified her as a target.

"Put a team on Lucia as well."

Leo's eyebrows lift. "The thief?" He looks at my expression and quickly nods. "Yes, padrino. I'll personally see to it."

There's a knock at the door, and Goran sticks his head in. "I'm sorry to interrupt, padrino," he says. "But Lucia Petrucci is here to see you."

She is? What a happy coincidence. I get to my feet, anticipation prickling through me. "We're done for the day. Goran, please show Lucia in."

My lieutenants file out. A couple of minutes later, Goran ushers Lucia in. "Little thief." She glares at me, and my smile widens. "This is an unexpected pleasure."

"Sorry I interrupted your meeting," she says through clenched teeth.

"No need to apologize, tesoro. I always have time for you. Would you like a drink?"

"No." She thrusts the box she's carrying into my hands. "You sent lingerie to me at work. The department assistant handed this parcel to me, and she all but demanded to know who the sender was. What the fuck, Antonio?"

I close in on her. "Do you like it?" She smells of lavender and roses, soft and subtle, and her eyes radiate pure fire. A woman of dazzling contradictions, Lucia.

"That's not relevant."

"No? I think that's the only question that matters." I lift the slip out of the box and hold it up. "It matches the color of your eyes." I tug her to me and turn her around so her back is pressed against my chest. "Try it on," I whisper into her ear.

"Are you out of your mind?"

Holding her like this, my erection presses insistently against her ass. "You know you want to."

"I told you to leave me alone."

"Not exactly." I kiss her neck, and she sucks in a breath. "You told me not to call you." I nibble her earlobe. "You told me not to drop by the museum unannounced. I listened."

"That's a technicality, and you know it."

"So you marched over here to throw the lingerie in my face? Liar." Her nipples are hard, and her breathing is shallow. Her body betrays her. A gentleman would pretend he didn't notice, but nobody ever accused me of being one. "Admit it, little thief. You want me."

Her voice is defiant. "Not even if you were the last man in Venice."

She's here and spitting fire at me, her eyes flashing like brilliant emeralds and her voice hard as a diamond. But I'm not holding her captive. She's free to walk out anytime.

My little thief likes the chase.

"Now, now," I murmur into her ear, my hand wrapping around her neck. "Is that any way to talk to me?"

She inhales sharply.

"You barge in here unannounced," I continue. Her hair is up in a prim knot, and I pull the hairpins out, one by one, dropping them on the floor with a small clink until her glorious tresses hang free. "Interrupt my meeting." I kiss the beating vein in her neck and lick that silky spot. "Throw my gift back in my face." I nudge her jacket aside and cup her breast through her sweater. "You've been a bad girl, Lucia. Do you know what happens to bad girls?"

Her voice is a whisper threaded with need. "They get punished."

"They do." I lean in, gliding my thumb over her lower lip. "Now, do you like the lingerie?"

"I do," she breathes.

"Good girl." I reach into the box for the panties and hold them up in front of her face. "Try it on."

"Why?" she challenges. "Are you going to give me the painting if I do?"

I chuckle. "No, little thief. I'll do better. I'll sit you on this desk, spread your legs. . ." I push her until her ass hits my desk, and then I hoist her up on the wooden surface and nudge her thighs apart. "And lick your pretty little pussy until you come."

She bites her lower lip. "And if I don't obey?"

"You'll leave here without an orgasm."

"I have fingers," she throws back. "I can take care of my own needs."

She's bluffing—she has no intention of leaving.

But so am I. Because I *have* to taste her. I *need* her to come on my tongue.

"Yes, you'll take care of yourself." I slide my hand up her thigh. Her legs fall open, the fabric of her skirt bunching around her hips. "But tell me, tesoro. Will you be satiated?"

She glares at me. "So arrogant."

"Guilty as charged." Leaning in, I cover her mouth with mine. I nibble her lower lip and lick the seam, demanding entrance. She parts her lips *and fuck*. She tastes like ambrosia, like the best kind of dark chocolate. Lush and delicious, with a hint of sweetness.

Addictive.

I palm her pussy. Her panties are drenched with her arousal. Hot male satisfaction explodes inside me. "And I think you like it."

She levels another glare at me but spreads her legs wider. I smother a grin. My sweet little thief is dying to be fucked. "You want this, tesoro? You know what to do."

The Thief

"Fine," she huffs. She slides off the table and lifts her sweater over her head. Underneath, she's wearing an ivory silk shirt, the fabric translucent, so I can clearly see the outline of her bra underneath.

She's so beautiful. The moon in a starless night sky, the quiet eye of a hurricane.

She reaches behind her back and undoes the button on her waistband. She starts to lower the zipper and looks up at me, an irresistible smile dancing at the corner of her lips. "Turn around."

"Shy?"

"Anticipation is the best foreplay, Antonio."

She has no idea. "I've been anticipating this moment for ten years."

She sucks in a breath, her eyes huge. "You can't say something like that to me," she whispers.

She's right. I can't. I *shouldn't*. I'm used to being in control, maintaining a poker face, and never revealing more than is strictly necessary. But with Lucia, everything is unexpected. I'm putty in her hands.

"What would you prefer I say?" I turn away. I'm not protecting her modesty; we both know I'm going to have her naked in minutes. No, this is for one reason and one reason only.

I need to shield myself.

"Should I tell you that if you aren't wearing those panties in the next minute, I'm going to bend you over my desk and spank that round little ass of yours?"

She doesn't reply, not immediately. Fabric falls to the floor in a rustle, and I spend a futile minute wishing for mirrors on the walls. "Okay, you can look now."

I turn around, and my cock turns into steel. She's wearing the panties and nothing else. Her breasts are perfect. Round and firm, her nipples are puckered and begging for my mouth.

"Show me." My voice comes out hoarse. "Turn around."

She does a little twirl, and my mouth goes dry. The moment I saw them in the store window, I knew the panties were perfect for Lucia. They're short enough that the curves of her ass cheeks peek out from underneath the fabric. She looks naughty, sassy, and completely fucking hot.

I'm practically drooling.

"I believe I owe you a reward." I crook two fingers at her. "Come here."

I lift her back onto the desk. Spread her legs. Suck those pertly puckered nipples into my mouth, lap them with the flat of my tongue, and scrape them with my teeth. Her skin is like satin, smooth and impossibly soft, and I could do this all day.

Except I keep catching tantalizing glimpses of her pussy, and I can't resist. Not much longer.

Pushing the gusset of her panties aside, I dip down and lick her. Fuck me, the way she tastes. Like honey and caramel and sin.

I lift her feet off the floor and place them flat on the table to give me better access to her slick folds. She's wet already, wet for me. "You like this, tesoro," I murmur, placing a kiss on her inner thigh. "You want me to chase you. To hunt you." I catch her clit between my lips, and her head falls back, eyes squeezing shut. A smothered moan escapes her clenched teeth. "Why not ask for what you want?"

I lean down and swipe her silky folds with my tongue, then lightly spank her pussy. She hisses and thrusts her hips into my face. Yes. I fight the urge to pull my cock out and plunge into her softness. Not yet. First, I promised her an orgasm.

"I should punish you," I growl. I slide a finger into her, and her muscles clamp tight around me. I slowly circle her clit with my tongue, and her breathing quickens.

She's slick and ready. Her thighs tremble as I increase the intensity, licking her clit with focused attention, adding another finger and thrusting. "Please," she groans, squirming. "Antonio. . ."

Hearing her moan my name is an aphrodisiac unlike no other.

"Please." She arches her back, pushing closer to

my face. I suck her clit between my lips, lashing at it roughly with my tongue. Her breathing is heavy, and her cheeks flushed. I run my hand up her leg, needing to touch her as she falls over the edge. My cock is pulsing with need, but I ignore it and focus on her pleasure, licking her over and over and thrusting into her with my fingers.

"Oh God," she cries out as she comes, her body writhing on my desk.

I'm *never* going to be able to work here without remembering her scent in my nostrils, her taste on my tongue.

Her thighs tighten around my head, and I push my fingers deep into her, twisting around to find her G-spot and doing my best to prolong her orgasm. I continue to lick gently until her shockwaves die down. I give her pussy one last kiss and straighten.

She's so beautiful, lying back on my desk. Her chest rises and falls as her breathing steadies. I kiss the curve of her shoulder. She looks hot and sweaty and satiated, strands of her hair clinging to her forehead. I fight the temptation to stroke them, to kiss her forehead, to drag her into my arms and never let go.

"Stay for dinner." It's phrased as a statement, but it's really a request. A plea.

She looks tempted, but she shakes her head. "I have to go." She straightens, her eyes resting on my erection. "But first, I need to return the favor."

Something sours inside me. She *needs* to return the favor. As if it's all tit for tat. Full, complete reciprocity. We're keeping score like sharp-tongued vendors at the market.

I hate it.

Lucia is willing to march in here to give me a piece of her mind. She'll happily moan out her pleasure and come on my tongue. But she won't eat a meal with me. Her answer is what I expected, but her rejection still stings. "No, you don't," I say curtly. "If you're done, leave. I have a meeting to get back to."

There's a flash of hurt in her eyes, making me

The Thief

feel like a complete asshole. Then the hurt changes to anger. "Fine," she snaps, jumping to her feet. "I'm leaving."

She tears the panties off her body as if they're made of sandpaper and dresses quickly in her clothes.

This time, I don't turn away. A better man would apologize, but what comes out of my mouth is, "Don't forget your lingerie."

"Fuck you."

"You can either take it, or it goes in the trash."

She gives me a truly poisonous glare. "You are such an asshole," she spits out. Grabbing the box of lingerie off my table, she sweeps out.

Leaving me in my office, my mouth smeared with her juices, with the realization that I want more.

More than the pleasure I coaxed out of her.

More than a grudging orgasm.

I want *everything*.

Damn it all to hell.

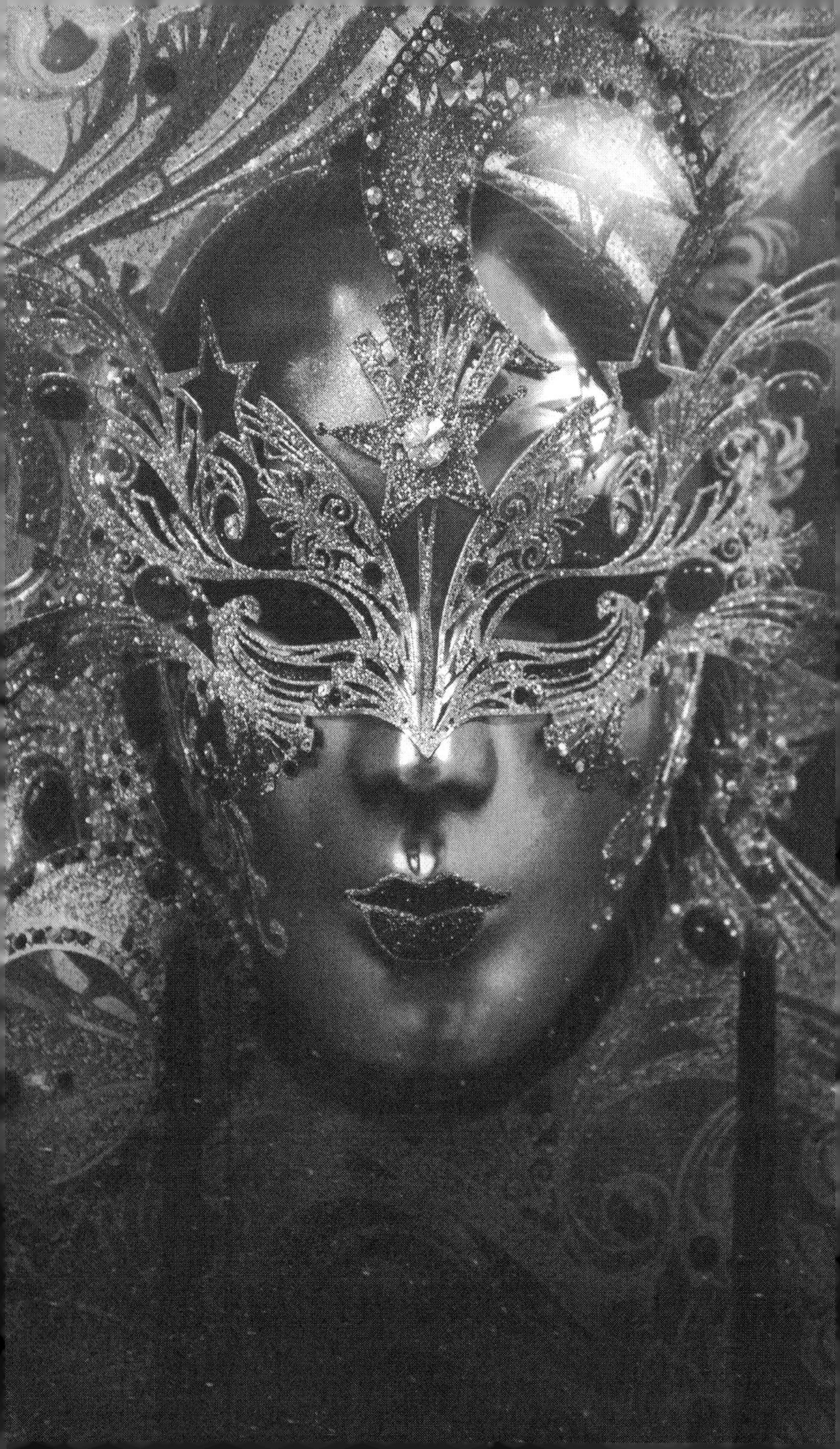

LUCIA

Chapter Eleven

I wake up Saturday feeling completely flat.

Walking away from Antonio yesterday evening was the right thing to do, but it doesn't feel that way. Instead, I'm struggling with the sense that I stomped on a frail seedling before it could grow into a beautiful flower.

It doesn't help that I wake up to an empty apartment. It seems like a metaphor for my life, bare and devoid of warmth. The only color in the place comes from Antonio's overflowing vase of flowers.

A blue-and-white ceramic vase, similar to the ones I admired in his house.

He bought me lingerie that matched the color of my eyes. I walked in on his meeting, and instead of being annoyed, he told me he always had time for me. Then he lifted me on his desk, spanked my pussy, and brought me to a screaming orgasm.

Damn it.

I'm finding it difficult to remember why I can't get involved with him. Fantasy Antonio is giving way to the real man; the trouble is that the real-life Antonio is alarmingly attractive.

He threw you out of his office.

Yes, he did. But only after I turned down his dinner invitation. Maybe I should be angry with him, but I know why he did it. After all, I'm an expert on self-preservation, on pulling away before someone hurts you.

If I had stayed, would we have fucked? Would I have spent the night in his bed? In his arms? Earlier this week, he invited me to the antique

The Thief

market. If I had stayed, would we have gone to the Piazzola sul Brenta together?

You're wallowing, Lucia. Enough. You made the right decision.

I jump out of bed, shower quickly, and trek to the farmer's market. My refrigerator is empty, and I'm determined to fix that. I might not have any furniture, but there's no reason I can't eat well.

I call Valentina on the way there to find out if she wants to join me, but her phone goes directly to voicemail. I leave her a message and dedicate myself to finding bread, vegetables, and, most importantly, wine.

It is a sunny day, clear, cold, and crisp. The market is busy, everyone taking advantage of the good weather. Young couples hold hands as they shop. Children dart between stalls. Mothers push strollers. Scenes of domesticity are everywhere.

My parents were happily married, and as a teenager, I always assumed I would be too. But when my parents died, I swore off love and avoided relationships. I never want to be as vulnerable, as broken as I was in the aftermath of their deaths.

But being back in Venice is disconcerting. Now that I'm home, I'm questioning my life choices. Meeting Antonio again makes me wonder what would happen if I let myself get involved with him.

A bouquet of out-of-season white roses catches my eye, and I stop to smell them. The vendor gives me a persuasive smile. "They're beautiful, aren't they?"

"They are. But too expensive for me." A fresh-faced young man is studying the flowers seriously, his expression thoughtful. Maybe buying something for his sweetheart and trying to decide what she'd like best?

I pass on the roses but get a small ivy plant in a yellow container. I head home to drop off my groceries and go to the antique market.

Alone.

Stealing a painting would snap me out of my

The Thief

funk. I looked at Valentina's list of targets, but nothing jumped out at me. I'm mildly tempted to steal Arthur Kincaid's entire Nazi-looted art collection, but even I know that's ambitious. That particular job requires a lot more planning.

Time is ticking by. It's the middle of November. I always steal a painting between November and February, but I haven't even identified who I'm going after this year. I'm letting myself get distracted by Antonio Moretti.

I wander through the market aimlessly, my thoughts churning. I'm tempted to buy a pair of hand-carved wooden and leather chairs from Morocco, but the price makes me change my mind. Same with a black and white rug. I linger over a pair of blue ceramic candlesticks but don't buy them either. What's the point? I'm not staying in Venice. I'll be gone by February.

My eyes keep returning to a painting of a red vase with yellow flowers. While I need furniture urgently, not art, I find myself buying it. I'm shaking my head at my folly as I walk out of the store.

That's when I notice something. The fresh-faced young man I saw at the farmer's market is here. He's paying for a cup of coffee at a nearby stall.

The hair on the back of my neck stands up. What are the odds? Following a hunch, I duck into a small restaurant and linger over my meal. An hour later, I emerge into the square.

He's still there. This time, he's examining a pair of shoes at an outdoor stall with a frown.

He's *tailing* me.

And only one person has a reason to have me followed.

Antonio Moretti.

A hot flash of anger surges through me. He told me to leave his office yesterday. How dare he put a tail on me? He's going to regret this. The gloves are coming off.

I quickly formulate a plan and then make a

The Thief

beeline for my tail. "Hi," I say brightly.

Consternation flashes over his face. "Signorina?"

"You work for Antonio, right? We had lunch plans at Quadri, but he's running a little late." I give him my most charming smile. "He told me to meet him at his house. Agnese is away, but Antonio said one of his people could let me in?"

The man responds just as I'm hoping he would. "Of course, Signorina Petrucci. I would be happy to escort you to Signor Moretti's home."

His name is Ignazio. He takes me to Antonio's house. A man comes up as he approaches the door. The two have a hurried, low-voiced discussion, and Ignazio turns to me. "Signor Moretti is not home," he says apologetically. "Stefano thinks he's in a meeting."

Everyone wants to feel like they are helping their boss out. Ignazio is young. Chances are, he's keen and eager to make a difference, and I'm going to take advantage.

I glance at my phone as if I'm reading a text

from Antonio. "Yeah, he's just finishing up." I do an exaggerated shiver. "I'll wait for him inside."

As I expected, Ignazio lets me in out of the cold. Poor kid. He's probably going to get into trouble, and I feel a little bad about it, but not enough to abandon my plan.

As soon as Antonio's front door shuts behind me, I hurry to his bedroom. I can't count on having too much time. Ignazio might be naive and easily fooled, but the other guy, Stefano, looked more alert. If Antonio doesn't show up in the next few minutes, he might even call him to check on my story. I need to grab the Titian and get the hell out of here.

As a happy coincidence, the painting I bought today is roughly the same size as the Titian. With a rueful grimace—I really did like the colors—I hang it in place of the *Madonna at Repose*. I hastily wrap the sixteenth-century masterpiece in protective packaging, then hurry out.

I've made no attempt to be sneaky. Antonio will

The Thief

know I'm responsible for the theft. But it doesn't matter. I'll stop home to grab my employee badge and then head straight to the museum. Once the painting is safely ensconced at the Palazzo Ducale, Antonio can kick and scream all he wants, but short of stealing it again, there's not a damn thing he can do about it.

Thirty minutes later, after an excruciatingly slow ferry ride from Giudecca, I climb the stairs to my apartment. I open the front door, grinning in triumph at my successful heist.

"Lucia," Antonio says, his voice silken. "If you wanted to see me again, sweet thief, all you had to do was ask."

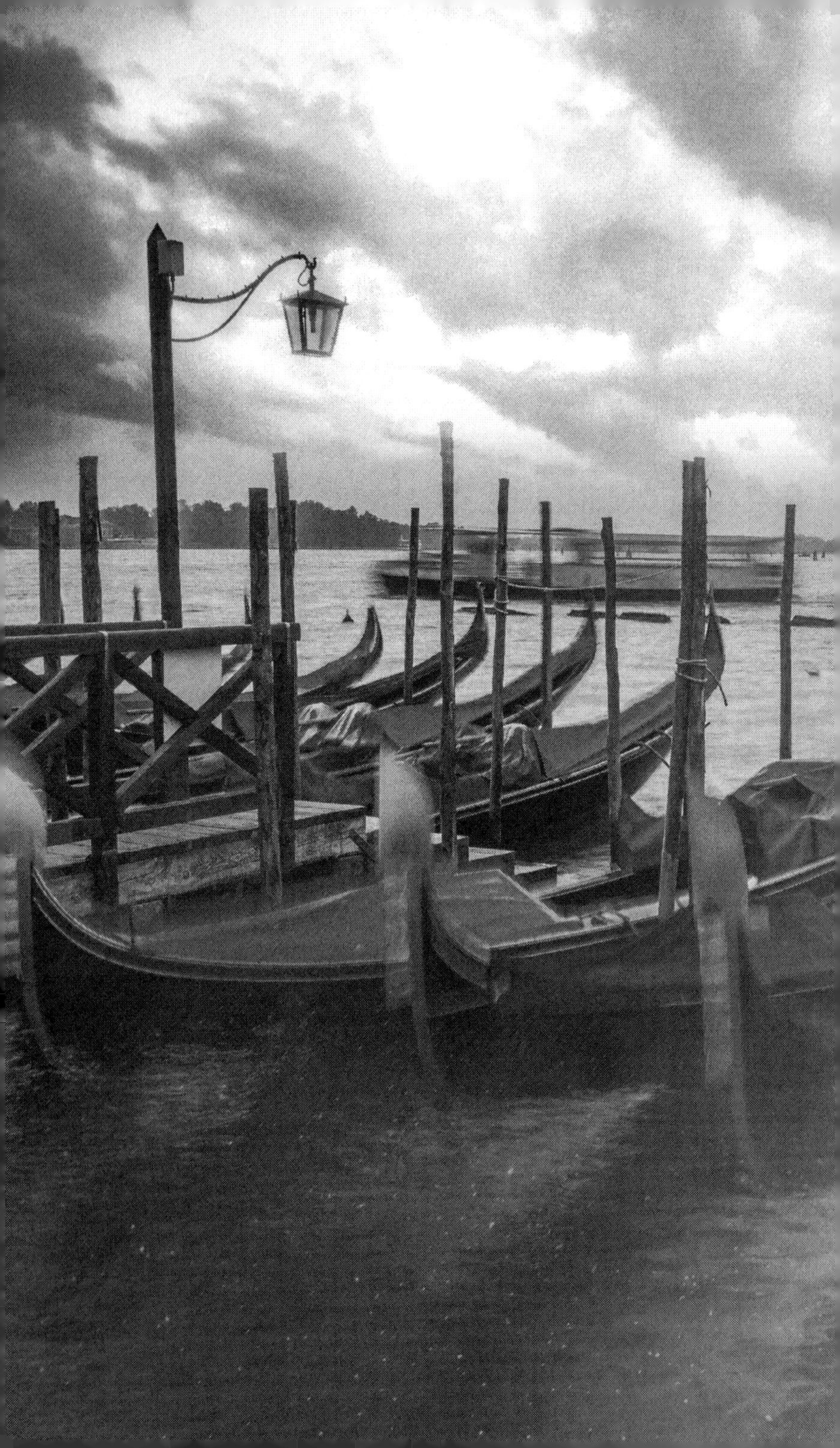

ANTONIO

Chapter Twelve

"What the hell are you doing in my apartment?" she demands. "How did you get in?"

Fuck me, she is stunning. Her cheeks are pink, her eyes shine like gems, and her hair cascades down her shoulders in glorious waves. Add in her crimson coat, and she looks like fire.

And she's going to burn you alive.

I remove my jacket and toss it on the room's only chair. "Your neighbor let me into the building, and I picked your front door's lock." I make a mental note to get Leo to upgrade her security. My thieving days are long behind me, but it was still laughably easy to enter her apartment.

"I should call the police."

I laugh out loud. "And how are you going to explain my painting in your bag? Are you planning on telling them you took it from my bedroom?" I shake my head. "I thought we reached an understanding about the Titian, tesoro. What brought on this attempt?"

"We didn't have an understanding about the Titian," she snaps. "And you put a tail on me. That's both creepy and invasive. What the fuck, Antonio?"

Ah. "A few weeks ago, I was approached by a member of the Russian mafia. They wanted to smuggle weapons through Venice. I said no."

I start to unknot my tie. "As much as I'd like to hope otherwise, that's not the end of things. We're preparing for war." I meet her gaze squarely. "You are important to me, Lucia. If something were to happen to you, I would react poorly." Talk about a fucking understatement. "We've been seen together in public. Your building has no security. Your upstairs neighbors are a couple in their eighties. Your downstairs neighbor works in Switzerland during ski season. His apartment is presently empty. You're an easy target. The security detail is for your protection."

"Oh." She digests my answer. "And this has nothing to do with yesterday—"

"If you're asking me if I assign a security detail to the women I sleep with, the answer is no. It's not usually dangerous to date me."

"I haven't slept with you."

"Yet." I undo my cuffs and roll up my sleeves. "I should have told you about Ignazio, but I didn't get a chance yesterday. I'm sorry about that." My voice hardens. "However, if you want me to apologize for worrying about your safety, that's not going to happen. I'm never going to apologize for protecting you. Not ten years ago, not now."

Her eyes track the movement of my hands. "What are you doing?"

My lips curl up. "I warned you there would be consequences if you tried to steal my painting." I start to unbutton my shirt. "Remember, Lucia?"

"You're going to fuck me. Whether I want it or not."

I roll my eyes. "Is that what you're telling yourself? That you don't want this?" I nod toward her front door. "I'm not stopping you from leaving. I'm not trapping you in here." I toss my shirt aside. "Stay with honesty, little thief, or go."

LUCIA

Chapter Thirteen

I *hate* him.

I *want* him.

Antonio drives me insane.

I can't let him walk out of here.

"This is my apartment," I spit out. "You're the one who should be leaving."

Antonio isn't a fool; he recognizes the consent in my words. His eyes turn hot. "Come here."

I step toward him, and the king of Venice closes

the gap between us.

He slams me against the wall. My back digs into the stucco, but I don't care. His fingers lace with mine, and he transfers his grip to my wrists, lifting my hands above my head and caging me in with the hard press of his body. His mouth finds mine, then he drags his lips down my neck, kissing the hollow of my throat, his lips warm against my skin. "Tell me why you're here," he breathes.

Because I ache for you. "I wasn't aware I had a choice in the matter," I say instead.

He nips my earlobe. "Liar," he says. His gaze rakes down my body, hot and searing. "Your nipples are hard." He shoves a knee between my thighs. "If I thrust my fingers into your cunt, I bet I'll find you wet, ready for my cock. Try again. Tell me what you want."

So smug. I *hate* the way my body responds to him. He makes me lose control, shreds my walls with laughable ease, and I *hate* how he makes me feel.

Hate it and *love* it, all in one.

Some of what I'm feeling must show on my face. Antonio laughs under his breath. "Is it so hard to ask for what you need?"

Yes. Because it's not just his cock that I want. I'm greedy for *him*. I want his attention. When he says he's been waiting for me for ten years, I want to believe him so badly it's terrifying.

I wriggle away from Antonio, shrug free of my jacket, and pull my sweater over my head. My T-shirt and bra follow. "Are you planning on fucking me, or are you just going to stand here and *talk*?"

His eyes blaze. I think I've provoked him for a split second, but then his lips quirk into a half-smile. He steps closer, close enough to obliterate the boundaries between us. Close enough that I don't know where he ends and I start.

My pulse pounds with anticipation and adrenaline. Antonio presses his lips to my neck, licking that fluttering vein. "I see you," he murmurs. "Your pulse is racing. You're nervous.

And it's not because you're trapped here. You know just as well as I do that if you wanted to leave, I wouldn't stop you."

I do know that. Whatever else he's capable of, whatever else he might do, he would never take me by force. Even now, when I slithered out of his grasp to take my shirt off, I didn't have to fight free. He let me go.

"That's not what you're afraid of," he continues. His hand cups my throat, and his stubble scrapes against my skin as he leans in to whisper. "You're nervous because you sense what I've known from the first time I kissed you." He unfastens the button of my jeans and lowers the zipper. Hooking his fingers in the waistband of my panties, he tugs both jeans and panties down in one fluid stroke. "This is not just sex. This is *more*."

My nipples are two aching peaks. A familiar heat blooms between my legs. I can pretend I'm unaffected by Antonio, but my body sends him a very different message.

"Shut up and fuck me."

"So demanding." He laughs under his breath. "Say please."

I like watching Antonio laugh. He's criminally sexy. Dangerously disruptive to my peace of mind. "You wish."

Pushing away from me, he takes off his belt. I don't move. I stay where I am, pressed against the wall, the sight of his taut muscles robbing the breath from my lungs.

He presses a finger into me, and I bite back a whimper. I was damp when I opened the door and saw him in my living room. Wet when he sternly told me there were consequences to stealing from him. Now, I'm *soaked*. It takes all my self-control not to push into his hand and press my aching pussy into him.

He holds his fingers in front of my face. They shine with the proof of my traitorous body's response. "I won't ask again, Lucia."

This time, there's a hard edge in his voice. What

would happen if I stayed defiant? Would he put me over his knee and spank me? But no, he knows I'd like that too much.

Or would he pull back entirely? Put his shirt back on and leave?

That thought sends a spike of fear through me. There's being stubborn, which I am, and being stupid, which I'm not. "Please, fuck me, Antonio."

His response is a low growl of approval. "Spread your legs, tesoro," he orders, cupping my breast and squeezing. "Open your mouth. Suck your wetness from my fingers."

His touch is like fire, and every time he lays a hand on me, I burn from the inside out.

Heat rushes through me as I spread my legs, exposing myself to him. I take his fingers into my mouth, tasting my desire on his skin. His eyes are dark with lust as he watches me lick him clean.

My own arousal grows, need building to a crescendo. I want more. I want him, and I want him now.

The Thief

He can read the desperation on my face. A smile brushes across his lips as he leans in close. "I'm going to fuck you now, Lucia," he says, his voice low and husky. "I'm going to pull out my cock and fuck you against this wall. Right here, right now."

"Yes," I pant. "Please."

His lips meet mine in a hungry kiss as he frees his erection. He gets a condom from his wallet and rolls it on, lifts my leg around his waist to pull me closer, and thrusts into me.

Every nerve in my body comes alive. With one hand, he holds my wrists in place above my head. He slams into me again, raw passion on his face. Each stroke is deep and brutal, and I choke back a gasp. My naked back scrapes against the stucco, and I don't care.

I wrap my leg around him and bring him closer. He's bottoming out with every stroke. Hitting my cervix. The sharp pain blends with the pleasure until I can't tell them apart. This is raw, animalistic passion.

It terrifies me.

I love it.

He grips my hips and shoves deep. His hand, the one that isn't holding my wrists prisoner, snakes between my legs. He finds my swollen, aching clit and pinches, and I gasp again, digging my nails into my palm to keep from screaming. A shiver of pleasure runs down my spine, making my toes curl.

"Lie to me," he demands, his voice low and husky. "Tell me you don't feel this." He thrusts deep. I'm swollen, aching, and a hair's breadth away from exploding. His mouth swallows my next gasp, his lips meeting mine in a hungry kiss. "Tell me this isn't special."

I don't form attachments. I can't—I can't afford the cost. When this ends—and it *will* end—it will shatter my already fragile heart.

Yet I can't find the words to tell him this doesn't matter. I can't pretend this doesn't affect me as deeply as it affects him.

The Thief

I can't lie that well. I'm not that good at pretending.

Antonio stares into my eyes, searching for the answers my mouth won't give him. His finger taps my clit, each touch sending a live current jerking through me. This time, he doesn't thrust—he pushes into me with deliberate slowness.

I stay stubbornly silent.

A smile tugs at the corners of his mouth. He leans in closer, his breath warm against my ear. "You don't have to say it, cara mia," he says. "I can see it in your eyes. The way you look at me, the way you respond to my touch."

He pulls out almost entirely before pushing in again. His finger makes a lazy circle around my clit, and then another. A shiver rolls through me. My body is on fire. I'm on the edge of release, swollen with need, shuddering with desire.

He doesn't let me come.

"Know this, though." He pulls out and slams into me. Hard. Powerful. Demanding. "I'm not the boy next door. I'm not sweet, and I'm not nice. What I am, Lucia, is ruthless in my desires." Another thrust. "I'm single-minded about what I want." His fingers strum my clit, playing me like a fine-tuned instrument. "And what I want is you."

His words are like lightning. Sizzling. Deadly. I'm shivering. Shaking. Every cell in my body is alive with the need for release.

"I'll ask you just once. If you don't want me, tell me to back off."

This is it. My out. I know Antonio will respect my wishes. He's not interested in my forced submission.

No, what he wants is far more dangerous.

He wants me. No doubts, no reservations. No obscured truths, no veiled lies.

He wants *everything*.

Antonio Moretti is not good for my peace of mind. But I can't make myself pull away. Precious little sanity remains because right here and right now, I want him to own every part of me.

The Thief

If I had any sense, I'd say no, but once again, *I stay silent.*

Another smile ghosts across his face. "Good," he says harshly. He lets go of my wrists and traces a finger down my cheek. His touch is gentle, almost tender, a stark contrast to his tone. "No closing your eyes, cara mia. Look at me when you come."

And then he's kissing me, deep and sweet, his tongue stroking mine in a rhythm that mirrors the pace of his thrusts. His hands are on my breasts, tweaking and tormenting my nipples. I can feel him everywhere; my body is melded to his. His scent. His taste. His strength.

He's a drug. A fever. An addiction. And he's consuming me.

His thrusts grow faster. More brutal. His fingers stroke my clit, and he buries his face in my neck, licking and biting me until I'm panting and moaning, lost in a sea of sensation and desire, crazy with the scent of Antonio in my lungs.

My orgasm barrels towards me with the force of a hurricane. My body trembles, and my muscles tighten, clenching with anticipation. It's so close... It's right there...

And then I'm coming apart in his arms. Thrashing, bucking, arching myself up and grinding my hips against his.

"That's it," Antonio growls, looking deep into my eyes, his stare burning through me like wildfire. "Take it all. Show me how much you want this. Show me how much you need it."

His thrusts speed up as he finds his own release. "Lucia," he says, a guttural sound of raw pleasure. I cling to him as I ride the aftershocks of my orgasm, my vision blurry and my body trembling.

Antonio wraps his arms around me and holds me close. We stay silent until the last shudders of pleasure fade away. When I finally pull away, his eyes linger on me, heavy with satisfaction. He reaches out and strokes my cheek with his thumb, the gesture both possessive and strangely tender.

I want to melt into that embrace, and that desire finally gives me the jolt of panic I need.

I thought I was going to get fucked into oblivion. But he gave me more than that. He didn't just give me his lust; he gave me passion. He didn't utter meaningless compliments; he gave me honesty. He didn't just fuck me; he offered precious intimacy.

He held nothing back.

It's so much more than I'm ready for.

But isn't this what you wanted? You weren't really annoyed about the bodyguard. You were just looking for an excuse to see him again. You didn't steal the Titian with the noble intention of returning it to the museum—you knew Antonio would make good on his promise. You wanted the chase.

But now that I've gotten a taste of Antonio, I'm addicted. We didn't even make it into the bedroom, and I'm already in trouble.

He notices me stiffen and watches me with

careful eyes. "The bathroom is down the hall," I mutter, avoiding his gaze.

"So I should clean up and leave?" A wry smile touches his lips as he pulls out the condom and ties it in a knot. "And here I thought you would invite me to spend the night."

He heads to my bathroom. When he emerges, his pants are zipped. A pang shoots through my heart, but I hold on to my panic. I have to throw him out before it's too late. He has to leave before he can break my heart.

He puts on his shirt, knots his tie, and slips his jacket over his shoulders.

"What about the painting?" I burst out and immediately wish I could take back the question. What the hell is wrong with me? Am I so bothered that he's leaving—a thing I asked him to do—that I'm reminding him about the Titian? "Aren't you going to take it?"

He shakes his head, an odd gleam in his eyes. "If I take back the painting, you'll make another attempt to steal it. Then what? I come over here and fuck you?" He fixes his gaze on me. "This game between us is entertaining," he says. "But the next move will have to come from you. You have my phone number, Lucia. If you want to see me again, call me."

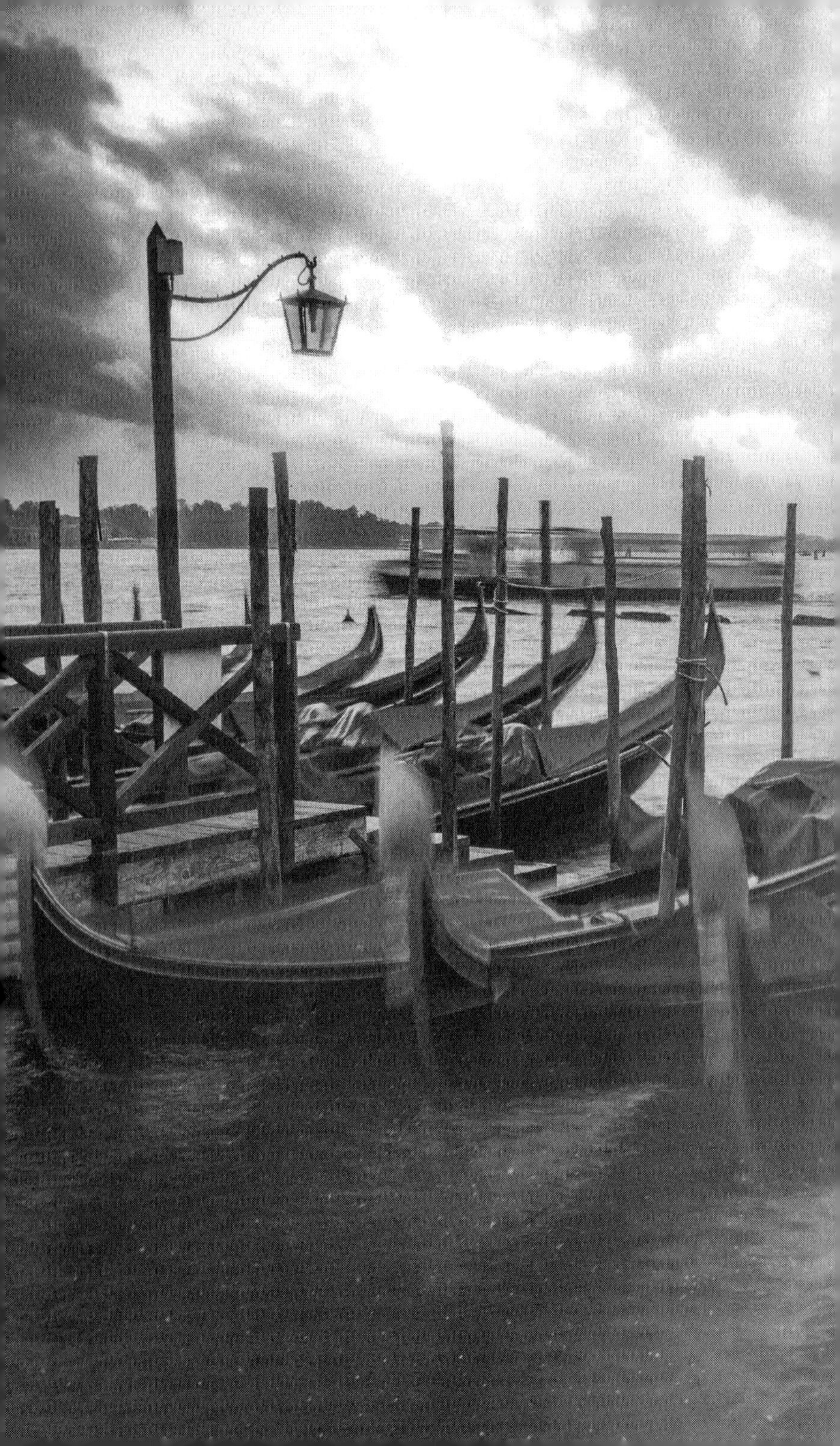

ANTONIO

Chapter Fourteen

For the first time, my house feels empty and alone. The objects I bought because they brought me pleasure feel like clutter. The bright, vivid colors around me fade as if worn out by spending too long in front of a strong sun.

Because of Lucia.

Her refusal to let me in settles in my gut like a lead weight. Tomas calls me with some questions about finances. I answer him on autopilot. When I hang up, I have no memory of what we discussed.

Dante reports on a conversation he had with an informant in Bergamo, and Valentina sends me an email detailing her efforts to track the Russians. I listen, I respond, and I do what's necessary. Normally, these details exhilarate me.

This evening, though, the walls feel like they're closing in on me, and I need to escape. Get some air.

I head outside. The moment I shut my front door, Rafe and Andreas fall into step behind me. Impatiently, I wave them away, and the men recede. They'll still follow me—Leo will have their hide if they leave me unprotected—but at least I can maintain the illusion that I'm alone.

I take my boat to Venice and walk for a couple of hours, maybe more, without a destination in mind. The night descends, and the fog deepens. Lights still shine behind cheerful cafes and vinotecas, but the streets are empty. Just the way I want it.

Eventually, my footsteps take me to the docks where, ten years ago, Lucia stumbled into my life.

There's chemistry between us. This afternoon's events play in a non-stop reel in my head, and my cock hardens in memory. That first thrust into her hot, wet cunt. Her moans. The curve of her neck as she threw her head back. The glazed expression of pleasure in her eyes as she came on my cock.

The shock that ran up my spine at the rightness of it all.

Ten years ago, the drunk girl about to fall into one of Venice's many canals hadn't avoided emotion. She'd been honest and raw. Splayed open and grief-stricken, but oh-so-real.

But in the intervening years, she's learned to protect herself.

I told her that if she wanted to see me again, she should call me.

Will she?

I doubt it.

Lucia's not blind to the attraction between us.

If I offered her something temporary and uncomplicated, she would accept. Like today, I know the sex would be off-the-charts amazing.

But *temporary* and *uncomplicated* is not what I want.

On an intellectual level, I can understand why she's keeping me at arm's length. Why she's so resistant to letting herself feel the connection between us. She's been hurt before and doesn't want to get involved.

My head is telling me to protect myself. Stop throwing myself at her. Follow through on my grand speech and leave her the fuck alone.

But my heart knows differently.

I have a reputation as a cold, controlled bastard. I'm not Domenico Cartozzi. I don't act on impulse. I don't swing wildly between moods, terrifying the people around me. I'm ruthless, yes, but I'm always logical.

But I've followed my heart in every pivotal moment of my life.

When I stopped Marco's abortive mugging of a drunk young woman on these very docks, even

The Thief

though everyone else turned a blind eye to his wild excesses.

When I gave him an ultimatum—leave Venice or else—even though he was the Padrino's nephew. His precious *nipote*.

When I spent the night in Lucia's hotel room, lying awake in the dark next to her sleeping body because I couldn't ignore the plea in her eyes when she whispered that she didn't want to be alone.

My heart knows what it wants. It knows that Lucia is precious, and the thing between us is rare.

Self-preservation be damned; I'm not going to let go that easily. This is the most important battle of my life, and I intend to win.

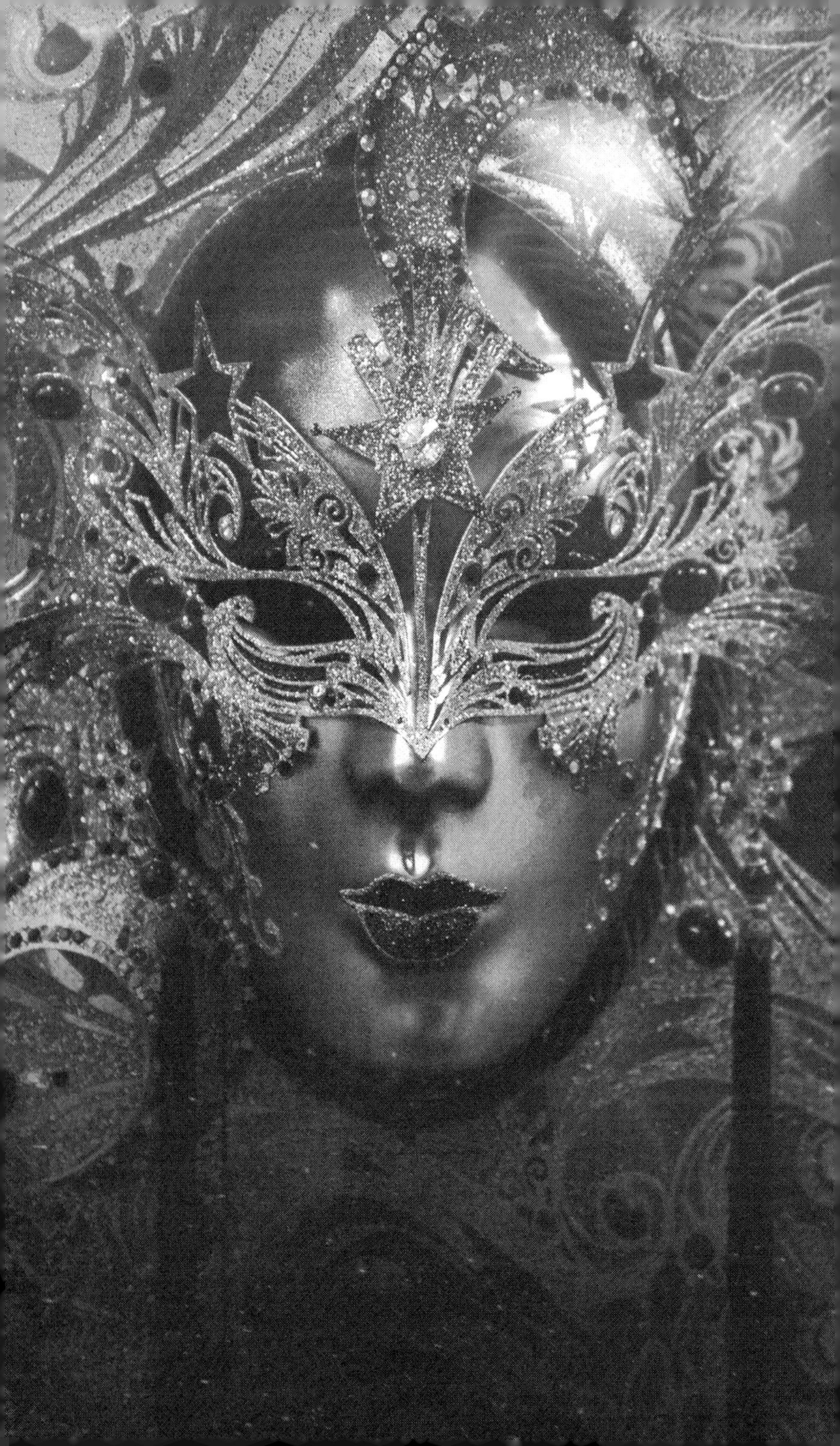

LUCIA

Chapter Fifteen

Valentina calls me back an hour after Antonio leaves. "I just got your message," she says. "Sorry, I didn't hear my phone. Are you still at the market?"

"No, I'm back home." I stare at the Titian on my wall. I should be triumphant about my successful heist, but I feel flat. *Again.*

The next move will have to come from you.

"What are you doing this Thursday? Do you have plans with Antonio?"

"Why would I have plans with Antonio?"

"Oh, come on," she says teasingly. "You marched into his house yesterday, and he dropped everything to be with you. And if that wasn't enough, Stefano told me you were at his house today as well, and, once again, Antonio interrupted a meeting and tore halfway across town to intercept you. Are the two of you an item now?"

As much as I want to tell Valentina everything, my best friend is a secret romantic. If I tell her about the last couple of days, she'll be planning our wedding.

"We are not," I say repressively. "I already told you—I have no intention of getting involved with Antonio. The only thing I'm doing on Thursday is my laundry."

"In that case," she says, sounding like she's smothering a laugh. "Want to go to a sex club with me?"

What? My mouth falls open. "Did you just say sex club?"

"Yes," she says, as if a sex club is a perfectly

normal place to go on a Thursday night. "I'm a member of Casanova. Angelica is having her second sleepover at her new best friend's house, which, after her bullying woes, seems like a reason to celebrate. I was so delighted when she asked me for permission that I didn't even care if it was a school night. Want to go with me?"

My brain is still stuck on *sex club*. As far as I know, Valentina hasn't dated since Angelica was born. I once asked her how she managed without sex, and she told me she had an outlet for that. I thought she meant a vibrator like the rest of us, but evidently, no.

Every day, I learn something new.

"Of course, if you don't think you should, because of your relationship with Antonio..." Her voice trails off suggestively.

I think of how bereft I felt when he left, how I've been staring moodily at the Titian propped against my bedroom wall for the last hour instead of returning it to the Palazzo Ducale.

"I have no relationship with Antonio," I say harshly. "Let's go to your sex club. What's the dress code?"

ANTONIO

Chapter Sixteen

Thursday evening, I'm having another meeting with Tomas when Dante walks into my office. "Sorry to interrupt," he says. "Tomas, can you give me a minute alone with the padrino?"

My senses go on high alert. Dante never pulls this kind of stuff. When the door closes behind us, I ask, "Kozlov?"

"No, something else." He hesitates.

"Spit it out, Dante."

He takes a deep breath. "It's about Casanova. Today is Thursday." His voice is flat. "Valentina just walked into the club."

Ah. Dante and Valentina have a complicated relationship. On the surface, the two of them are unfailingly polite to each other and work well as a team. But there are undercurrents between them. Roberto, the father of Valentina's child, was Dante's brother, but Dante had no idea at the time about the abuse Valentina suffered at Roberto's hands. And when he found out the truth...

Nobody knows what happened the night Roberto died. The official story from the Carabinieri was that there was a tussle between Roberto and another man, and Roberto's gun went off. His death was ruled an accident.

The other man, the one the Carabinieri didn't name? It was Dante. Was the death an accident? I've never asked, and Dante has never said.

Valentina credits me with rescuing her from

Roberto, but it's not me she needs to thank.

My second-in-command has always been a little in love with Valentina. But he's never made a move in the years since his brother's death. Dante still feels guilty about Roberto's abuse, but it's more than that. He blames himself for not spotting the signs.

Instead, he silently watches Valentina visit Casanova and tortures himself, imagining what she does there.

My lieutenant will not appreciate my sympathy. "You want a drink?"

He looks up, and I realize I didn't do a great job keeping my emotions off my face. "I'm not here to drown my sorrows in drink," he says, biting off each word with precision. "I'm here about Lucia Petrucci."

I can't quell my instinctive flare of panic. "Did something happen to her? Is she okay?"

Dante meets my eyes. "Valentina didn't walk into Casanova alone. She walked in there with Lucia."

He starts to say something else, but I don't hear him. I'm already moving toward the exit.

Liam Callahan, the club manager, stops me when I walk into Casanova. "Signor Moretti," he says politely. "May I have a word with you, please?"

Very few people know I own Casanova. I keep it secret for a reason—people will hardly visit if they know I'm privy to their innermost desires. When it opened, I put Liam in charge.

Liam takes the running of Casanova seriously. In the three years he's been the manager, he's built a reputation for running the best and safest club in Italy. Maybe all of Europe.

I hired Liam because I trust him to enforce the rules consistently and fairly and because he's incapable of being intimidated. *Even by me.*

"Of course, Mr. Callahan. Why don't we head to your office?"

The Thief

In his office, Liam leans back and surveys me with narrow eyes. "You haven't been to Casanova in over a year. What's going on?"

Liam's office overlooks the club floor. I look out his floor-to-ceiling window, searching for Lucia's dark hair. "It's been over two years, actually."

"I see I need to be blunt. Why are you here, Antonio?"

"I'm interested in one of your guests. Lucia Petrucci."

He waits silently for me to continue. "I didn't realize she'd be here." What is she doing? Is she looking to slake her desire for me with another man? I go hot and cold at the thought of Lucia with someone else. "Did she sign up to be a member?"

"I'm not going to answer that." His expression makes it clear that he doesn't care if I own the club; I'm still going to have to follow the rules, or he'll ban me from the premises. "We take privacy seriously here."

"I'm not here to make a scene," I assure Liam.

"I heard Lucia was here, and. . ."

And I wasn't thinking straight. I just ran down here like a lovestruck, jealous, possessive fool.

"Hm." He takes in my expression, and an amused smile fills his face. "I never thought I'd see the day when Antonio Moretti lost his head over a woman." He gestures to a spot on the club floor. "She's at the bar. Far left side."

I look, and sure enough, there she is. She's wearing a black dress that hugs her curves, and even from this distance, she looks radiantly beautiful.

And the men around her are closing in like sharks.

"You know the rules of the club," Liam continues. "You're welcome to approach her. If she turns you down, you respect her decision."

"Of course."

He takes in the tension in my shoulders, and his smile grows. "Go on down before you explode."

Lucia has moved away from the bar by the time I go downstairs. She's sitting at a booth with

The Thief

Valentina, sipping a glass of wine.

And they're not alone. Enzo Peron is with them, and Lucia is laughing at something he's saying.

I bite off a swear. Enzo Peron is Venice's chief of police, and I'm her biggest criminal. He's also family, the brother of my heart, and one of my best friends.

Is he interested in Lucia?

Talk about complicated.

I detour to the bar and order a glass of sparkling water. A floor show starts, and a woman straps her submissive to a Saint Andrews Cross. She warms him up with a couple of spanks, and then she starts to crop him.

I don't watch them. Instead, I watch Lucia's reaction.

She's not shocked. She's not freaking out. She leans forward imperceptibly, her tongue swiping over her lower lip.

She's turned on.

Okay, that's it. Fuck Enzo. I can't stay away any longer. I walk over to them. "Hello, Lucia."

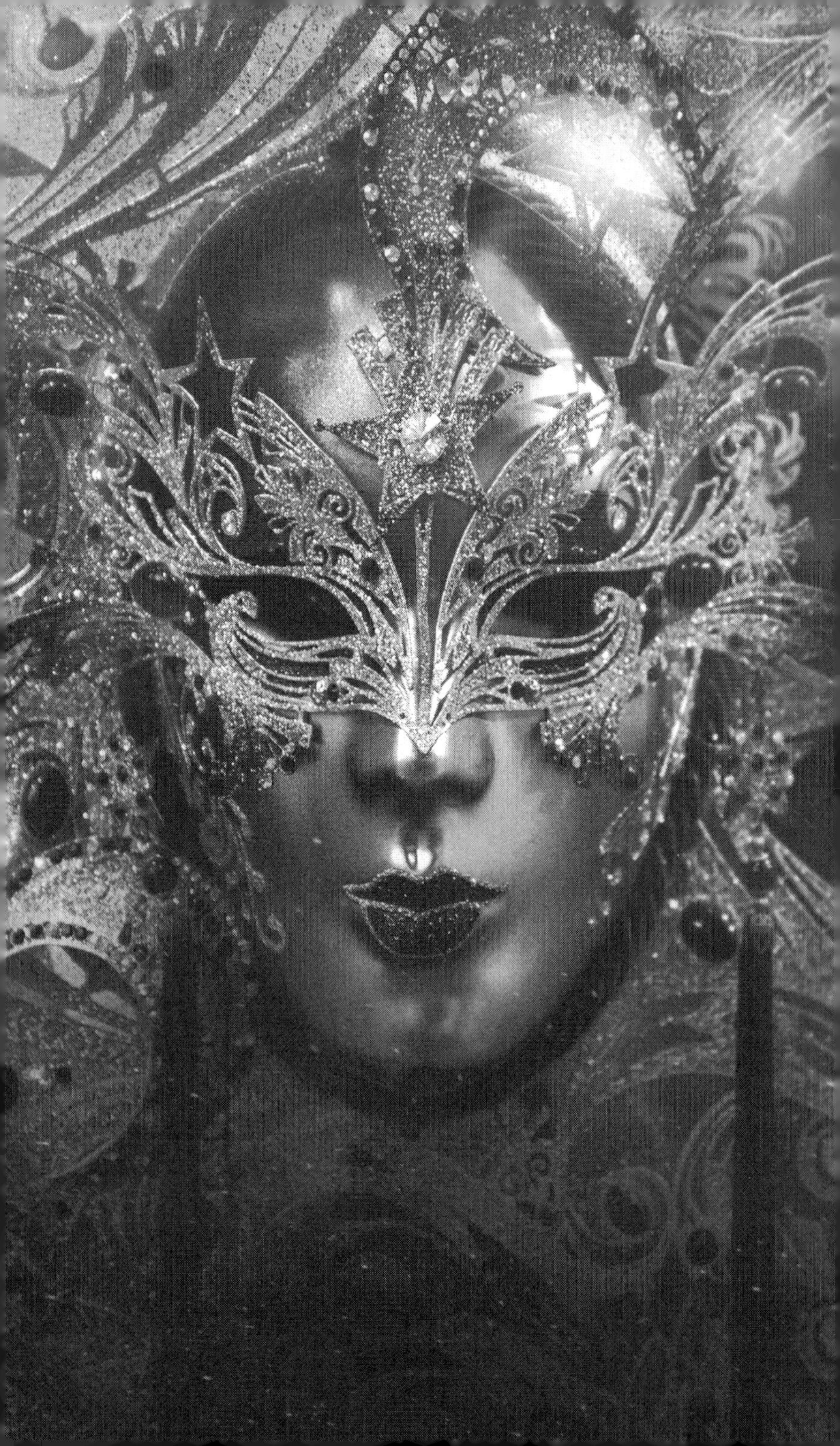

LUCIA

Chapter Seventeen

Casanova is... *wow*. It positively reeks of luxury and opulence. Everyone here looks effortlessly elegant. I used to visit a sex club in Chicago during my self-destructive phase, but Casanova looks nothing like Asylum.

Valentina introduces me to a few people at the bar. One of them is Enzo Peron. "Enzo is the chief of police," she says with a sly grin. "He's a good person to know." She turns to him, her smile widening. "Enzo, join us at our table?"

I frown at her. What is she doing? The chief of

police is a good-looking man—tall, in fantastic shape, and much younger than I expected someone in his position to be. But he's not doing anything for me, and I'm pretty sure the feeling is mutual.

Admit it. Antonio's ignored you all week, but you're still thinking about him.

Valentina is not done with her matchmaking efforts. "Lucia just moved back to Venice," she says. "She works as a curator at the Palazzo Ducale. Enzo loves art, Lucia. You should show him around the museum sometime."

I am going to strangle my best friend. "It's not that exciting," I murmur. "And I'm only here on a four-month contract."

A shadow falls over Valentina's face. "Right. I forgot. You're leaving in January."

"February. After Carnival." I feel like a jerk reminding Valentina my time here is temporary. Some days, it's hard for me to remember that. The first few weeks were disquieting. Memories of my parents haunted every street corner. But as

The Thief

Christmas approaches, being back also reminds me how much I missed being away. Venice is and will always be the home of my heart. It's nice to text Valentina a hundred times during the day without having to account for the time difference. It's delightful to eat dinner with her and Angelica and listen to my goddaughter chatter about her day, her friends, and the pony she wants to buy when she turns thirteen. She wants to learn to knit. Valentina doesn't know how, but my mom taught me, and I promised to teach Angelica. Will I have time to do all that before I leave?

"You've moved back to Venice?" Enzo says politely, dragging me back to the present. "How long were you away?"

"Ten years." A crew is setting up a Saint Andrew's Cross in the center of the floor, and a woman in a skintight leather outfit leads a man to it and straps him in place. Goosebumps rise on my skin. I want to be that guy, bound tight, knowing that punishment is coming.

The two of them are staring at me. I should probably make conversation. "You sound Venetian, Enzo. You're from here?"

"I grew up in Venice, yes," Enzo replies. "But like you, I moved away for a while."

"Enzo returned home a couple of years ago," Valentina adds. "He was a rising star in Rome, and we're lucky to have him."

The star in question looks faintly discomfited. "She's exaggerating."

The woman circles the man, slow and intent, a predator toying with her prey, and then flicks the crop in her hands. The sound of the crack fills the room. My breath catches. My attention narrows to the scene unfolding before me, and there's an ache in my core. I don't just want to be that person in the middle of the room. I want Antonio to dominate me. To promise me pleasure and pain in equal measure. I want—

"Hello, Lucia."

I jump. As if my need has summoned him here,

The Thief

Antonio Moretti is standing in front of me.

I blink.

He's still there.

Not a figment of my imagination, then. "Antonio? What are you doing here?"

I'm gaping at him. I realize that. I don't care. He's the last person I expected to see at Casanova. What are the odds? It's like getting on a plane and discovering that the guy sitting next to you is gorgeous, rich, and single. It just doesn't happen.

Valentina is trying not to smirk. "Hello, Antonio," she purrs. "What a surprise to see you here."

"Valentina." His eyes meet Enzo's briefly. "Peron, you're looking well. Lucia, could I talk to you for a moment, please?"

Enzo has an unreadable expression on his face. He must know who Antonio is; everyone in Venice does. Which makes this a very awkward meeting. Enzo is the chief of police, and Antonio operates on the wrong side of the law. I don't think the men will come to blows, but why take a chance?

I slide out of my seat. "I need a drink. Buy me one?"

We walk to the bar. Every set of eyes in the room is on Antonio. Unlike most of the men here, he's dressed casually in dark slacks and a sweater. His hair is tousled, and his eyes look tired. But no matter how he's dressed or how weary he appears, everyone at Casanova pays attention. Antonio is *the* power in Venice. They'd be foolish to ignore the apex predator in their midst.

He pays for my drink, then draws me into a quiet corner. "What are you doing here?" I ask as soon as we're out of earshot.

"I'm here because of you." There is a hint of wariness in his eyes. "Dante told me you were at Casanova, and I charged over here like a fucking fool."

He looks disgruntled by his admission. And I'm so surprised by his honesty that I start to giggle. All week, it felt as if a giant hand was squeezing my heart. But now, that pressure lightens, and a giddy sense of anticipation grips me. "Were you jealous?"

His lips tilt up in a wry smile. "Extremely." He takes the drink from my hand and sets it aside. He turns me so my back is pressed against his chest. His arm wraps around my waist and draws me closer. "Do you want to make me jealous, Lucia?" he says, his voice a warm caress. "You're playing with fire, little thief."

The room recedes to the background. "Am I going to get burned?"

"Mmm." He kisses the side of my neck. I inhale sharply, my breath catching on a hitch. "Are you interested in Enzo?"

Is he serious? I'm practically grinding my ass into his crotch, and he thinks I want someone else? "No, you idiot. I'm interested in *you*."

His thumb slides over the swell of my breasts. "I haven't been to Casanova recently, but I'm pretty sure they still have private rooms. Want to find one?"

My pulse is racing. My throat is dry. But I've never been more ready, more certain of a decision. "Yes."

"What are your limits?"

"No needles, no blood, nothing that breaks the skin. And nothing weird."

He raises his hand for an attendant. "Weird?"

I feel myself blush furiously. "Nothing icky. No water sports, that kind of thing."

His eyes dance with amusement. "Agreed," he says. "How about some light impact play and oral?"

The outline of his erection presses against his slacks. I laugh softly. This is more familiar ground. "You want me to suck your cock."

His hand cups my ass. "No," he corrects, his voice deliciously stern. "If you ask very nicely, I'll *let* you suck my cock. But first, I'm going to insist you come on my fingers and on my mouth." His lips curve in a half-smile. "Shall we get started?"

LUCIA

Chapter Eighteen

A club monitor walks us through the rules and then hands us each a clipboard. There are several pages of disclaimers before we can use the private room, but Antonio scrawls his signature on the bottom without reading any of the fine print.

I raise an eyebrow, surprised by his inattention. "Aren't you going to read it?"

"I own the club. But more importantly," he

adds, fixing me with a meaningful look, "right now, I don't give a fuck about paperwork."

A shiver runs through me, restless excitement bubbling through my body. I flip through the pages quickly and sign as well. Does it surprise me that Antonio owns Casanova? Not even a little. The monitor finishes up her safety instructions and leaves.

Antonio looks at me. "Ready?"

I think about how many times he's spanked me in my dreams. "You have no idea."

His hand engulfs mine. "Tell me."

Blood rushes to my cheeks. "I fantasized about you punishing me for stealing from you."

A light dances in his eyes. "I think I can do that."

Spanking games with the dangerously attractive Antonio Moretti. *Hell, yes.*

He pushes the door open. The room that greets us is sparsely decorated. There's no carpet on the cement floor, no art on the wall. A heavy wooden desk sits in the center, and several chairs are propped against the wall. A crystal bowl offers lube and condoms.

Antonio's blue-gray eyes rest on me. "What's your safeword?"

"Red."

"Red to stop, yellow to slow down and check in?" he clarifies.

I nod.

An enigmatic smile covers his face. "Do you know what happens to thieves who steal from me?"

Just like that, with one question, the air between us charges with erotic anticipation. "No, Sir, I do not." My insides tighten. "What are you going to do with me?"

"I'm going to bend you over my desk, hold your hands behind your back, and spank your ass." He tilts his head to the side. "Take off your dress, Lucia."

I step into the room. Antonio takes my hands

and tugs me forward, and I stumble against his rock-hard body. He wraps his arm around my waist, steadying me. "How many drinks have you had?"

"Just a half-glass of wine. It won't interfere in my ability to safe word."

"Okay." He lets go of me and takes a half-step back. His expression turns forbidding. "I believe I told you to take off your dress, Lucia. Since you're having trouble following instructions, I think I'll have to punish you."

Need zaps through me, an electric current shocking my body. Antonio is so deliciously stern—I love it. "I'm sorry, Sir," I whisper.

"I'm not interested in your apologies." He moves behind me and unzips my dress, his fingers brushing my skin. His gentle touch is a sharp contrast with his harsh words. "And I'm not interested in your excuses."

My dress falls to the floor in a pool of fabric.

My underwear isn't anything fancy. A plain

The Thief

black bra and matching cotton panties. But as I step out of the dress, Antonio sucks in a breath, and the heat in his eyes makes me feel like the most beautiful woman in the world.

"Gorgeous," he says. His hands grip my hips. "Every single time." His eyes never leave mine. "Take off your bra and panties, please."

He's seen me naked before. But there's something about this roleplay that changes the dynamic between us and amplifies the intensity. I'm inexplicably nervous as I undo the clasp of my bra, and my palms are sweaty as I take off my panties.

When I'm naked, Antonio leads me over to the desk and pushes me down on it. "Hands on the table."

My aching breasts are crushed against the wood, sending a fresh surge of heat through me. I obey his order, bringing my hands up in front of me and setting my palms flat on the surface.

"Good girl," he murmurs appreciatively. His

hands slide over my ass, and it takes everything to hold still. I want to push against him. Feel his fingers on my clit, his mouth between my legs. . .

His nails scrape my skin, and I can't hold back my whimper. Need effervesces through me like bubbles in champagne, and though I do my best, I can't hold still.

Antonio pushes down on the small of my back. "Stay where you are," he commands.

"I'm trying." There's a plaintive whine in my voice that makes me flush.

He chuckles. "Try harder." He moves his hand between my leg, and I bite my lip as arousal surges. "Here's how this is going to work, Lucia. Punishment first, then pleasure." He kneads the flesh of my ass. "How many spanks, do you think? Ten? Twenty? It was a very valuable painting."

"A very valuable painting that doesn't belong to you," I say snarkily. "I'm just making sure it's reunited with its actual owner."

Mistake. His fingers sink into my hair. "Did I

give you permission to speak?" he asks, his voice dangerously mild.

"No, Sir," I say contritely. I'm definitely going to get punished for being a smart-ass. "I'm sorry."

"Twenty, I think."

Gulp. Should have kept my mouth shut. A frisson of fear goes through me, one that vanishes as Antonio slides one finger and then another into my pussy.

So good. So mouthwateringly, toe-curlingly good.

He circles my throbbing clit. "You don't have to count them," he says, as if his touch isn't driving me insane. "You can yell, you can cry out. But you need to hold still, and you need to keep your hands where they are." He grazes his fingernails down my back, a light touch that has me biting back a moan. "If your hands move, I'll have to start over."

"I understand."

Whack. The first spank is just hard enough to warm me up but not hard enough to hurt. "Thank you, Sir," I say automatically. It's been a long time since I've done this. Too long. I take a deep breath, close my eyes, and sink into sensation.

"Such a good girl," he says. "So polite." His hand descends on my left buttock. I whimper at the sting, but then he strokes my skin, and the pain morphs into a rush of pleasure. "When did you first know you were into kink?"

I turn my head around to give him an incredulous look. "Seriously? You're asking me questions *now?* And you expect me to give you a coherent response?"

I'm punished—rewarded?—with another hard spank. "Are you incapable of doing two things at once?" He dips a finger into my pussy and finds me dripping. "Answer me, Lucia."

It isn't an order. I don't have to tell him anything. But I want to. Of all the people in the world, Antonio will understand.

"I was a wreck after my parents died. I blamed myself. How could I not have realized how sick my mother was? Was I so self-involved that I missed all the signs? I kept replaying every conversation we'd had. The last time I talked to them, I had a test to study for, so I couldn't talk much. If I'd stayed on the phone, would they have told me the truth?" I take a deep breath. "Those memories haunted me, and I couldn't let it lie. I just kept circling back to them, poking at them like a scab."

He rests his hand on my back, just for an instant, but his touch feels like the forgiveness I haven't been able to give myself. "I was pretty self-destructive," I continue. "I took stupid risks. The first painting I stole..." I shake my head at the memory of that first unplanned job. "It's a miracle I didn't get caught. I probably would've landed in jail within a year, but then I found kink."

His finger brushes over my clit, and I gasp and squirm. He stills me with a couple of hard strokes. "How?" he asks calmly.

My ass is throbbing, the stinging of my flesh fueling my arousal. "My college roommate had an older boyfriend who belonged to a kink club. I tagged along one day."

"And you liked it." His lips kiss my reddened skin. I inhale sharply, so turned on that I can't think. "Spread your legs wider."

I obey. I feel him kneel and then part my folds. A thrill shoots through me as he puts his mouth on me. Tendrils of desire snake through my body as his tongue licks its way to my clit. I moan, and he pulls away, punctuating his withdrawal with a spank. "Keep talking," he orders.

The message is clear. If I keep revealing hidden pieces of myself, then he'll bring me to orgasm. I almost sob from sheer frustration. "I liked it," I say. "I didn't think I would, but it was cathartic. Being tied up, being helpless, it filled a void in me."

He kisses my inner thighs, his hands holding my hips in place. "If somebody else was punishing you, you didn't need to punish yourself."

That is so insightful that I almost safe word the

hell out of there. This isn't what I signed up for. I was prepared for some spanking games, some sexy role-play where the big bad mafia guy takes the wicked little thief in hand, punishing her for stealing his painting by making her suck his cock.

(Not that it would have been a punishment.)

This, though? Antonio Moretti is peeling my layers like an onion, and it is terrifying.

But the word 'red' doesn't cross my lips. Instead, I confess my darkest thoughts to Antonio in a sex club while being spanked. "Yes," I whisper between the blows. "I should have known. I should have been here. I should have never gone away to college. My selfishness made this happen."

Something shocking happens as the words spill out of my mouth. I feel lighter. I feel free. Antonio alternates between punishing and pleasuring me as I bend over the table, my breasts mashing into the wooden surface. My legs stay parted as the most powerful man in Venice kneels between them, making me come with his fingers and mouth.

He's making me fall apart.

Hot desire knifes through my body. I'm shaking. "Please," I beg. I'm so turned on. My body is on fire.

"What do you want, little thief?"

I need release. I need his cock. Contradictory desires dance through me, and I can't choose. He thrusts two fingers inside me again, and his thumb flicks my clit, lightly at first and then harder. He grabs a fistful of my hair. "Tell me what you need."

"I need to suck your cock."

"So tempting." He sucks my clit between his lips, and I bite my cheek to keep from screaming out loud. "But I believe I promised you an orgasm first."

Oh, fuck. Shivers roil my trembling body. Antonio's tongue works magic on my clit, and I gasp, writhe, and shudder. He thrusts his fingers into my wet heat, and desire blazes through me. "Please," I beg, my voice breathy and needy. "Please don't stop."

"I wasn't planning on it, tesoro." He strokes in

and out of my pussy, and his tongue circles my clit over and over, a pulsing rhythm that takes me to the edge of an orgasm. "The way you taste," he growls. "I could get addicted to you, Lucia."

I feel dizzy. Wave after wave of pleasure batters my body, but I know I can't come. Not unless he allows it.

"Antonio..." My knees are shaky, and my muscles are taut with strain. The feel of his mouth, his tongue, devouring me... It's making me liquid. "I want... I need—"

"To come? And you're asking for permission like a good girl?" There's warm approval in his voice as he pulls away from me and straightens, which confuses me until he flips me over onto my back. "I want to watch you fall apart."

"Yes, Sir."

He kneels between my legs again, yanking me closer so my ass is on the edge of the desk. His hands spread me open, and his gaze is scorching hot. "Beautiful," he murmurs. "Fucking perfect."

He puts his tongue on my clit again. "Come whenever you want, Lucia."

Every time he licks me, my body jerks like I've touched a live wire. I rock my hips into him, and he laughs and holds me steady. He fucks me with his fingers and pleasures me with his tongue, and it doesn't take long for the dam to burst. Sizzling heat sears me, and the blazing inferno of an orgasm burns through my body.

He licks me until the wracking shudders cease. I lie there, half on the desk and half off, lazy and sated. "Wow," I murmur. "That was. . ." *Spectacular.*

He chuckles as he gets to his feet, wiping his mouth with the back of his hand before kissing me in a hungry, open-mouth kiss. His erection is a hard bar against his woolen trousers. I brush my hand against it. "Want me to suck your cock?"

He gives me an amused look. "Is that how you ask?" he teases. "Where are all the pleases and thank-yous now, Lucia? I let you come, and all that politeness disappears?"

I laugh at his grumbling tone. It's so strange how comfortable I am with him. Every time I'm with Antonio, it just feels. . . right.

What the hell, Lucia?

He just read me like an open book. He gave me the best orgasm of my life. He growls orders at me in a way I find irresistible, but he always treats me respectfully. He listens to me, truly listens.

I'm catching feelings for Antonio Moretti.

I could very easily fall in love with him.

And that thought fills me with a buzzing sense of panic.

This is about hot sex. That's all it can ever be.

I slide off the desk and sink onto my knees, looking up at him from lowered lashes. "Thank you for my orgasm, Sir. Please, may I suck your cock now?"

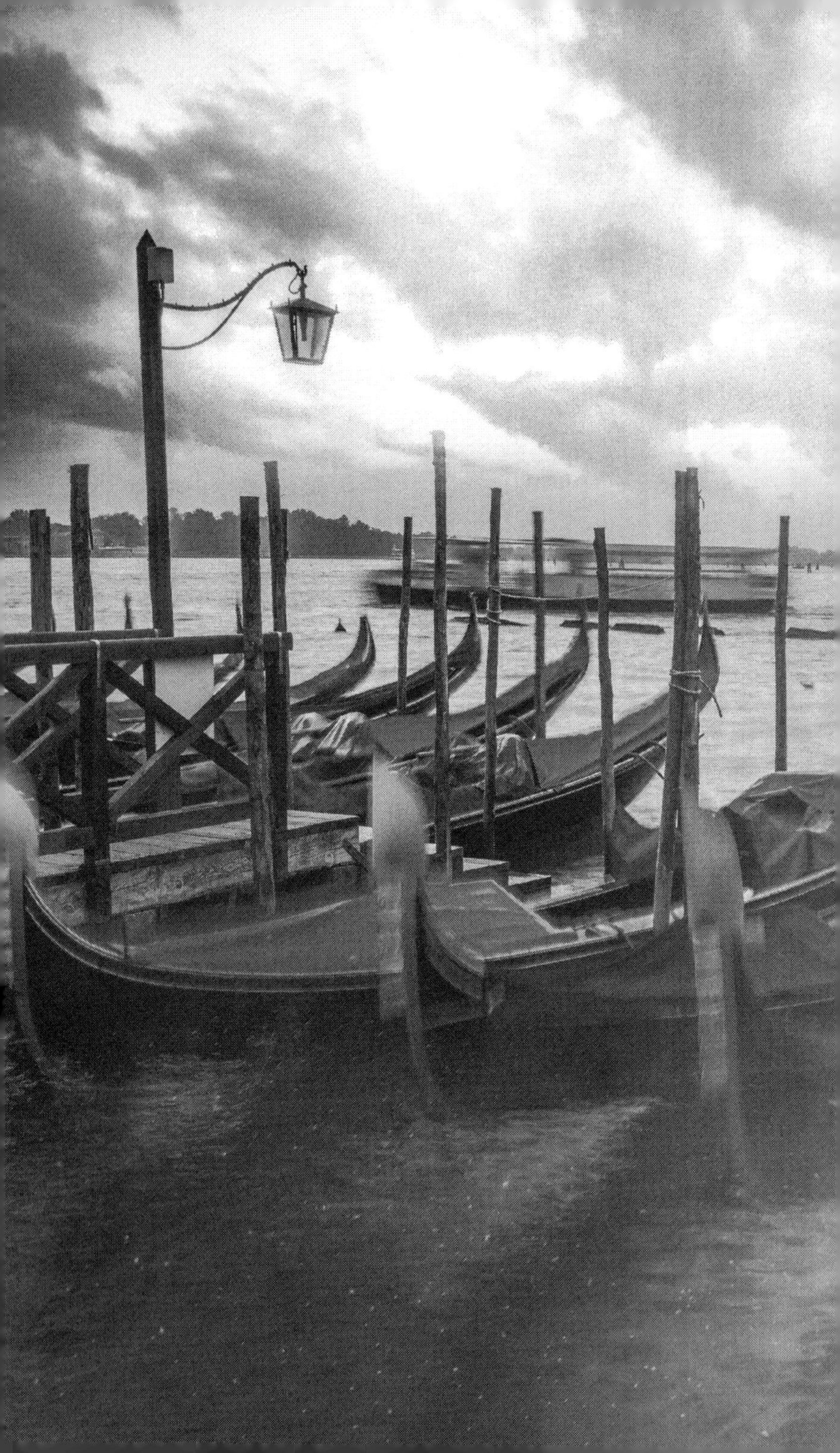

ANTONIO

CHAPTER NINETEEN

We had a moment of almost intimacy, and then she pulled away. Now we're back to sex games.

Are you surprised by that?

Lucia's doing what she always has. When intimacy threatens, she retreats to protect herself. If I weren't ten kinds of a fool, I'd do the same thing.

But something prevents me from putting up my own walls. Something keeps me battering hers. Maybe it's because she's so vibrantly alive when she lets her guard down.

Or maybe it's because I'm so fucking turned on by the prospect of her mouth on me.

She looks up at me from on her knees, her eyes bright with arousal, a devilish smile playing across her lips. Her body is soft and curvy and perfect. Her dark hair spills down her back in wild tangles. My cock throbs and drips with precum. My balls ache. I'm not thinking straight—I cannot. Not now. Not with her kneeling before me, her lips ready for my cock.

I lower my zipper, and my erection springs out, ready and eager for her smart, sassy mouth. I sit back on the chair and beckon to Lucia. "Come here."

She starts to get up. I'm dangerously close to losing control, and that won't do. Not at all. I shake my head sternly. "Crawl to me."

A shiver runs through her body. She moves to me, sinuous and graceful, sexy beyond belief. She settles between my thighs and looks up at me through her lashes. "Please, may I suck your cock, Sir?" she asks again.

Oh, fuck, yes.

I bend down and kiss her, cupping her chin in my hand. "Such a good girl," I praise. "You want my cock, little thief?" I wrap a hand around the base of her neck and tug her closer. "Take it then. Wrap your pretty little lips around it."

The tip of her tongue darts out and licks the precum off my head. Desire rocks through me. I grip the arms of the chair and let out a hiss. "Deeper," I order.

She obediently parts her lips and engulfs my head in her mouth, taking me in. The feeling is indescribable. The warm silkiness of her tongue stroking my cock, the tight suction of her cheeks, the exquisite friction as she bobs her head on my length... I can't take it. My toes tingle, and my balls tighten. I'm on the brink far too soon.

"I'm close," I warn her.

She takes me deeper in response.

Well, fuck. I move my hips, thrusting into her mouth with fast, short, shallow strokes. She feels incredible. I'm about to pass out. I grab the back of her head, brace myself, and explode into her mouth.

I fetch her a velvet robe—Casanova does not skimp on the amenities—and pour her a glass of sparkling water.

She looks up at me with a smile. "Thank you. That was. . ." Her voice trails away. "Are you in a hurry, or can we stay here for a bit?"

"I have all the time in the world." *For you.*

She sips her water. "Can I ask you a personal question?"

"Yes."

"The Titian, why didn't you try to sell it?"

Whatever I thought she was going to ask, this wasn't it. "Maybe I couldn't find a fence willing to handle such a hot item."

She surveys me thoughtfully. "No, you didn't try. I checked with Signora Zanotti. She said it had never come up in the marketplace."

The Thief

I can't pretend Alvisa Zanotti is out of touch. The woman is a legend. She might be retired, but she's kept her ear to the ground.

"When I was fourteen, I tried to find my parents. I wanted to know who they were. I guess I wanted to understand why they would abandon a baby."

Her voice softens to a whisper. "And?"

"My father was a thug. My mother, an addict. They were both dead by that point. But my mother had family. A brother who was married with two children. My cousins."

She gets to her feet and moves toward me, sitting on my lap. She tucks her head on my shoulder and wraps her arm around my waist. "What happened next?"

"My uncle didn't try to pretend I wasn't my mother's son. Evidently, I look like her." A bitter smile touches my lips at the memory. "He gave me a hundred euros and warned me to stay away from his family."

Her body goes stiff. "You were *fourteen*."

"I was a troubled teenager. I kept running away from foster homes. If he took me in, I would disrupt his perfect family." I lift my shoulder in a shrug. "I can understand that."

"You were a child in need," she says in outrage. "His nephew. His own flesh and blood. How could he turn his back on you?"

My heart is warmed by the fire in her voice. I kiss her hair. "Save your pity, little thief," I tell her. "My life turned out just fine. Anyway, when I saw the painting—" I search for the right words. "Have you ever looked at a painting and felt a sense of recognition in your gut? It sounds ridiculous, but that Titian spoke to me, and I couldn't part with it."

"You let me steal it?"

She phrases it as a question, and I counter it with one of my own. "You haven't taken it back to the museum. I like the painting you left me as a replacement, by the way. The canvas practically

The Thief

crackles with energy. It's very *you*."

"I'm energetic?" She bites her lip, and I'm hard again. Fuck me, I wish we were in my bedroom. I want to push her down on my bed and discover all the places her energy might be better applied. "Interesting choice of compliment. I know you're the king of Venice, and women throw themselves at you all the time, but still, you might consider working on better ones."

"Women throw themselves at me all the time?" I move the robe aside and kiss her shoulder. "You sound jealous, cara mia."

"Of course not. I have no claim on you."

She still doesn't get it. I open her mouth to correct her assumption, but before I can speak, her stomach growls loudly. "Have you eaten?" I demand.

"Not really."

"In that case, we're going to dinner." I lift her to her feet. "According to Ignazio, you like Quadri."

She winces. "That poor kid. I strong-armed him to let me into your house. Is he in trouble?"

I shake my head. "No, it's not his fault. This one is on me. My men have standing orders to let you into my house whenever you want."

Her eyes widen. She opens her mouth to say something and then closes it. "It's after ten. Quadri will be closed by the time we get there."

I laugh. "As you pointed out, tesoro, I'm the king of Venice. They'll stay open for me."

Valentina isn't around when we emerge from the private room. We get our coats, and I call Quadri to give them a heads-up that we'll be dining there. While I'm doing that, Lucia checks her phone. "No message from Valentina," she says when I finish my call. "It's weird that she'd leave without telling me."

"Maybe she went into a private room."

"With whom?"

"Enzo?"

She shakes her head at once. "No, she's not

The Thief

interested in him." A frown furrows her brows. "I should go to her place, make sure she's okay."

"Hang on."

I text Dante, asking him if he knows where Valentina is. He responds immediately.

> Migraine.

"She's not feeling well," I tell Lucia. "She went home."

"Valentina's sick?"

Lucia sounds on the verge of panic. I squeeze her hand reassuringly. "She gets migraines. She's been getting them ever since Angelica was born. The attacks usually last a few days, so she'll be fine by the weekend. Dante's got Angelica."

"Dante?"

"My second-in-command. You met him outside my house the first time you visited."

She thinks back. "Broad shoulders, short dark hair, light gray eyes? Why is Angelica with him?"

She noticed the color of his eyes? "He's her uncle." She's still looking freaked out. "Are you okay, Lucia?"

"I'm fine." She gives me a bright, false smile. "Let's go to dinner."

We arrive at Quadri. The restaurant isn't closed yet, but it's definitely emptying, and only a handful of people linger over dessert.

The maître d' leads us to my usual table, and a waiter arrives a moment later with the wine list.

"Wine?" I ask Lucia.

She shakes her head. "Just water for me, please."

"Same for me, thank you."

The waiter fills our glasses and sets menus in front of us. "I recommend the tasting menu."

"Sounds good." The waiter takes our order and retreats. When he's gone, Lucia eyes me. "I didn't know Dante was Angelica's uncle. How is he related to Roberto?"

From the way her voice changes when she mentions Valentina's asshole ex, she knows Roberto used Valentina as a punching bag. "Dante is his brother."

"Valentina said you rescued her. And Angelica has never mentioned her father." Her eyes widen. "Did you kill Roberto?"

If Dante hadn't taken care of it, I would have. "Would it bother you if I did?"

She bites her lower lip. "I don't know. Your world is very different from mine." She glances around the room, her gaze landing on my men. "I don't usually need bodyguards following me wherever I go."

"It's not that different," I point out. "Your parents were thieves."

"But they took care to shield me from it." Her lips quirk. "They tended to do that. Shield me from things."

I think about the secrets her parents kept and the circumstances of their deaths. The wounds have cut deep and left permanent scars.

Scars I want to kiss.

Scars I want to erase.

"They weren't wrong to protect you from the mafia." I think back on the old days, the way the organization functioned when Domenico was in charge. We walked around on pins and needles, waiting for him to explode. But I was always ambitious. I clawed my way up the ranks and became his second-in-command, but everyone knew that to be Domenico's right hand was to walk around with a death sentence hanging over your head.

Those memories are in the past. I push them away. The present, where I'm dining in a nice restaurant with a complicated, fascinating woman, is far more compelling.

"I didn't kill Roberto. Valentina always assumed I did, but she's wrong. Dante took care of it."

She leans forward, clearly surprised by my revelation. "Why haven't you told her?"

"Dante doesn't want me to."

"And you're okay with that?"

"It's his story to share. I keep people's secrets."

She surveys me for a long moment. "Tell me a secret, Antonio."

"You want to play games? I'll make a deal with you. An answer for an answer."

"That's a dangerous game."

"Afraid to play?"

Her eyes sparkle at my challenge. "Okay, I'll bite. Tell me something about yourself, something real."

"I ran away from my foster home when I was fourteen. I went to see my uncle, which you know didn't go well. I lived on the streets, and the hundred euros he gave me didn't last long. I was soon desperately hungry. I tried stealing some fruit from a vendor and got caught. An old thief saw me. He was a master of his craft, and I think he was offended at how bad I was. So, he taught me how to steal properly."

"And you became very good at it."

I grin. "The best."

"So modest," she teases.

"I got sick the winter after I stole the Titian. No matter how many blankets I piled on myself, I couldn't get warm. Enzo and Tatiana begged me to sell the painting, but I wouldn't. They railed at me and called me a sentimental fool, but I stayed stubborn."

"Enzo, the guy I met today? Enzo Peron, the chief of police? And Tatiana Cordova?"

"We grew up together. Enzo and Tania are the family of my heart. You'll like them."

"Are they the ones who think your house is too cluttered?"

She remembered my throwaway comment from weeks ago? I have to work to keep from grinning. "They are, yes." Sensing an opening, I push. "Would you like to meet them?"

She lowers her lashes, hiding her expression from me. "I was just making conversation."

Fuck. I pushed too hard, and she's retreating again. I will myself to be patient. We're interrupted by the waiter, who sets a couple of bowls in front of us, each with a small, beautifully plated portion of fish. "Tuna carpaccio with radicchio and white truffle," he announces. "*Buon appetito.*"

Lucia tries a forkful. "Oh God, this is good," she moans in appreciation. "I'm biased because I'm hungry, but oh my God. This is *delicious*."

She moans, and my cock stirs in anticipation. She dips her fork in the sauce, and the tip of her tongue darts out to taste it. My vision goes hazy. Lucia is the sweetest temptation. Everything about her is fascinating.

And I want to know all her secrets.

"My turn," I announce. Her expression turns immediately wary, but she doesn't need to worry. I've learned my lesson. *For now.* "You seem concerned about being seen with me. Were there any side effects from my visit to the Palazzo Ducale?"

Her shoulders relax. "That's what you want to know? Half the people at work are convinced I'm your mistress, and the other half only care about your donation. Thankfully, Signor Garzolo belongs to the second category."

I feel a sudden rush of anger. "Who thinks you're my mistress?"

"Why do you want to know? So that you can threaten them?" She rolls her eyes. "I'm not going to tell you, Antonio."

"It doesn't bother you?"

She shrugs. "It is what it is. You're the king of Venice. People are going to talk."

I still don't like it. She takes in my expression, and a smile darts on her lips. "You're glowering. Our poor waiter looks terrified. Let's change the topic. It's my turn again to ask a question. I looked you up. According to the Internet, you've dated a string of women, but you've never been in a relationship."

"Is there a question there?"

"Is that true?"

"Yes."

She leans forward, barely paying attention to the second course. "Why?"

"I've never met anyone I want to be in a relationship with."

"That's not a real answer," she accuses. "You're telling me that in that long line of women, there's never been anyone you could see yourself settling down with? Why not?"

"Maybe I've been haunted by the memory of a girl with green eyes and a bottle of vodka."

Lucia sucks in a breath. "Oh." Her voice is unsteady. "It's your turn."

"Why do you avoid relationships?"

She fiddles with her napkin. "You already know why."

"Do I? Tell me again."

"Love is pain, Antonio. Love is loss. I've already lost everything once. I won't risk it again."

"Instead, you panic when your friends get sick. But we all die in the end, Lucia. Death doesn't discriminate. It's what we do with the time we have that counts." I hold her gaze in mine. "I'd rather take a chance on love than go through life without it."

LUCIA

Chapter Twenty

I want to protest. Tell him that he doesn't know what he's talking about. I want to insist that he cannot possibly understand how I feel.

But that's not true, is it? Unlike me, Antonio never knew his parents. He doesn't have the good memories to comfort him on bad days. He hasn't known the warmth of a mother's hug, the strong grip of a father's steadfast love.

Is he right? Am I being a coward? Is it better to dive in and risk heartbreak?

I eat the rest of my meal in silence, my thoughts in turmoil. The waiter sets dessert in front of us and glides away. "You're pensive," Antonio says.

I give him a wry smile. "You gave me a lesson in perspective. I'm absorbing it." I glance at the plate in front of me. A cream and fruit extravaganza is nestled in a delicate bowl of spun sugar. "This is so pretty. I almost can't bring myself to eat it."

"Come here." He pats the space next to him. I sit at his side, and he pulls me into his body so my back rests against his chest. He feels warm, solid and comforting.

He kisses the side of my neck, his stubble prickling against my skin. Sensation layered upon sensation, and I love it.

He holds out a spoonful of the cream extravaganza. "Open your mouth."

I've already come. I should be satiated. But hearing his words, a shiver of pure arousal runs through me.

I exhale slowly. "Funny," I quip. "When I imagined you saying those words to me, it was under very different circumstances."

He growls deep in his throat, and his grip around me tightens. "Do you know what it means to be the king of Venice?" he rasps into my ear. "I could fuck you right here, right now, and nobody would utter a word of protest."

Desire rushes through me in a tidal wave, leaving me tight and aching. "Is exhibitionism one of your kinks?" I swallow the dessert he's holding out and moan. It's not quite an involuntary reaction. The dessert is delicious, but I'm deliberately exaggerating my response. I'm playing with fire, and I'm ready to combust.

"Not with you. If anyone here looks at you, I might kill them."

If I had any sense at all, those words should terrify me. But they don't. They're fueling my need like an accelerant poured on an already raging fire.

And he can sense it.

"Are you finished with dessert?" he demands. He gets to his feet and yanks me up. "Let's go. I'm going to take you home, tie you to my bed, and fuck you until you can't walk straight."

Saturday, we didn't make it past my living room. This time, he hurries me up the stairs at his house and pushes open his bedroom door. I barely have a moment to glimpse my painting on his wall before he strips me naked and throws me down on the bed.

Saturday, when we fucked, it was hard, fast, and urgent. Not today. Antonio sheds his clothes and covers my body with his. His kisses are long and drugging, his cock thick and hard between my thighs. His fingers linger over my curves and caress the contours of my body. He tweaks my nipples, and I bite back a gasp of pure pleasure.

His answering chuckle is rich with male satisfaction. "I like that reaction."

So smug. I flip him on his back and straddle him. "Do you?" I lower myself until I feel the pressure of his cock against my entrance. "What about now?"

His eyes turn hot. Inviting. "Are you going to ride me, tesoro? Give me a second to find a condom."

I wait impatiently. He sheathes himself, then grips my hips, urging me back onto his cock. I could slide down, impale myself on him, and the pleasure would be exquisite. But I stop myself, shifting back and forth on his erection, rubbing my swollen, aching clit against his shaft.

Antonio groans, low and deep. "Tease," he accuses, his voice rough with need. His blue, blue eyes hold me captive. "Stop fucking around and take my cock like the good girl you are."

He holds my hips and thrusts upward in a brutally deep stroke. He bottoms out, the head of his cock hitting my cervix, and shock frissons through me. "Yes," he hisses, his eyes clenching shut. "Just like that."

Saturday, I was shockingly wet and aroused, my pussy slick around his thick cock. I'm just as soaked today. Possibly wetter. He holds me in place and fucks me, each thrust a punch, and my body welcomes the deliciously decadent abuse. I move in synchronicity with him, lifting myself up and slamming down onto his hard length, need burning through me like an inferno. I'm shaking, panting, desperate. And so is he. His thrusts speed up, turning wild, ragged. We're both on the brink of climax. "Please. . ."

"No." Sweat beads his forehead as he reasserts control. He releases his grip on my hips and tugs me down, rubbing my nipple between his thumb and forefinger. "Not yet. I promised myself I'd take it slow."

I huff out a disbelieving laugh. "Slow? You were slamming into my cervix. Forget slow. Fuck me hard."

"So demanding." He follows his fingers with his mouth, sucking my engorged nipples between his teeth. His teeth scrape my skin with just enough pressure to spread heat all over my body. "I'll fuck you as I please. Slow or fast, gentle or rough. And you'll like it."

He's not wrong. "So cocky." I lift my hips and sink onto his shaft, excruciatingly slow, inch by inch, and he groans and throws his head back. "Two can play this game, Antonio."

"It's not a game, tesoro. Not now, not ever. Not with you." His lips twist into a half-smile. "It's all too real."

He's spanked me tonight. Put his mouth on my pussy and brought me to a screaming orgasm. I got on my knees and sucked his cock. And my appetite still isn't slaked. I want him to tie me up and possess me. Spank me some more. I want him to cage me in with his body and fuck me until I can't walk straight.

He's right. This isn't just about sex. Try as I might, I can't deny that this is far deeper than raw, carnal desire. There's a connection between us, a live wire with the power to electrocute me.

Saturday, Antonio told me to lie. He ordered me to tell him that what we had wasn't special, and I stayed silent, frozen between my fear and the truth.

Not today.

Today, for the first time, I don't fight his assertion. "It is," I whisper. "It's all too real." I close my eyes. "I want you too much. I'm walking on a tightrope without a safety net, and I'm scared."

"You don't have to be." He doesn't sound triumphant at my admission. He sounds... He sounds like he understands. Like he truly gets me. His thumb slides over my lower lip. "I'm here for you, little thief." His mouth crashes into mine, his fingers tangling in my hair. Heat radiates through me as he flips me on my back and thrusts deep. "Let me be your safety net, and I will never let you fall."

Our gazes collide. He drinks me in, his eyes hungry, and I forget to breathe. "Antonio," I whisper.

"Lucia." He pulls out, props himself up on his elbows and slides into me oh-so-slow. "My sweet little thief. You take my breath away. Every single time." He kisses me, hard and hot. "You undo me. I can't go a moment without thinking about you." His callused hands wrap around my breasts, squeezing them with just enough pressure to make me whimper. "In my bedroom, your painting reminds me of you." His fingers tease my nipples, tugging and pinching the tender nubs. "In my office, I can't look at my desk without remembering you coming on my tongue."

A full-body shudder runs through me. Blood leaves my brain as he speeds up his thrusts. My toes curl, and my back arches. "Antonio," I whimper. "I'm so close."

His face is etched with desire. "Wait for me, tesoro."

Always. "Yes," I whisper. A wish and a promise rolled into one. "Yes."

He kisses me again, his tongue plunging into

my mouth, deep and possessive. His hips rock into me. His cock is thick and hard, stretching and filling me. He groans, his voice a guttural sound of need. "Come for me, little thief."

He thrusts hard, and I shatter. My orgasm explodes over me, searing and scorching, wave after wave of pleasure pushing me over the edge. Antonio's right there with me. He buries his face in my neck, trailing hot kisses down my shoulder, and in perfect connection with me, he finds his release.

ANTONIO

Chapter Twenty-One

We take a break to drink a glass of wine and eat a platter of cheese and fruit, and then we're at it again. I tie her to my bed with silk rope and make her climax, then she straddles me, riding me until I come, hot and hard, her name on my lips.

We collapse on the bed, temporarily sated. I tuck her next to me, and she rests her head on my shoulder. Then I notice her wrists. The rope has left its marks, and her skin is red and irritated. I stroke them gently. "I'm an idiot."

She laughs. "Is this where I jump in to contradict you?" She kisses me. "I wanted it. Besides, you already know I like a little pain with my pleasure."

I carefully press my lips to her reddened wrists, one after the other. "I should have been more careful." I shake my head ruefully. "You drive all thought from my brain."

I scoop her into my arms and lift her up, ignoring her squawk of surprise. "Antonio," she yelps. "What are you doing?"

"Running a hot bath for you."

A smile breaks out on her face. "What a good idea."

I draw a bath for her. She tests the temperature and gets in. She winces a little as the water hits her abraded skin but settles back with a sigh of pleasure.

"Do you want to be left alone?"

"Hang on," she says teasingly. "Is Antonio Moretti actually offering me a choice?"

I bite back my smile. "I am sometimes capable of not being an asshole. Not often, so don't get too complacent."

She rolls her eyes. "Complacent? Never." She tilts her head to the side. "No, I don't want you to go. This tub is big enough for two. Join me?"

It's a simple question. It shouldn't mean as much as it does. But my mother abandoned me in a church, and when I found her family, my uncle paid me to go away.

So, when Lucia holds out her hand to me and beckons me into the tub, it means a lot.

I feel *chosen*.

It feels good. It feels vulnerable.

"Move over," I tell her. I open the refrigerator and pull out a bottle of chilled, sparkling water. "Do you want a drink?"

"You have a refrigerator in your bathroom." She

shakes her head with a laugh. "Of course you do. Yes, thank you."

I hand her the water and sit in the tub behind her. She leans back against me. We don't talk much, instead taking turns sipping from the bottle. "This must be an amazing view in the day," she murmurs, looking out the window. "You can see the basilica from your bathroom. And the Palazzo Ducale." She twists around to look at me. "You started from nothing. This is. . . impressive."

"I can be a single-minded bastard."

Lucia entwines her fingers in mine. "I hadn't noticed," she says dryly. "This is nice."

It is. The warm water is soothing, and a rare sense of contentment settles over me. The stresses of daily life drift away like dust on the wind, and what's left behind is Lucia.

I kiss her neck and stroke her nipples—my fingers can't stop touching her. "All those years away," I murmur. "I always wondered what you were doing."

"You didn't look me up?"

I shake my head. "I'll chase you now, tesoro, and without apology, because it's a game we both know we're playing. But compiling a dossier on you because I'm interested in you? That seems dangerously close to stalking, and I've seen the harm that obsessiveness can do." I trace a circle over her arm. "Instead, I fantasized about you.

Her muscles tense. "You did?"

Judging by her reaction, I'm treading on dangerous ground. Yet, *recklessly,* I continue. "In my daydreams, you were the damsel in distress, and I would rescue you in a hundred different ways. But those were the fantasies of a boy lusting after a girl." Lucia isn't a girl. She's all woman, and I can't get enough of her. "The reality is so much better."

"Is it?" She leans forward, breaking away from my embrace to lift herself out of the tub. "I should go."

Damn it. This again? I make a noise of protest. "Stay."

"I can't. I'm turning into a prune."

"The prettiest prune Venice has ever seen."

She laughs out loud. "First, I'm energetic, and now I'm a prune? Ah, Antonio. Your compliments overwhelm me." She dries herself and wraps a fluffy towel around her body. "It's really late. I need to get back."

I could ask her to stay. I could insist. God knows I want to. But something inside me rebels at the idea. I want her to stay because she *chooses* to.

"I'll take you home."

"You don't need to do that. I'll be fine."

"If you think I'm letting you walk home alone at three in the morning, Lucia, you don't know me at all."

"I won't be walking home alone," she points out. "You've assigned bodyguards to me, remember?"

"This isn't up for negotiation, tesoro."

She rolls her eyes. "So bossy," she says affectionately. "Okay, King of Venice. Let's go."

She has reason to be afraid of love, I tell myself. She took a step toward me today. I just need to be patient.

LUCIA

Chapter Twenty-Two

I'm a mess on Friday. I slept less than three hours and can barely keep my eyes open, but that's not the only reason. Thoughts of Antonio consume my mind.

Telling him I needed to leave was a reflex born from fear. The moment he said he fantasized about me, I panicked. *Again.* Because I fantasized about him too, and I wasn't ready to admit it. I wasn't ready to admit that the reality was far better than my imagination.

Antonio asked me to stay, yes. But if I'm being brutally honest, I wanted him to pull his King of Venice act and *demand* I spend the night with him.

If you want Antonio, stop playing games and tell him how you feel.

I'm in a daze when my phone rings. My cell phone, not the one in my office. Antonio, I think, answering without looking at the screen.

It's not Antonio. It's a male voice I don't recognize. "Signorina Lucia Petrucci?"

"Yes?" I glance at the screen. The number isn't familiar, either.

"My name is Rocco Cacciola. I head the Conservation Department at the Uffizi. You applied to a job here?"

"I did?" I ask and then want to smack myself. The Uffizi in Florence is arguably the best museum in the country, and I sound like an idiot. "I mean, yes, of course I did."

The Thief

"It was last August." Signor Cacciola sounds like he's smothering a laugh. "I found your resume interesting, but we already had a candidate in mind for that role. I have an opening coming up that I think you'll be perfect for."

He goes on to describe the job, and it's *perfect*. If I had to describe my dream job, it would be the role Rocco Cacciola is dangling in front of me.

"I'm very interested," I say when he's done. "What are the next steps?"

"You'll have to formally apply for the role. You can do that on our website. And please do that this week, Lucia. There are three people on the hiring committee, and I'm one of them. If the other two are convinced you're right for the role, we'll invite you to Florence for an interview. If all goes well, you'll be working at the Uffizi in March."

March.

Only three months away.

We finish our conversation, and I hang up. I stare at the screen in front of me, lost in thought.

Florence is only a couple of hours away from Venice, but if I accept this role, I'll have to say goodbye to my weekly dinners with Valentina and Angelica. I can't drop by their place at the drop of a hat; I'll only be able to visit on weekends.

And Antonio? What about him?

This was always temporary, I tell myself. You knew that. Your contract at the Palazzo Ducale was for four months. That's how long you were going to stay in Venice. That's why you haven't bought any furniture. Why you're still sleeping on a blowup mattress.

Except Venice is increasingly feeling like my home again.

And I'm not sure I want to leave.

After texting Valentina and making sure she's up for company, I go see her. "Why didn't you tell me you got migraines?" I demand as soon as she opens the door.

"Hello to you too," she replies dryly. "Come on in. Do you want something to drink? I just made myself a cup of tea."

Valentina always has the best tea. "Yes, please."

I enter her apartment, take off my boots, and hang up my jacket. "Who told you about my migraines?" she asks as she pours me a cup of something that smells like vanilla and caramel. Yum. "Antonio?"

I nod, and her eyes dance with mirth. "Tell me more," she says in a singsong voice. "Tell me about the very intimate dinner you had at one of the nicest restaurants in the city."

I settle on her couch and tuck my feet under me. "You're changing the topic."

"I get migraines," she replies. "I started getting them when I was pregnant and have been getting them ever since. I've been to a neurologist and done all the tests. Nobody can find anything wrong. It's just one of those little annoyances of life, that's all. And I didn't tell you because I knew you'd freak out." She eyes me pointedly. "Just like you're doing now."

It doesn't sound like one of life's little annoyances to me. It sounds like a big deal. But I don't have any perspective about people getting sick. As Valentina has rightly pointed out, I tend to panic and overreact. "Antonio said that Angelica was with Dante. Why did I have to hear he's her uncle from someone else?"

Surprise flashes across her face. "I thought you knew. I didn't tell you? Sorry, Lucia." She sips her tea. "Yes, she's still there. Whatever else I might think of him, he dotes on her."

My eyes narrow. "What you mean, whatever else you might think of him?" Her expression turns unreadable, and awareness hits me in a flash. "Oh my God. You like him, don't you?"

She avoids my gaze. "I do not. It's just good for Angelica to know her family."

Wow. Talk about complicated relationships. There are layers upon layers here, a tangled mess of a situation. Valentina was in an abusive relationship with Dante's brother, Roberto. Dante killed him, but Valentina doesn't know. She's clearly conflicted. If she found out what Dante did, would it make a difference in how she feels about him?

Valentina is my friend. I love her like a sister, but I'm not going to tell her what I learned. Antonio told me what he did in confidence, and I don't feel right about betraying his trust. And, for all I know, it could make the situation worse, not better.

I drink my tea in silence. "So," Valentina says after a long pause. "You and Antonio. Are you guys together now?"

"I don't know."

She tilts her head to one side and gives me a searching look. "Well, that's an improvement from 'absolutely not.' Why the uncertainty? Is he giving you mixed messages?"

I shake my head. "No, he's extremely clear about his intentions." And his directness is more refreshing than I thought it would be. With Antonio, I never have to doubt if he's interested. When he looks at me, I have his complete, total attention, and it's a heady, addictive feeling. "It's me. I just don't know..." My voice trails off as I gather my thoughts. "His life is dangerous. He has armed guards following him. I have a security detail on me now." I spread my hands in a helpless gesture. "I don't even understand his world. It's too much."

Valentina snorts. "You're full of crap, you know that? Every time you steal a painting, you put yourself in danger. And the people you steal from. Do you really think they would hand you over to the police if they caught you? Of course not. You know that, and it's a risk you're willing to take. Because what you're doing is important to you."

"What are you saying?"

"I'm saying that what Antonio does is important. He grew up on the streets, Lucia. Nobody knows the dark, gritty underside of this city like he does. And because of that, he works really hard to make things better." She gives me a pointed look. "Like you, he puts himself in danger because it's worth it."

"You're making him sound like a crusader or something," I grumble. I want to maintain my illusions and pretend that Antonio and I are nothing alike. But Valentina is no fool, and there's truth in what she's saying. "Let's talk about something else. Like the painting I'm going to steal."

A smile tugs at the corners of her mouth. "You're not interested in the Titian anymore?"

The Titian is propped against my bedroom wall, but I haven't told Valentina. She'd never stop teasing me if she knew. "You're the one who told me not to steal in Venice."

"And you did so well listening to me," she responds dryly.

"Ahem. Anyway, I've been looking at the possibilities. How about Gavin Powell?"

"Is that the British asshole living in Hungary?"

"The same." *Asshole* is putting it mildly. Gavin Powell is a men's rights activist. On his podcast, he expounds upon how women are naturally subservient to men, advocates treating your wife like garbage, and throws in other racist dog whistles. He lives in exile in Hungary because he's wanted on rape charges in the UK.

Perhaps more relevant to my purposes, he owns a stolen Jacopo Bassano. The painting was stolen three years ago from a museum in Turin in a brazen smash-and-grab. Powell funded the heist, which means that if I steal his Bassano, he can't very well report the theft. Not unless he wants Interpol to ask him some deeply uncomfortable questions.

"A satisfying target," Valentina says with relish. "I thought you might pick him, so I went ahead and did a full assessment." She opens her desk drawer and hands me a USB key. "Here you go. Everything you ever wanted to know about Gavin Powell, and then some. Be ready to shower once you read the sordid details; I know I did."

"You're the best."

Signora Girelli, my downstairs neighbor, is struggling with the door when I get to my apartment building. Her fluffy poodle, Sasha, is nestled at her feet, her leash tangled up around Signora Girelli's ankles. "Let me get that for you," I say, hurrying up. I hold the door open while she untangles herself and scoops the dog up.

She enters the lobby and presses the button for the tiny three-person elevator. I clear my throat. "Signora Girelli? I don't think the elevator is working." It stopped working the week after I moved in. I've been trying to get a maintenance guy to fix it with no success.

She turns to me with a smile. "Oh no, dear. Someone was in here earlier today to fix it. Your furniture delivery people used it."

It takes me a minute to register her words. "My what?"

"Furniture." She pats my arm. "I'm so glad you're settling in."

I mutter my thanks, my brain whirling. What is Signora Girelli talking about? Does she have me confused with someone else? But no. She might be in her eighties but is alert and chatty, and her mind is as sharp as it was ten years ago.

I unlock my apartment door, push it open, and freeze in my tracks.

My living room is transformed. The rug I liked at the antique market last Saturday is spread on my living room, the black-and-white pattern a vivid contrast to the wooden floor. The Moroccan chairs I admired are placed by the window, with a wooden side table between them.

On the table, nestled between the blue ceramic candlesticks I fell in love with, is a huge bouquet of winter-white roses, their delicate aroma filling the air.

Antonio Moretti strikes again.

I stare at the furniture. Brush the soft petals of the roses with my fingertips and bury my face in their fragrance. Everything I saw on Saturday in the market—everything I admired—is here. This is a display of wealth and power, yes. But it's so much more. This is about paying attention to my needs. Understanding what I want.

He's always done that. Ten years ago, he gave me exactly what I needed. He walked with me in the middle of the night, offering me companionship while letting me grieve. And now, this little corner of my house looks like *home*.

What about the Uffizi?

I head to my bedroom. My air mattress is gone, deflated and folded in a corner. In its place is a bed, a duplicate of the one in Antonio's bedroom. Same dark wood, same slatted headboard that I can be tied to.

My knees weaken at that thought, and my nipples perk up. Liquid desire runs through me in a molten torrent.

I call Antonio. He picks up on the first ring. "You broke into my house," I accuse him.

"Not personally." I can hear the smile in his voice. "Do you like the flowers?"

"They're beautiful. Why did you buy me furniture?"

"I needed a table to set the vase on, but you didn't have one."

I have to fight to keep from laughing. "That's almost reasonable. And the rug, chairs, and bed? Why those?"

"The table and chairs were a matched set," he says. "The rug, because your floor was cold. As for the bed..." His voice lowers suggestively. "Your air mattress isn't going to be sturdy enough for the things I want to do, Lucia."

He says my name like a caress. I wet my lips. "You can't buy me stuff."

"You keep telling me what I can and cannot do, little thief. Do you not like the furniture? It can be replaced."

"I love everything."

"Then I don't see the problem."

Argh. He is really the most aggravating person. And yet, I'm grinning like an idiot. "Do you?" I hesitate, then plunge forward. "Do you want to grab dinner sometime next week? There's a trattoria in my neighborhood. It's not fancy, but—"

"I'd love to. When?"

"Tuesday?"

"I'll pick you up at seven."

I hang up, sit in my new chair, and breathe in the aroma of the roses. I just invited the King of Venice to dinner. Valentina's right. Whether I admit it out loud or not, I'm involved with Antonio Moretti.

And that thought both terrifies me and thrills me in equal measure.

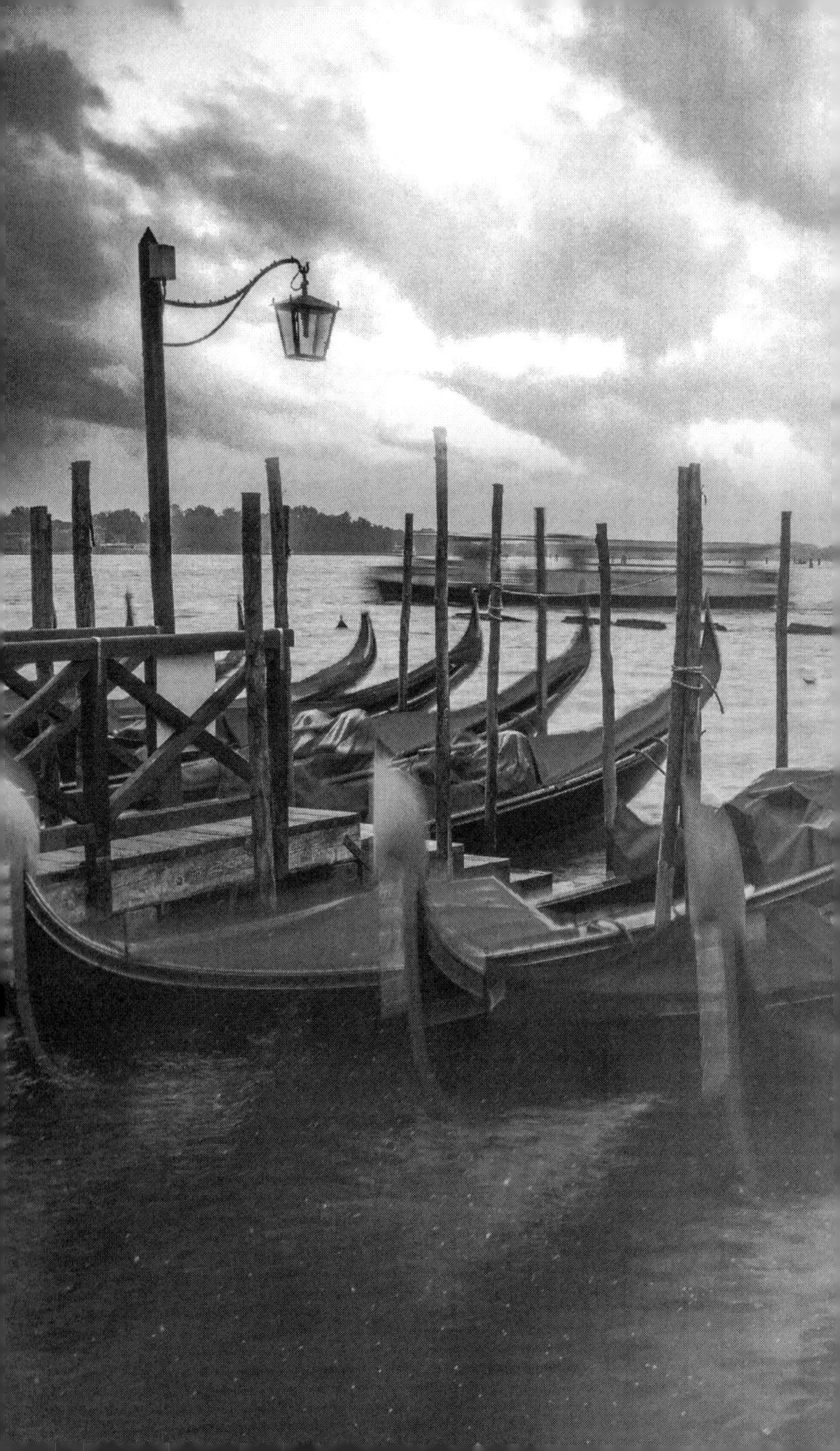

ANTONIO

Chapter Twenty-Three

On Sunday, Enzo and Tatiana show up for our monthly lunch. "What happened last week?" Enzo asks as he hangs up his jacket. "You canceled on us at the last minute. Anything I should be concerned about?"

"It's not work, Enzo," Tatiana says, leading the way into the kitchen. "Look at Antonio's face. He looks almost cheerful." She pours herself a glass of wine, filling it to the brim, and perches on the counter. "It's the girl." A slow smile breaks out on her face. "Tell me everything."

Tania seldom drinks during the day, which means something is wrong. I look at Enzo, wondering if he knows what's bugging her, and he gives me a slight shake of his head. I sigh inwardly. I've learned from experience that there's no point pushing her for answers. Tania will talk about what's bothering her when she's ready and not a second before.

"I see Enzo has been talking."

Enzo chuckles. "You marched into Casanova, glared daggers at me, and dragged away the woman I was talking to. Of course I told Tania."

Both my friends are staring at me with expectant looks on their faces. I drag a hand through my hair. "Fine. Her name is Lucia."

"Yes, yes, I already know that," Tania says, with an impatient roll of her eyes. "She's Venetian, moved back home after ten years abroad, and works at the Palazzo Ducale."

I give Enzo an irritated look. "You ran a background check on her?"

He looks unrepentant. "Let's see," he says,

ticking off on his fingers. "First, you show up at Casanova, which you never do because you don't want anyone to find out you own it. Second, you scene with a woman at the club. Something you've never done."

"Third, you bailed on us last week," Tania adds. "You never cancel our monthly lunches."

"So yes," Enzo finishes. "I looked her up. Stop glaring at me. You'd do the same thing if I were seriously involved with someone."

He's right. I wouldn't stop at a simple background check, either. Since our time on the streets, I've watched out for Enzo and Tatiana, and they've watched out for me. We're protective of each other, the three of us. We had to be.

"Fair enough," I concede. "Fill your plates, and I'll answer all your questions over lunch."

My housekeeper made sopa coada for lunch. Some recipes call for pigeon, but Agnese's version is closer to a hearty soup made with beans, vegetables, sausage, and chicken. "Ah, I see Agnese is back," Enzo says appreciatively as he digs in. "Thank heavens. I was a little nervous about this meal."

I make a rude gesture in his direction. "I know how to cook."

"And when was the last time you cooked for someone?" Tania prods. "Have you cooked for Lucia? Is it that kind of relationship?"

"Not yet." A flaw that needs to be rectified. "And yes, I want it to be."

"This is a first. You finally decide to get seriously involved with someone, but from what I can see, she doesn't commit." Enzo frowns. "I don't like it."

"She has her reasons for that." I set my jaw. "More importantly, it's none of your business. You're my family, and I want you both to like Lucia. But your approval isn't required."

Enzo pulls out his wallet and hands Tatiana a ten-euro note. It takes a second for it to sink in. "Seriously?"

I demand. "You were betting on my reaction?"

"Oh, come on. Let us have our fun." Tania pats my hand. "Tell us about Lucia. What do you like about her?"

"*Everything.* Lucia is not afraid of me. She's not interested in my money or my influence. She doesn't want anything from me." I draw in a breath. "People see me, and they see the head of the Mafia. The power and the wealth. Not Lucia. She just sees me."

And I'm in love with her.

"You should see the sappy expression on your face," Enzo says. "It's a little nauseating. You have it bad, my friend."

"It'll be you one day."

He laughs. "Oh, I very much doubt that. But I'm delighted for you. I hope she makes you very happy. Why didn't you invite her to join us today?"

Lucia won't even spend the night. Meeting my friends? It's way too soon for that. Not that I'm going to tell Tania and Enzo that—the two of them are already bristling with over-protectiveness.

"She had other plans," I lie. "Soon."

"Good." Tania leans forward, setting her glass on the table. "I can't wait to meet her."

Tatiana's already gone through her first glass in record time and is midway through her second. And these aren't small pours. "Are you going to tell us what's wrong with you?"

She avoids my gaze and busies herself with her food. "You're changing the topic. We were talking about Lucia."

"You've been here for less than thirty minutes, and you're more than three-quarters of the way through that bottle of wine. You know how nosy Enzo is. If you don't tell us what's wrong, he might be forced to find out a different way."

"Fine," she snaps. "If you really must know, I auditioned for a role yesterday."

"And you didn't get it?"

"Oh, I got it." Her voice has a forced calm. "Well, as long as I was willing to suck the director's cock for the role."

A cold rage fills me. "Who was the director?"

She sighs. "And this is why I didn't say anything. Let it go, Antonio."

I glance at Enzo. His face is expressionless, but I read the fury in his eyes. He nods slightly, and I let myself relax. He'll take care of it.

Tatiana leaves right after lunch—she has a flight to catch for a shoot in London. Enzo lingers for a bit longer. "There are more guards out front than normal," he says. "What's going on?"

I consider how much to share. "A high-ranking member of the Gafur OPS approached me a few weeks ago to smuggle weapons through Venice into France. I turned them down."

"You're not involved in this? At all?"

"You know I don't like guns." It's more than that. Even though Gafur swears the weapons are going somewhere else, guns have a way of showing up where they don't belong. I don't want that for my city.

Enzo heaves a sigh of relief. "Thank fuck. The entire thing is a powder keg, and it's going to explode at any moment."

"It's on your radar?"

"Yes. The Russians are working with Salvatore Verratti. The DIA has been building a case against Family Verratti for months. They're almost ready to make an arrest."

"You're sure Verratti is involved with the Russians?" I press. Valentina has been searching for proof, but she's come up short. Salvatore is being very careful.

"I'm dead certain." His expression is grim. "Be careful, Antonio. Verratti is broke and desperate for his partnership with the Russians to work. If you turned them down, it's not only Gafur you have to worry about."

I'm extremely aware that our friendship puts Enzo in ethical dilemmas from time to time. He's gone out on a limb and warned me, which means the situation is much more serious than I thought. "Thank you."

The Russians aren't the only threat. I need to watch out for Verratti's men as well.

And they blend in a lot better than Ilya Kozlov and his goons.

I call Dante once Enzo leaves. "Do you still have Angelica with you?"

"No, I just dropped her off with her mother. Why?"

"Head back there. I need everyone here for an emergency meeting. Joao, Tomas, Leonardo, and Valentina. You can serve as Valentina's protection."

"You want Valentina too?" he asks sharply. "Okay. Her neighbor can watch Angelica for a couple of hours."

"No." I don't think Salvatore Verratti would stoop to attacking a child, but I won't take any chances. "Bring her too."

Dante digests that, and his voice turns grim. "Yes, Antonio."

Twenty minutes later, I stare at the five people assembled in my office. My top lieutenants, the people I trust in a crisis. "The Russians aren't forcing Salvatore Verratti to cooperate with them," I tell them. "He's working with them of his own free will. The situation has suddenly become a lot more serious. Until this is resolved, everyone stays in Giudecca."

Valentina turns pale. She's the only one in my inner circle who doesn't live nearby. Her apartment is in Dorsoduro, a difficult neighborhood to secure. Too many university buildings, too many students. "Valentina, you'll have to move. You and Angelica can stay—"

Dante leans forward. "They'll stay with me."

Nobody will protect the two of them better than my second-in-command. But Valentina and Dante have a stormy relationship, and I want to make sure I'm not putting her in an uncomfortable situation. "Valentina?" I prompt. "Does that work for you?"

Her expression turns unreadable. "Yes."

"Leo, nobody goes anywhere alone."

"I'll see to it," my security chief replies calmly.

"Good. That's it, everyone. Be careful. Keep your eyes open, and don't take any chances. Leo, hang on for a minute. I need a word."

My people are protected. Tatiana is safe in London. Enzo can take care of himself.

Which leaves Lucia. I've been seen in public with her; now, because of me, she's at risk. And that's something I'm never going to let happen.

The room clears out. I turn to my security chief. "Lucia Petrucci lives in Castello. How safe is she?"

Leo frowns. "She doesn't work for us; she's only a target because she's connected to you. Things will be easier if you break things off with her." He nods, warming to that idea. "Can you do a scene in Casanova with someone else? Everything that happens in the club is supposed to be confidential, but you're too juicy a topic of conversation. It'll get out."

Do a scene with another woman when I'm in

love with Lucia? Is he out of his fucking mind? "That's never going to happen."

Leo hears the frost in my voice and realizes he's walking on very thin ice. He grimaces. "My apologies, padrino. I wasn't thinking clearly." I nod, accepting his apology, and he continues. "Can she move in with you?"

Lucia in my house, in my bed. Waking up next to me every morning, her glorious hair spread out in a riotous tangle over my pillowcases, her eyes sleepy, her body soft and warm. For a brief insane second, I want it so badly that it clouds my judgment, and I'm tempted, so tempted, to order her to live with me whether she's ready or not. It is for her own safety, after all.

But then, common sense reasserts itself. Just last night, Lucia invited me to dinner. She's scared and cautious, but she's slowly letting me into her life. Her trust is fragile, and the last thing I want to do is trample all over it. "Can you protect her where she is?"

The Thief

"We upgraded her building security yesterday when we fixed her elevator, but there are other complications. The ski instructor downstairs rents his unit to tourists when he's not at home. He hasn't had any bookings this month, but a couple from Germany will arrive next week. The week after, a family from Canada. Same with the building across the street. Half the units there are tourist rentals. There are always people coming and going. It's a security nightmare."

A sniper could hide in the building across the street and take a shot at Lucia. My stomach clenches. "Rent the units, all of them. Buy the buildings if you need to, if that's what it'll take to secure them. I don't care how much money you have to spend. Put our best people on her, Leo. Keep her safe."

According to Enzo, Salvatore Verratti is broke and desperate. But if he knows what's good for him, he'll stay far, far away from Venice. If he threatens the woman I love, I will end him.

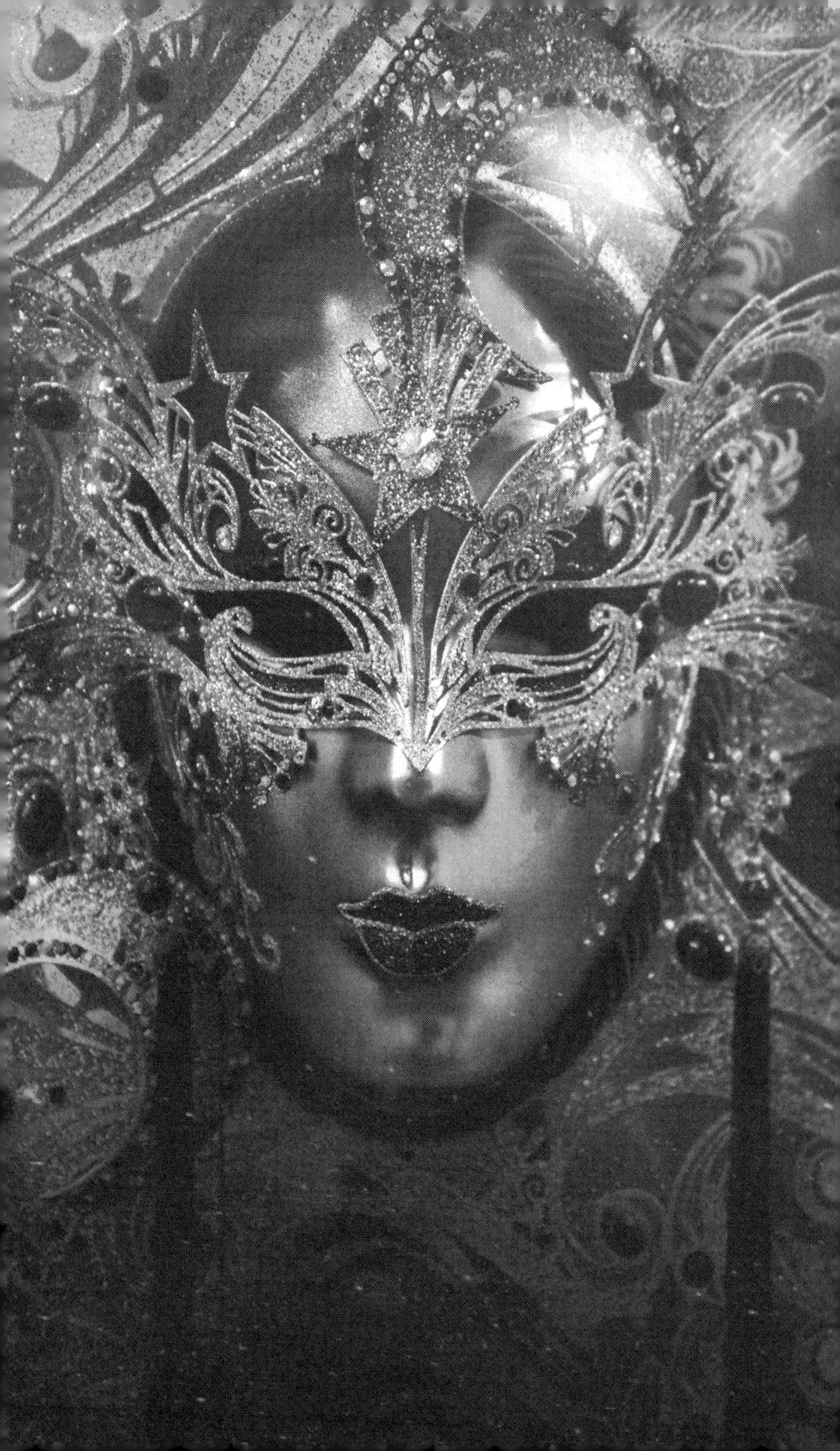

LUCIA

Chapter Twenty-Four

Most women have that one male coworker who is a condescending, sexist jerk. At the Palazzo Ducale, that role is filled by Felix Mayer.

Dr. Mayer, the assistant curator in charge of acquisitions, is in his mid-fifties. He always turns to me in meetings and says, "Would you mind taking notes, Lucia?" Two weeks ago, when our department assistant was out sick for a day, he asked me to bring him a coffee. Yeah. For real. For almost a minute, my brain struggled to process iron control, I said, "Dr. Mayer, I'm your colleague, not your assistant. The coffee is in the break room. Get it yourself."

Evidently, my response hurt his feelings. Ever since the incident, we've maintained an uneasy peace. I do my best to avoid him, and he alternates between pouting like a child and ignoring me. I've heard through the grapevine that he expects me to apologize for being mean to him. Like that's going to happen.

Given all of that, it's something of a surprise that the first person I see when I get into work Monday morning is Felix Mayer, holding a box of pastries in his hand.

"I stopped by at the bakery on my way in," he explains, holding out the sugary treats as a peace offering. "Please, have one."

"Thank you." Is this his version of an apology? *Whatever.* I take one, hoping he'll go away, but he doesn't.

"I wanted to make sure there were no hard feelings from our conversation a couple of weeks ago."

You mean the conversation where you demeaned me and asked me to bring you coffee? I bite those words back. "Okay," I say instead. "If you'll excuse me, Dr. Mayer. I have a busy day ahead of me."

"Yes, yes, of course." He makes no move to leave. "What are you working on, Lucia?"

I summon up patience and answer his question, and he pretends to listen. Five excruciating minutes later, he departs my office.

Twenty minutes later, Nicolo Garzolo wanders in.

Dr. Garzolo never seeks me out. He hired me to digitize the collection, but he's not interested in my work and has largely ignored me since I started.

Evidently, today's my lucky day. "Dr. Garzolo, good morning."

He enters my office and settles himself in the chair across from me. I not-so-patiently wait for him to explain why he's here, but he doesn't say anything, so I prompt, "Is there anything I can do for you?"

"I came by to see how you are doing." He looks around the tiny, windowless space. A glorified closet, really. "You don't have a lot of light here. We should find you a better office."

It finally dawns on me what this is about. Venice is a small city, and I was seen having an intimate dinner with its most prominent resident. I am now *somebody*.

Dr. Garzolo was happy to ignore my existence. Felix treated me like I was his assistant. But now that I'm connected with Antonio Moretti, things are different. Everyone is suddenly very eager to curry favor with me.

I repress the desire to laugh hysterically. What are they trying to achieve? What do they think I can do for them? Does Dr. Garzolo think that Antonio will increase the size of his donation to the Palazzo if the sex is exceptional? What's the end goal here?

The Thief

Resisting the urge to scream at the top of my voice, I mutter something suitably polite and get my boss out of my office as quickly as possible. Then I duck out for a quick cup of coffee, hoping the chill in the air will calm me.

I'm not going to lie—a very large part of me wants to call Antonio to yell at him.

For what? My conscience prods. *You want to blame him because your co-workers are being nice to you? It's not Antonio's fault that your colleagues want to suck up.*

I'm still fuming though, so I text Valentina.

> What are you doing tonight?

> Why?

> My coworkers are assholes. I had dinner with Antonio, and suddenly everyone's kissing my ass. Can I swing by after work to vent?

> I can't this evening. Need a favor. Calling you now.

"What's going on?"

"Long story," she replies. "Is there any way you can duck out early from work today, pick Angelica up from school, and keep her at your place for a couple of hours?"

"Sure thing," I respond. Valentina sounds stressed. "Is everything okay?"

"It's fine. Thanks, Lucia. I'll let Angelica's school know you'll be picking her up. Heads up, Dante will probably be there too."

There's an edge to her voice when she says that. "Are you sure everything's fine?"

"Dante's not the problem, if that's what you're asking," she responds. "As for the rest, I'll fill you in tonight."

When I get there, Antonio's second-in-command, Dante, is already at Angelica's school. "Signorina Petrucci, good afternoon," he says. "I'll be walking

The Thief

back with you and Angelica."

"Okay." I'll admit it—I'm wildly curious about Dante. Whether or not Valentina acknowledges it, he's important to her. And she's my best friend. I wasn't here for her the last time she was in a relationship, so this time around, I'm going to do my due diligence and make sure the guy she's interested in isn't a jerk. "Call me Lucia."

"Lucia." He spots Angelica, and a smile touches his lips. "There you are, monkey."

Angelica is clearly thrilled to see him. "Uncle Dante," she squeals, her face breaking out into a wide smile. "You came to pick me up. And Aunt Lucia." She pauses for a moment, and her expression turns worried. "Where's Mama?"

Dante responds before I can. "She got held up at work," he says, his tone warmly reassuring. "Lucia and I volunteered to pick you up."

"Yep," I confirm. "I hope you like hot chocolate, kid, because that's all I have to drink at my house." Hey, I'm not above bribery.

"Hot chocolate?" Her eyes shine. "I love it."

"What did you do at school today?" I ask her on the walk back.

"We learned about zebras," she responds. "And I had a surprise math test." She sounds as excited by the surprise math test as when I offered her hot chocolate. She's her mother's daughter, alright. "Did you know that zebras can run as fast as sixty-five kilometers per hour?"

Dante and I listen to animal facts on the walk back home. Well, I listen. Dante glowers at every tourist who gets too close to us. I want to ask him what's going on, but I'm conscious of the fact that Angelica has sharp ears, so I hold off.

"You have new chairs!" Angelica exclaims as soon as I open the front door of my apartment. "And a new carpet." She spots the roses, which are still fresh, and makes a beeline for them, burying her face in their scent. "And pretty flowers. Look, Uncle Dante."

"They *are* beautiful," Dante agrees with studied

blandness. No doubt he knows exactly who they're from. "Now, what shall we do? You can either tackle your homework or. . ." He pulls a Lego kit from his bag. "Want to build a pirate ship?"

He *is* good with her. I leave them to their construction and head into my kitchen to make hot chocolate. A few minutes later, Dante knocks at the door. "I've been sent to tell you that Angelica would like whipped cream on her hot chocolate," he says. "If you have any."

Whipped cream is *essential*. "I do." I glance at the man. "What's going on? Can you talk about it?"

He considers for an instant and then nods. "The Russian threat has escalated," he says. "Valentina and Angelica are moving in with me until we take care of this issue."

"For how long?"

"Two weeks, maybe. A month at most."

Dante's interested in Valentina—I'm absolutely convinced of it. He should look pleased about the move, but he looks almost tortured.

"The threat has escalated? Antonio didn't say anything."

"That's not surprising, is it?" Dante's tone is matter-of-fact. "The padrino is going to protect you—he's always done that. But he also wants to shield you from the worst of his world."

"What do you mean, he's always protected me?"

He winces. "I shouldn't have said anything."

"Please?"

He sighs. "Ten years ago, when you first met Antonio, there was a man who hurt you, yes?"

I nod.

"That was Marco," Dante responds. "Antonio told Marco that if he ever stepped foot in Venice again, he would personally kill him. Unfortunately, Marco was the *padrino's* nephew. As you can imagine, that created a bit of a situation. But Antonio being Antonio, he wouldn't back down."

"Oh." I did not know that.

"You are important to him," he says. He gestures to the stove behind me. "I believe the hot chocolate is ready. Where are your mugs?"

Dante takes the hot chocolate out to Angelica. I stay in the kitchen, needing a moment to digest everything.

It's a lot.

Valentina moving in with Dante is a big deal. There's real danger here—that much is obvious. And Antonio is at the center of it. He's the biggest target.

He could have asked me to move in with him. He could have *insisted*. But he didn't. All the flowers, lingerie, and over-the-top furniture purchases aside, he's letting me set the pace of our relationship.

I close my eyes and let myself dream about living with Antonio. Sitting with him in the kitchen, morning sunlight streaming in through the French doors, talking about art over multiple cups of coffee. Walking through antique stores, picking up eclectic pieces that catch our eye. Bantering with him about who really owns the *Madonna*.

But that's only one side of the coin. The flip side is that Antonio will always be in danger. He will always have armed bodyguards following him around. He will always have a security team monitoring his house.

If I'm with Antonio, then this will become my life. If I'm with Antonio, I have to be prepared for the possibility that he could vanish like my parents did. One moment, he could be alive and the next, gunned down in a hail of fire.

Am I ready for that? Am I ready to open myself up to the possibility of love when love leads to crippling loss?

Do you really have a choice?

No, I don't. I'm too invested. His death would flay me open. Even if I broke things off with Antonio this very instant, even if I never set eyes on him again, it's too late.

I've done the thing I warned myself against.

I've fallen in love with Antonio Moretti.

LUCIA

Chapter Twenty-Five

Shockingly, after realizing I've fallen in love with Venice's most dangerous man, I don't book the first flight out of Italy. Instead, I turn my closet inside out, obsessing about what to wear for my date.

A black, knee-length, fitted sheath dress gets discarded as too business-casual. I try on a soft, cream-colored sweater dress that hugs my curves in all the right places, but knowing me, I'm likely to ruin it spilling pasta down my front. Finally, I settle on an emerald-green wrap dress. The V-neck is deep, the dress nips in at my waist, and the skirt is full and flowing, falling just above my knees. The fabric is a blend of silk and wool jersey, and it feels warm against my skin.

Tuesday evening, I take more time with my make-up than usual. I pull out all the stops—foundation, mascara, blush, and a bright red lip. I spend almost forty-five minutes trying to put my hair in a chic up-do before I give up and leave it down. In a concession to the cold, I pair my dress with knee-high brown suede boots and add a wrap for extra warmth.

My doorbell rings exactly at seven. I put on my mother's pendant, take one final look in the mirror, and head to the living room to answer the door.

Antonio is there, wearing an impeccably tailored suit, a white shirt, and a subtly patterned tie. His hair is brushed, he's freshly shaved, and he looks fantastic.

The Thief

Not going to lie—I want to drag him inside and ravish him.

He takes in my appearance, and heat touches his eyes. "You look lovely." His eyes trail down my body and rest on my boots. "Those heels look like weapons."

I flash him a grin. "I guess you'll have to remember to behave." Those are fighting words to a man as dominant as Antonio. I might as well wave a red flag to a bull.

"Why would I do that? It sounds boring." He reaches into his jacket and pulls out a flat box roughly the size of my hand. "I have something for you."

"That looks like jewelry." I give him a wary glance. "Antonio, you can't keep buying me things."

"So you say." He hands it to me. "Open it."

I glance at his face. Whatever is in the box, it's important to him that I like it.

I flip the lid open.

It's a bracelet. But not just any bracelet. Six

rubies, each the size of my thumb, are cradled in intricate filigree, with golden tendrils twisting and curling around the gemstones like vines. The rubies glitter and shine against the gold, catching the light with every movement.

I swallow. This jewelry has been designed to match my mother's pendant, which I wear daily on a chain around my neck. The filigree work is identical. The color of the stones is a perfect match.

This is... incredible.

I look at the man standing in front of me. "You had this custom-made," I whisper.

He nods carefully. "Yes. Do you like it?"

"I love it." I blink the tears away before they have a chance to fall. If my mother were still alive, she'd pull me aside and tell me that Antonio is a keeper. "When did you commission it?"

"Show me your arm." I extend my right hand toward him, and he fastens the bracelet around my wrist. "I had it made the day you stole my painting from Daniel Rossi's apartment."

The Thief

"Again, it's not your painting," I say automatically. Then his words sink in. "The day I stole the Titian from Daniel Rossi's apartment? But that was only the second time we met. You didn't know me at all. How did you know I'd sleep with you? Was I that much of a sure thing?"

"Not at all." He winks at me. "I like to think positively, like the self-help books recommend. Manifest."

I have to struggle not to laugh. "Manifest?"

"Exactly," he agrees. His expression turns serious. "I didn't know you'd sleep with me, Lucia. I hoped you would, yes, but I would never take you for granted." His fingers stroke my wrist. "I commissioned this because I thought you'd like it." A pause. "I would do anything to make you happy."

I touch the bracelet. It probably costs more money than I've ever made in my life, but that's not why I'm struggling to keep from tearing up. After all, Antonio is the richest person in Italy. He has plenty of money.

But, like the furniture he bought me, like the blue and white vase filled with hyacinths he sent me at work, this is *thoughtful*. He knows how important my mother's pendant is to me, and he's given me a gift that complements it.

He wants me in his life, but he also wants to be in mine.

I can't find the words to express how much this bracelet means to me, but I look up, and the tenderness in his eyes tells me that maybe I don't need to. "Thank you," I whisper. "It's beautiful."

He offers me his arm. "Shall we?"

La Buona Tavola is one of many small trattorias that dot the Campo Santi Giovanni e Paolo. From the outside, it looks indistinguishable from the dozens of small restaurants in Venice. But true insiders know better. Claudia Marino is an amazing cook, and her food is to die for.

The Thief

Four bodyguards surround us on the five-minute walk to the restaurant. Two in front, two in the back. Antonio looks faintly unhappy but otherwise ignores them, and taking my cue from him, I do too.

"Can you walk in those?" Antonio asks, glancing at my boots. "They look uncomfortable."

They are hideously uncomfortable, and no, I can't walk in them for any distance. Although if I say that to Antonio, he's more than capable of carrying me. "I'm tougher than I look."

"I know." He takes my hand in his and frowns. "Lucia, you're freezing." He removes his coat and drapes it over my shoulders.

Warmth hugs me. "Thank you." I come to a stop outside the restaurant. "We're here. It's not as nice as Quadri, I know—"

He chuckles. "I grew up on the streets, cara mia. I remember pressing my nose to the windows of places like this, fantasizing about a future where I could afford to order anything on the menu." He squeezes my hand. "Also, Signora Marino is a great cook."

"You've been here before?"

"Not in years. How do you know it?"

One of Antonio's men enters the restaurant to check it out for threats. We're supposed to wait until he gives us the okay to enter. Once again, I do my best to ignore the heightened security. "I've known Claudia and Miriam since I was a child. My mother used to babysit them. We were here the day they opened this place." I smile at the memory. "I was thirteen. I didn't want to be here; I wanted to stay home and watch TV. But Claudia bribed me with apple fritters."

Antonio's bodyguard comes out and nods to us. "Shall we sit by the window?" I ask with slightly forced cheer. The over-the-top precautions are getting to me. "La Buona Tavola is a seat yourself kind of place."

He gives me a careful look as if to gauge the extent of my irritation. "Sure." He pulls my chair

The Thief

out for me. "I'm sorry about this."

I'm about to tell him it's fine when another bodyguard walks into the restaurant. "Padrino, may I—"

"No," Antonio snaps without looking at the guy. "Go away."

The man retreats without another word. Antonio looks frustrated. "Once again, I'm truly sorry." He grimaces. "This is not how I wanted this date to go."

I place my hand on his. "It's fine," I say. "It's your life. I get it."

"It's not normally my life." He runs his hand through his hair. "This is temporary, I promise."

I smile at him. "I'm starving. Let's get some wine and order some cicchetti?"

"Sure."

Another man walks into the restaurant. "Padrino, I'm sorry to interrupt. May I have a word, please?" It's phrased as a request, but his tone makes it clear he's not going away until he talks to his boss.

Before Antonio loses his temper entirely, I give him a little wave. "Go. I'll be fine."

With a frown, he gets up. The guy pulls him to the back and says something in a low voice. Antonio responds, his expression annoyed. The guy throws up his hands in the air. It's like watching a play, so I'm almost disappointed when Claudia's sister Miriam bustles up to me and interrupts my view.

"Lucia!" she exclaims, bending down to kiss my cheeks in her typical exuberant manner. "You're very dressed up today. What's the special occasion?" Without waiting for me to respond, she continues, "A half-liter of wine to start and some cicchetti? Our specials today are bigoli con l'anatra, and risotto al limone con gamberi e zucchini. Or do you feel like soup? The creamy pumpkin soup is very good today."

"Umm, I'm here with someone." I gesture in Antonio's direction. "Can you give us a few minutes?"

She glances at Antonio and does a double-take.

The Thief

Her mouth falls open, and her eyes go wide. "Is that?" she whispers, her voice trailing off.

"Antonio Moretti." *Crap*. Antonio is the head of the Mafia. Do they still require 'protection' money from local businesses? I wasn't thinking about this when I invited him to dinner. Should I not have brought him here?

"That's who you're here with?"

I nod mutely. Claudia and Miriam have known me since I was a baby. They can be a little protective of me, so I'm pretty sure I know what Miriam is going to say. She's going to remind me that sensible women do not hook up with violent, dangerous men. She's going to warn me to stay the hell away from Antonio.

"Miriam, I'm so sorry. Do you want us to leave?"

"Leave?" Her face breaks into a huge smile. "Why? Just wait until I tell Claudia who's eating with us tonight. She's going to be thrilled."

I'm missing something. "You know who Antonio is, right?"

She rolls her eyes. "Am I an ostrich? Of course I know who he is, Lucia." She lowers her voice. "A few years ago, Bruno fell in with the wrong crowd and got into trouble with the carabinieri."

"He did?" Bruno is Claudia's twenty-year-old son. He's quiet and serious and wants to be a doctor. I can't imagine him running afoul of the law.

"He might have gone to jail if the padrino hadn't intervened," she says solemnly. "And Bruno's not the only person he's helped." Her eyes shine. "Signor Moretti will always be welcome here. *Always.*"

She hurries to the back, undoubtedly to tell Claudia about the celebrity in their midst. Antonio finishes his conversation and returns. "Leo, my head of security, insists we move away from the window." He looks pained. "I'm so—"

"Sorry," I finish. We need to move away from the window because a sniper could shoot Antonio through the glass. My stomach does a weird flip, and my palms go damp. It's one thing to know that Antonio's life is dangerous. It's another thing entirely to be confronted with the proof of it.

He does his best to keep his face expressionless. "This isn't what you thought you were getting into. I'll understand if you need to leave. You'll be safer that way."

Leaving would be the smartest thing to do. But I'm past that. Maybe I was past that when I asked him to stay with me ten years ago.

I get to my feet and lace my fingers in his. "Stop apologizing. It was cold by the window anyway."

I can't decide between the risotto and the steak, so Antonio suggests we get both and share. Claudia pops up with a platter of cicchetti and a complimentary bottle of wine. She fusses over Antonio, promises to make him a meal to remember, gives me an approving nod, and disappears into the kitchen.

Once we're alone, I lift the bottle of wine. "I've

known Claudia and Miriam all my life, and I don't get free wine," I grumble. "Then again, I've never kept Bruno out of jail."

"Is that what Miriam said to you?" Antonio looks uncomfortable. Hang on, is he blushing? I love it. "She's exaggerating."

"You don't even know what she said."

"I can guess." Yup, he's definitely blushing. "All I did was make a couple of phone calls." He gives me a stern look. "And you're having entirely too much fun at my expense."

Oops. "Guilty." I pour us both some wine and sip the complex red. It's glorious. Claudia really is pulling out all the stops. "Maybe I'm looking to get punished."

A smile curves at the corners of his mouth. "Are you, now?" Our food arrives before he can elaborate on how he'll make me pay for my teasing. Pity. There's nothing like anticipation to make a spanking even sweeter.

The Thief

"How's your work going?" Antonio asks as we share dessert. It's an orange liqueur-flavored panna cotta served with chopped kiwi, passion fruit, and mango. I'm really too full to eat it, but I saw it on the menu and couldn't resist. "Any blowback from our Quadri meal?"

He's frighteningly astute. "Let's see. Dr. Garzolo, who has spent most of his time ignoring my existence, offered to give me a bigger office with a window. And my most sexist co-worker, who usually expects me to bring him coffee and take notes, brought me pastries. Dating Antonio Moretti comes with its perks." I roll my eyes. "Dr. Garzolo, I understand. Felix, though? I can't even. Does he really think I'm going to turn to you when we're in bed and say, 'Do you know who's really good at acquiring fine art? Dr. Mayer.'"

His eyes narrow. "Felix Mayer," he says. "Good to know."

I glare at him. "Do. Not. Do. Anything. This is my problem, and I'll handle it."

"Mmm."

"I'm serious, Antonio."

He lifts his hands up in a placating gesture. "I won't do anything without your knowledge," he says. "I promise."

I set my fork down. "I can't eat another bite."

He gestures for the check. I attempt to pay, but he won't hear of it. Claudia and Miriam tell him the meal is on the house, but he won't listen to them either. "The food was even more delicious than I remember," he tells them. "I'm delighted Lucia suggested we eat here tonight."

We head back outside. It's gotten even chillier, and Antonio immediately drapes his coat back over my shoulders. "About your punishment," he says. "I hope you're not done for the night because I have plans for you."

My insides quicken. "What kind of plans?"

"Plans that involve you spending all night tied up to my bed."

"Oh, that's a pity." I paste a disappointed look

on my face. "Because I was going to invite you to spend the night at my place."

For a fleeting second, shock fills his eyes. We're both extremely aware that it's the first time I've invited him to my house. Then a neutral mask once again slides over his face. "I can be flexible."

I give him a teasing smile. "Can you, now?"

"Of course," he says loftily. "When the situation calls for it, I can adapt. It's always wise to consider new information when making a decision."

I have to struggle to keep a straight face. "What kind of new information?"

"Your place is less than five minutes away." He kisses me, quick and hard. "Four, if we hurry. So walk faster, Lucia."

You haven't told him about the Uffizi, my conscience prods. I dismiss it. It's too soon to have this discussion. I don't even have an interview yet.

But the feeling of guilt persists all the way home.

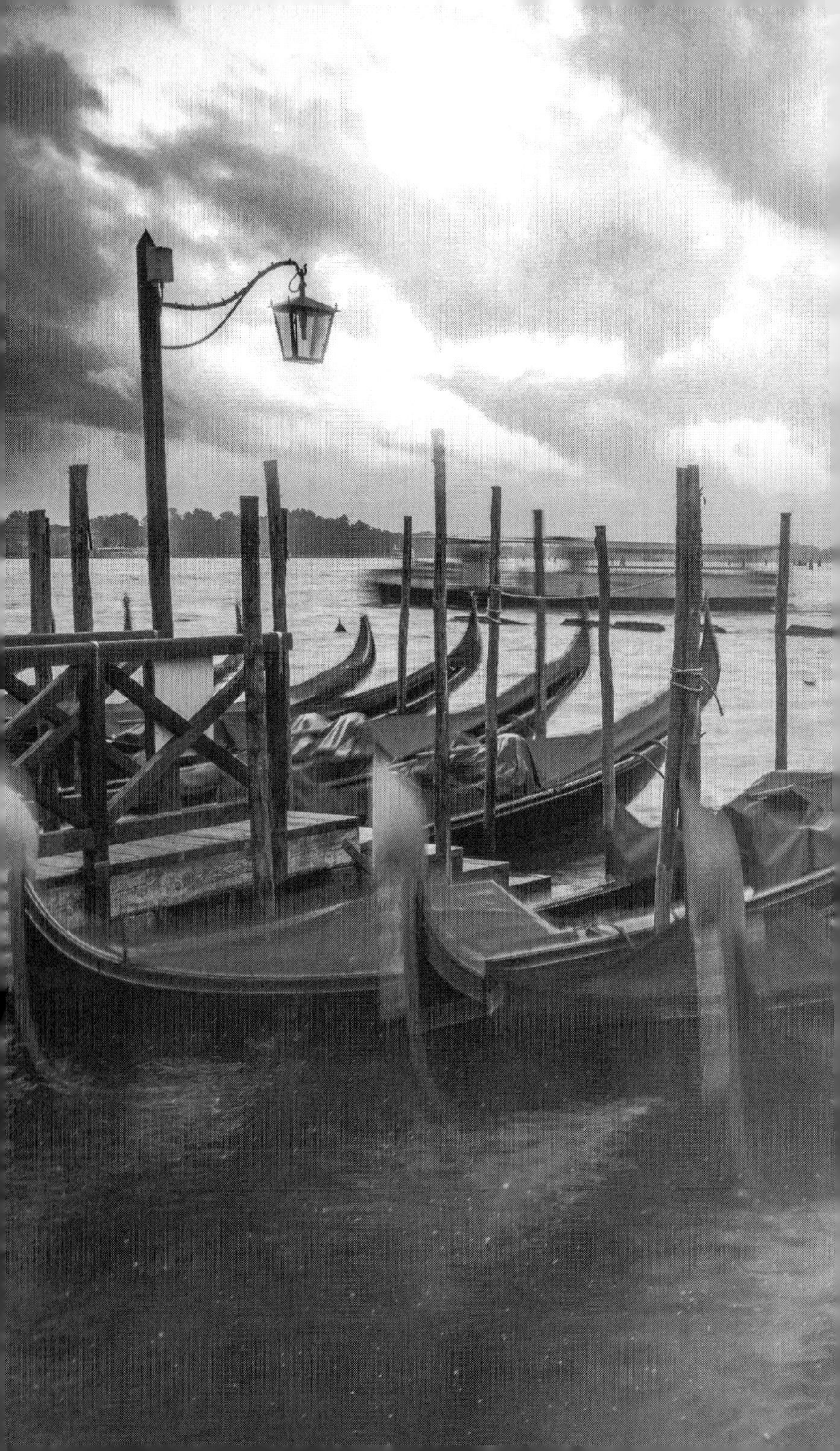

ANTONIO

Chapter Twenty-Six

When we reach Lucia's building, my guards separate into pairs. One set stays at the front of the building, and the other two announce their intention to stand guard outside Lucia's front door.

"Take the stairs," I order, stepping into the elevator and hitting the button to close the door before they can protest.

We fall on each other as soon as the doors close. I kiss Lucia's neck, shoulders, and soft lips as the ancient elevator creaks all the up to her apartment.

I only let her go so she can open her door. We step inside, and I hurry her into her bedroom. "The dress is nice. Lose it."

"Yes, Sir." She winks at me and loosens the tie at her waist. Her dress falls open, and I suck in a breath. She's wearing the lingerie I bought her. The green bra hugs her breasts perfectly, and her nipples are erect under the lace. I glance at her matching panties, and I go hard. The last time she wore those panties, I lifted her onto my desk, pushed the gusset aside, and feasted on her. My cock remembers.

"What do you think?" She twirls around.

"They're nice. Take them off."

"I'm sensing a theme here, Antonio," she says teasingly. "It sounds like you want me to get naked."

"Not entirely. Keep the boots on." I pull her to me and kiss her deeply, my hands roaming over her body. She moans into my mouth. I nudge her to the bed and push her onto the soft sheets. I'm so turned on that my vision blurs.

I undress quickly and join her. She runs her hands over my chest. I lean down to kiss her again and then move down her body. I kiss her breasts through the lace, then impatiently push the bra cups down and suck her nipples into my mouth, alternating from one side to the other. She arches her back and moans in pleasure.

I move lower. I kiss her stomach and hips, then slide my fingers between her legs. She's already wet. Soaked.

"You want my mouth on you?" I circle her clit with my fingertips, and she shivers. "Take what you want. Ride my face, tesoro."

We change positions. Lucia laughs breathlessly as she shimmies up my body. Grabbing the headboard, she straddles me, her pussy over my face.

Fuck, yes.

I grab her ass and pull her down onto my mouth, pressing my tongue against her clit and stroking the tender nub. She throws her head back. "That feels so good," she gasps. "Can you breathe down there?"

I laugh into her delicious pussy. "Don't worry about me, tesoro. This would be the most pleasurable way to die."

I dive back in, flicking her clit with my tongue and sucking her pussy lips between my teeth. She grinds down on me, her juices dripping down my chin. She squirms on my face, trembling as I squeeze her breasts, pinch her nipples, and feast on her.

Her thighs quiver, trapping my head in a vice. Her juices gush into my mouth as she comes, and I hold my tongue flat against her and savor every last quiver.

"Wow," she murmurs. She collapses against me, her eyes heavy-lidded, her cheeks flushed. She looks well fucked. Well-loved. "That was... amazing." She rolls onto her back and sits up. "You always go down on me," she says. "I want to suck your cock."

Happy to oblige. I lean against the headboard, and she nestles between my legs. She closes her lips around me, taking my cock deep. Her mouth is hot and wet. Her cheeks hollow as she sucks, her tongue swirling around my shaft, and pleasure gathers in an electric storm at the base of my spine.

When the sensation becomes unbearable, I pull free and draw her to her hands and knees, sheathing myself and taking her from behind.

We've made love before, but somehow, it's different this time. This time, I know I'm in love with Lucia. This time, we'll fall asleep next to each other, and when I wake up tomorrow morning, she'll be here. With me. And knowing that makes all the difference in the world.

White-hot pleasure builds inside me as I thrust into Lucia. I'm close. I urge her onto her back to look into her brilliant green eyes as I fall apart. I come with an intensity that shakes me to my core.

I eventually untangle myself from her to dispose

of the condom. "You want something to drink?"

"Yes, please." She sits up in bed, and the sheet falls to her waist, revealing her round, perfect breasts and tight, pert nipples. Her cheeks turn pink. "You're staring at me."

"I can't help myself. What would you like?"

"Water. I can get up."

"Stay in bed," I urge. "Still or sparkling?"

"Sparkling, please."

I walk into her kitchen. I half-expect her refrigerator to be empty, but I'm wrong—it's filled with food. Something eases inside me at the sight of the fresh vegetables, the jars of pesto, and the half-eaten loaf of bread on the counter. When I was here a week and a half ago, Lucia had no furniture. She lived out of a suitcase, and it seemed like she was ready to leave Venice at a moment's notice.

But the food. . .

The food gives me hope.

The Thief

I wake up before Lucia the next morning. I tiptoe out of bed, take a quick shower, and head to her kitchen to brew a pot of coffee.

Silvio and Omar have relieved Goran and Stefano. I take them cups of coffee and warn them I'll be here for a few hours.

Going back inside, I can hear Lucia moving around. A few minutes later, she emerges from the shower wearing a dressing robe, her hair damp. "The smell of coffee woke me up." She smiles at me. "Hey there."

She looks soft and dewy. "Hey yourself. I took some out to my guys. I hope you don't mind."

"Really? That's very nice of you."

"Try not to sound so shocked, Lucia. You could hurt my feelings."

She laughs, then stands on her tiptoe to kiss me on my lips. "You're full of surprises. Is there any coffee left?"

"Of course. Are you hungry? You have eggs. I can make you an omelet."

"You made coffee, and you're offering to cook me breakfast? Somebody pinch me."

We fall into an easy conversation as I chop green peppers and mushrooms and beat the eggs. "What time do you have to be at work?"

"Nine," she says. She watches as I pour the whipped eggs into a pan and scatter the vegetables on top. "You really do know what you're doing."

"Thank you." I leer at her. "I thought I did some of my best work last night. I'm happy to hear you agree."

She rolls her eyes. "I'm talking about your expertise in the kitchen, not in bed."

"Those are fighting words, tesoro. A man might feel compelled to respond." I flip the omelet, turn off the heat, slide it onto a plate, and place it in front of her with a flourish.

She takes a bite. "Delicious." Her expression turns serious. "What are we doing, Antonio?"

"Eating breakfast." I meet her gaze squarely. "Do you want a label on us, Lucia? I want to be your. . . the word boyfriend makes us sound like teenagers. I want to be your partner."

"You're talking about a relationship."

"Did you think one night with you would be enough? Yes, of course, I'm talking about a relationship. Lucia, since I saw Arthur Kincaid's security footage of you, there's been no one else for me. You are the only woman I want. The only woman I *need*."

She bites her lower lip. "Is it too soon? We've only really known each other for three weeks."

Has it really just been three weeks? I try to remember a time when I didn't know Lucia and draw a blank. It feels like I've known her forever.

I put down my fork. "Do you want something else?"

"No, I don't." Her reply is immediate, and a flash of relief shoots through me. A slow smile spreads across her face. "So. . . We're in a relationship now."

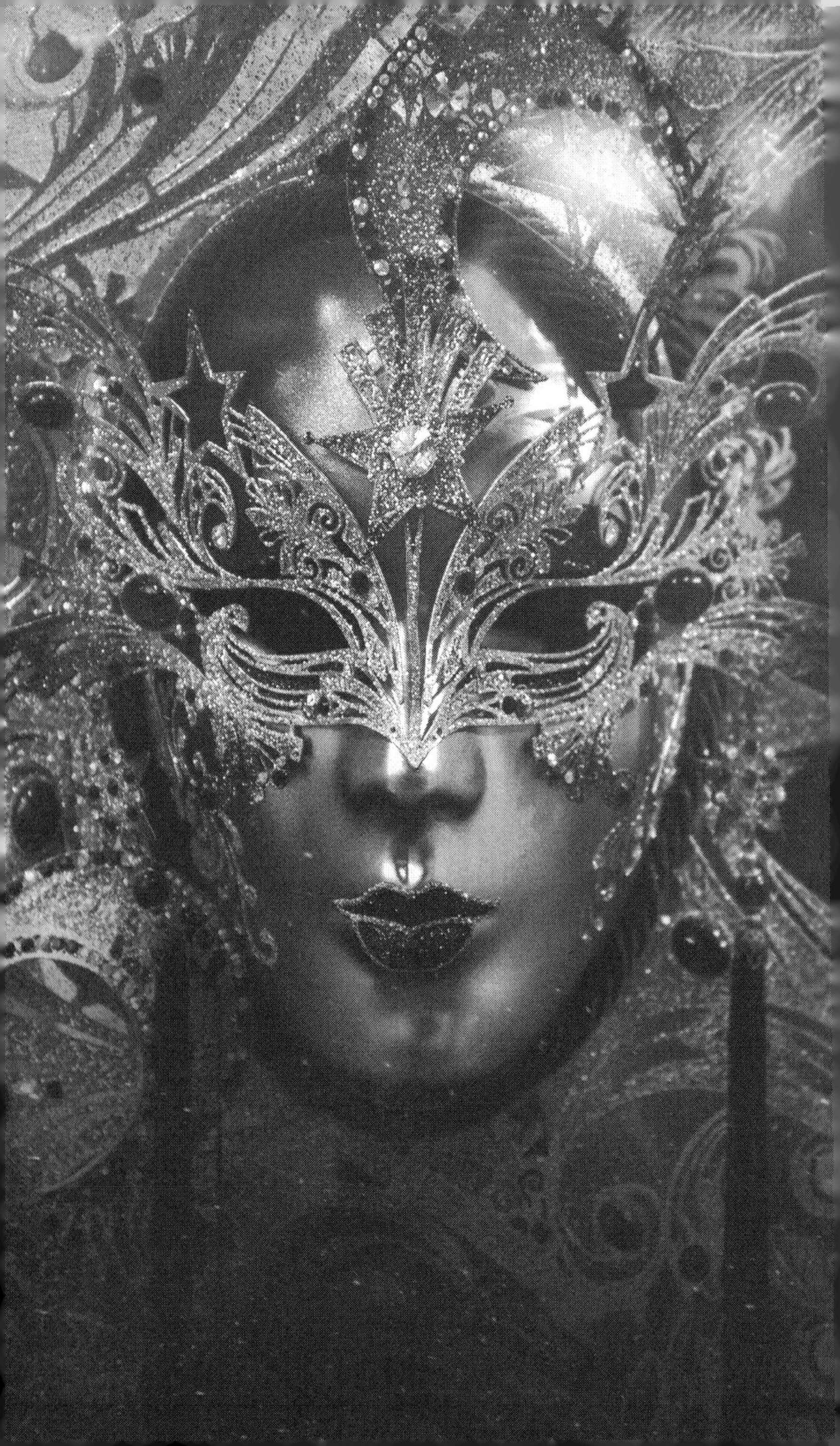

LUCIA

Chapter Twenty-Seven

Florence *is only a couple of hours away from Venice*, I tell myself as Antonio walks me to work. *And there's no guarantee the Uffizi job is going to come through.* No need to worry about it. *Yet.*

Two weeks go by, and I settle into my new relationship. Most evenings, I spend with Antonio. On the rare occasions we're not together,

I miss him fiercely. After ten years of suppressing my emotions and living in a world devoid of color, I'm suddenly living in a rainbow, and it's a little terrifying.

When my parents died, I did countless reckless things and took many stupid risks. But nothing beats the sheer peril of embarking upon a relationship with Antonio Moretti.

I'm already scarred. My heart has been broken into jagged pieces. I've done my best to put it back together, but my glue is brittle, and my recovery is tenuous. Falling in love with Antonio is the most dangerous thing I've ever done because if this thing between us shatters, so will my heart. And this time, I won't be able to put it back together.

Yet, like a moth to the flame, I flutter towards him, unable to help myself. I throw open the doors and invite him into my life. I ask him to come with me to my parents' storage unit. "I don't think I can brave it alone," I confess. "If you're not too busy—"

His reply wraps around me with the warmth of

The Thief

a handmade quilt. "I always have time for you, Lucia."

I find old albums in the storage unit, and we spend an evening looking at photos of my teenage self. I went through quite the goth phase, and Antonio laughs at my surly expressions. I get my revenge when I meet Enzo and Tatiana, and they tell me stories about Antonio's teenage exploits. "Remember his skinny pants?" Enzo asks.

Tania turns to me, her eyes dancing with glee. "He looked like a chicken in them," she tells me. "And one time, he bent to get something that fell on the floor, and they split."

I can't stop giggling. "You're ganging up on me," Antonio grumbles, putting an arm around my waist. "I don't like it." But I know he's lying. Enzo and Tatiana are his family, and he's delighted we're getting along.

Antonio's housekeeper, Agnese, is also very excited he's dating someone. "I'm so glad he found you," she gushes. "The padrino is a good man, and he's been alone too long." She makes me tell her a list of my favorite foods, and soon I'm eating Risi e Bisi three times a week. On weekends, when she's off, Antonio and I cook for each other. I've never cooked a meal for a man before. It feels decidedly intimate.

I love it.

On the first Thursday in December, Angelica has a ballet recital. Valentina, Dante, and I attend, and when Angelica comes on the stage in her little pink tutu, my heart feels like it's going to burst. Valentina's daughter has called me Aunt Lucia her entire life, but I've always felt like an impostor. I'm acutely aware that I've bribed my way into her affections with presents and candy, but I've never been there for the day-to-day stuff. Now, attending her recital, I finally feel worthy of the title.

In short, everything is perfect. Well, as perfect as it can be given the looming Russian threat.

Antonio does his best to conceal it, but he's stressed. The constant presence of bodyguards is getting to him. Enzo reassures us that Salvatore Verratti's arrest is imminent, and this time will soon be over, but as the days tick on, nothing happens. Antonio is not the only one affected by this. Valentina's living with Dante and is a stressed-out mess. We're all on edge, and I just want things to go back to normal.

Three days after Angelica's concert, Antonio and I have our first disagreement as a couple.

Antonio *really* doesn't like the idea of me going to Budapest. "I asked Valentina about Powell," he says. "Lucia, this guy is a piece of shit."

"Exactly." Knowing Antonio, he's asked Valentina for a copy of the dossier, read it cover to cover, and has already formulated three ways of retrieving the stolen Bassano, all of which involve me staying safely in Venice. "That's why he's my target."

"You already stole the Titian from me."

"That doesn't count."

"I don't see why not."

"It just doesn't." The guys I steal from—and they're almost always men—are horrible people who deserve to be robbed. Antonio is... more complicated than that. So much so that I still haven't returned the painting to the Palazzo Ducale. The masterpiece sits inside my bedroom closet. Antonio saw it there when he opened it to hang up his shirt, but he didn't press for an explanation, and I didn't offer one.

"Lucia, Powell is a piece of shit who's got the Hungarian police in his pocket. This is exceedingly dangerous. People who get on the wrong side of him disappear."

"Sounds like someone I know," I tease.

Antonio looks disgusted. "I am nothing like Gavin Powell."

I stand on tiptoe and kiss him. "I know that. I was just messing with you."

"No, you were trying to change the topic." He

The Thief

runs his hands through his hair. "I want to go with you, but I can't. Powell has a contact in the border agency. If I enter Hungary, there's a chance he could find out. And even if I travel incognito—"

"You can't," I cut him off. "You can't leave Venice right now." Antonio has eyes and ears everywhere in Venice. Outside the city, not so much. There's an active threat, and this is the safest place for him.

"I can't, but not for the reasons you think." He sounds frustrated. "Being with me puts you in the crosshairs of any number of people. As much as I hate to admit it, you're safer without me." He surveys me with serious eyes. "Is there anything I can say or do to get you to give this up?"

He is the king of Venice. If he decreed it, I wouldn't be able to leave the island. But, as he's shown time and time again, Antonio has no desire to control me. Except in bed, where I welcome it.

"I won't take any risks," I tell him. "I promise. I have a good plan."

He kisses me, deep and hard, like he never wants to stop. His eyes are hot and possessive, and his mouth claims mine. His lips and hands roam my body and send a message. I've seen Antonio's dominant side, but this feels different. The boundaries between us dissolve, and the walls we've erected to protect ourselves shatter.

"I don't doubt your abilities," he says finally, drawing back from me. "But that doesn't change how I feel. I'm afraid for you."

"I get that," I say softly. That kiss has wiped thought from my mind. "Thank you for not interfering."

He lets out a breath. "Take my plane."

"You own a plane?" Why am I surprised? I shouldn't be. Antonio owns construction companies, vineyards in Conegliano, Soave, Treviso, and Valpolicella, houses in most of Europe's major cities, and much more. He's wealthy on a scale I don't understand. "Thank you for the offer, but I'll be flying commercial. I've already bought my ticket."

He huffs in displeasure. "Will you at least let me upgrade your flight?"

All things considered, he's being extremely reasonable. I kiss him again to let him know I appreciate his restraint. "Yes, Antonio," I say sweetly. "I'd love to be upgraded. Thank you very much."

According to Valentina's dossier, the art thieves who stole the Bassano also walked away with three other paintings from the museum in Turin. Powell sold those but kept the Bassano because he didn't need the money.

That was three years ago. But times have changed. Powell's been banned by every major social media platform, drying up his podcast revenue. Lured by the prospect of fantastical returns, he invested the money he inherited from his family in cryptocurrency, but that market has since crashed. Basically, the guy is hurting, and he's being forced to sell the Bassano to cover some of his losses.

He set up a private auction and contacted a list of buyers who are receptive to the idea of acquiring stolen art. And, to reassure them of the painting's authenticity, he sent the Bassano to be appraised.

I plan to steal it from the appraiser. Specifically, I'll take a page from Antonio's book and replace the real Bassano with a fake. The appraiser will be able to tell the difference, but will he communicate that to Powell? Not a clue. Not my problem.

The job is a piece of cake. Everything goes according to plan. I get in, grab the painting, and get out. Forty-eight hours after I left Venice, I'm back at Marco Polo airport, the Bassano safely in my backpack, waiting in front of the baggage carousel for the ski equipment that was my cover for the trip.

That's when I feel someone staring at me.

I turn around and see a man in his mid-thirties.

The Thief

He's a few inches taller than me, his face weathered and lined. His thinning black hair is slicked back, and a dark beard covers his jawline. He's wearing a heavy woolen overcoat with the collar turned up. When he realizes I've noticed him, he turns away into a coffee shop.

I'm positive I've never seen him before, yet he somehow seems familiar. One of Antonio's men, maybe? After the incident with Ignazio, Antonio's security guards haven't tried to hide their presence. I've met the people guarding me. Ignazio, Marta, Benito, Manuel—I know what they look like, I've been introduced to them, and I know how to contact them.

Frowning, I look for him again, but he's nowhere to be seen. My bag is here, though. Lifting it on my shoulder, I head toward the exit.

Antonio is waiting for me outside the airport, leaning against a black limo, holding a bottle of chilled prosecco and two glasses. The moment I spot him, a wide smile breaks out on my face.

Despite everything happening—how busy he is

and his disapproval of my Hungary trip—he came to pick me up.

I feel special. *Loved.*

I practically throw myself in his arms. "I can't believe you're here. You braved the airport for me?"

"This is quite a reaction." Laughing, he hugs me back, then takes my luggage and puts it in the trunk, waving off his driver's help. "Of course I did." I slide into the car, and he follows me. We get underway, and then Antonio kisses me, long and passionately. "Welcome home, cara mia." He holds up the wine. "A toast to your success?"

Home.

Venice hasn't felt like home in a very long time. But here and now, sitting in a car with Antonio and sipping champagne he brought to celebrate my success, I finally feel like I'm exactly where I'm meant to be. I'm home.

Later that evening, I check my voicemail and find a message from Rocco Cacciola.

"The hiring committee has reviewed your application," he says. "We'd like to invite you to Florence to formally interview for the job."

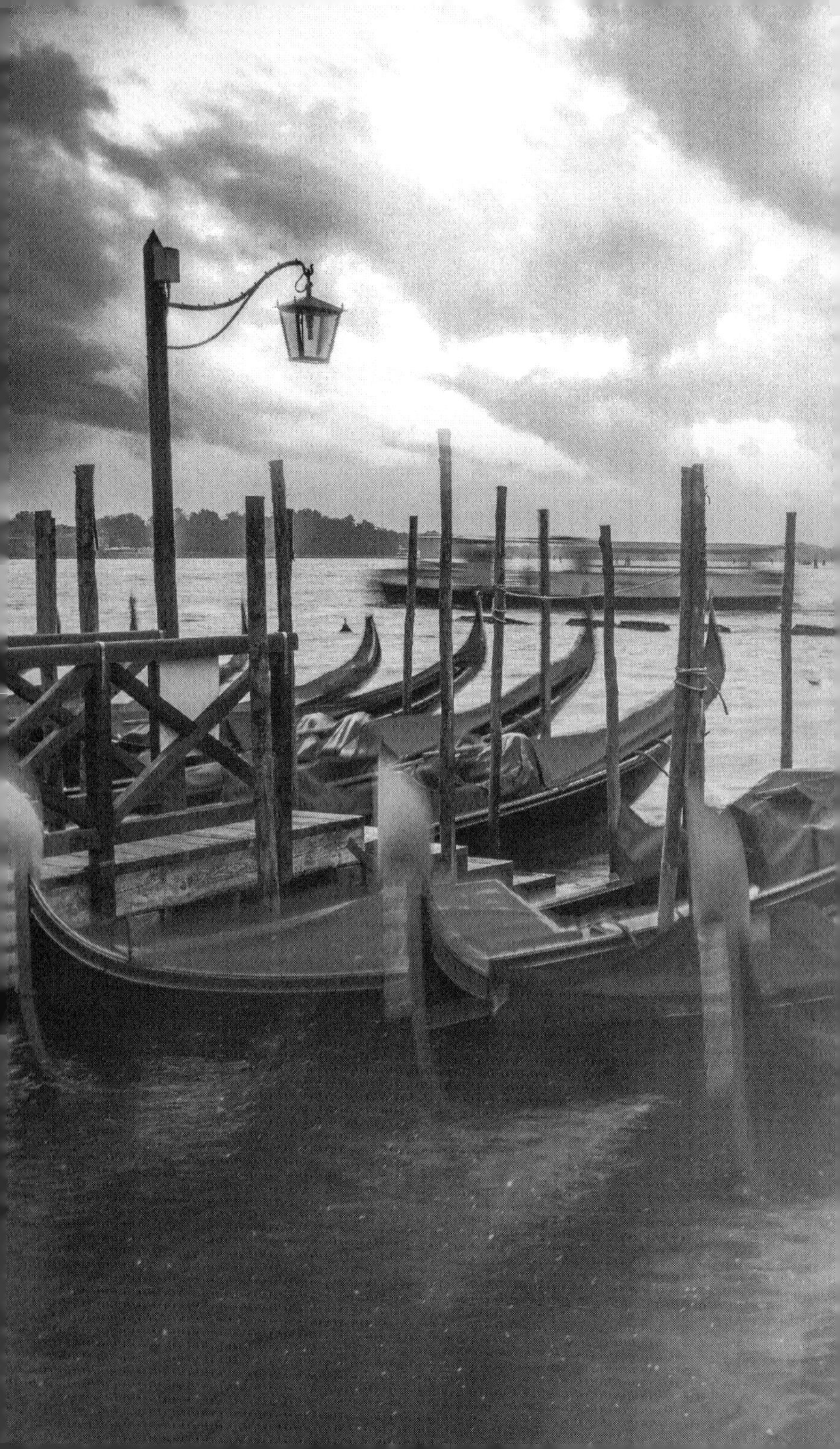

ANTONIO

Chapter Twenty-Eight

"Are you going to the gala?"

The day after she gets back from Hungary, Lucia and I are in my living room. It's after dinner. Agnese is gone for the evening, so it's just the two of us. The drapes are drawn, and the fireplace is lit, filling the room with softly flickering light.

Lucia's lying on my lap and watching something on TV. I should be paying attention—God knows it took us long enough to agree on what we wanted to watch—but I'm mostly watching her.

"What gala?" I ask, playing with her hair.

"The Palazzo Ducale annual donor gala. I was in the break room today getting a cup of coffee, and Dr. Garzolo tracked me down there to ask if I was going." She sounds mildly disgruntled. "He doesn't care whether I'm there—this is about you."

Every year, the palazzo hosts a glittering reception for its donors. They wine and dine us hoping we'll keep giving them money. I answer Lucia's question with one of my own. "Were you planning on going?"

"It's a work event. My presence isn't optional."

There's something in her voice. In the way she's avoiding my gaze. "You want me to go with you?"

"It's a security risk," she replies. "Leo wouldn't like it."

"Leo's not in charge. I am." A smile breaks out on my face. The gala is a big, glittering affair, and everyone who is anyone in Venice will be there. Not to mention all her coworkers. "You want me to go to the gala with you."

"Don't sound so smug. I just don't fancy the idea of dancing with Nicolo Garzolo. Or, heaven forbid, Felix Mayer."

I ignore that. "You want to be seen in public with me," I tease. "You want the world to know I'm besotted."

She snorts. "Besotted. Please."

"But I *am* besotted, cara mia. And I want the world to know." I kiss her forehead. "Do you need a dress?"

"No." She twists around and fixes me with a glare. "Do not buy me a dress, Antonio. I'm dead serious. I'll take care of it."

"If you insist."

She maintains her glare for another beat, and then her expression softens. "Thanks for coming with me."

She's seen the real me, the person behind the facade. I don't have walls around her. The guardrails are gone. She's seen the hurt boy and the angry teenager. She knows the thief that stole because that was the only way I could eat, and she's met the man who toppled the padrino to protect his people.

And she's still here. She's choosing me. Thanking me for accompanying her to this stupid gala. In truth, I'm the one who should be thanking her.

LUCIA

Chapter Twenty-Nine

What am I doing? I love Antonio, and I know he cares about me. Things are going well between us. Really well.

And yet, I call Rocco Cacciola and schedule an interview for the first week of January.

And yet, I keep the whole thing a secret from Antonio.

Why? I'm not sure. It's almost like I think my

happiness is temporary. Deep down, I expect the rug to be yanked from under my feet. And when that happens, when life hits me with a tidal wave and drags me out to drown, the Uffizi will be my life jacket.

Before I knew Antonio was going to the gala, I planned on wearing my navy-blue dress. The knee-length cocktail dress has a conservatively high neckline and delicate lace panels on the side to give it some interest. It's the perfect garment for a curator to wear—polished and sophisticated while still letting me move through the palace with ease.

However, now that I'm going as Antonio's date, I need to up my game. I text Valentina.

> Help. I need a dress.

She calls me back immediately. "A dress for what?"

"I'm Antonio's arm candy to the Palazzo Ducale gala."

"You are?" She sounds surprised. "And Leo cleared that?"

"I don't think Leo knows yet." Antonio's security chief has one goal—to keep us safe—and he's extremely single-minded in its pursuit. If Leo had his way, we wouldn't leave the house until this threat was over. "I asked Antonio about it, and he said, and I quote, 'Leo isn't in charge. I am.'"

I don't add that Antonio kissed my forehead and told me he was besotted with me and wanted the world to know. That moment is just for me.

"He's going to flip his lid," she predicts. "Which will be interesting. I've known Leo for a very long time, and he never loses his cool."

"Can we get back to my dress? I loftily announced that I'd buy my own dress. The gala is next week. I'm running out of time."

"I know just the person," she replies. "Rosa Tran. You remember Rosa? She was a few years behind us in school."

I search my memory. "Quiet, skinny, always had a sketchbook with her?"

"That's her. She went to design school and apprenticed with several Parisian fashion houses. Then, a couple of years ago, her mother got sick, so she moved back to Venice. She has a boutique on Calle del Traghetto in Dorsoduro."

Calle del Traghetto is close to the university and is littered with trendy shops, bars, and restaurants. Good for Rosa. "Do you think she can fit me in?"

Valentina laughs. "You're going to a gala as Antonio Moretti's date. Rosa isn't going to pass up the chance to dress you. I'll call her and make an appointment."

The Thief

Rosa studies me with narrowed eyes. "Green is the obvious color, of course," she murmurs. "But one must always try to do the unexpected. What about your jewelry—do you have that picked out?"

I show her my ruby pendant. "I'll wear this. I always do. And there's a matching bracelet."

"There is?" Valentina asks immediately. Should have known she'd pick up on that. My best friend doesn't miss anything.

"Antonio gave it to me."

"Do you have it with you?" Rosa asks.

I shake my head. "I have a picture." I pull out my phone and show Rosa and Valentina the bracelet Antonio had custom-made for me. Valentina whistles under her breath. "If those are real rubies," she murmurs, "this bracelet is worth—"

"Don't tell me," I interrupt. "I don't want to know. It'll just freak me out." I turn to Rosa. "What do you think?"

She zooms in on the bracelet. "I have the perfect dress."

The dress Rosa brings out is gold. "The fabric is a metallic lamé," she says. "Try it on."

I change into it, and Valentina zips me up. "Oh, wow."

I look in the mirror, and my mouth falls open. This *is* the perfect dress. The metallic fabric catches the light, shimmering delicately as I move. The bodice is draped, clinging lovingly to my bust and falling in soft folds over my arms. The skirt has a high side slit, and the hem pools on the floor. The dress is reminiscent of the togas worn by Greek goddesses but in a modern, updated way.

"What do you think?" Rosa asks.

"Yes," I say. I feel like a magical creature, a fairy goddess sheathed in glowing fire. "Yes, yes, yes."

I open the door for Antonio. He starts to say something, then stops mid-sentence when he looks at me. His heated gaze roams my body, taking in the dress, my pendant, and the bracelet. "You are a vision."

"You don't look too bad yourself." This is the first time I've seen Antonio in a tuxedo. It's beautifully tailored and fits him impeccably, and the effect of all that jaw-dropping perfection makes me light-headed.

His lips curl into a slow smile, and I know he's tempted to skip the gala entirely. He's not the only one. But Rosa gave me a steep discount on the dress because she's counting on people seeing it and seeking her boutique, so as much as I want to blow off the evening, I can't. "Shall we?"

"Oh, fine," he grumbles, offering me his arm. "If you insist."

***

The gala is a glittering affair, taking place in the ornate halls of the palace. The decor is inspired by the Renaissance era. Rich velvet drapes hang from the wall, and gilded accents are everywhere, illuminated by a thousand flickering candles. Elaborate floral arrangements featuring Venetian roses, peonies, and lilies dot the room, filling the air with their delicate aroma.

I walk through these halls every single day, but tonight, the space has been transformed into something intimate, sensuous, and magical.

We walk into the grand ballroom arm in arm. Heads turn at our entrance, and whispers fill the air. People stare openly. Everyone here knows Antonio, and I feel the weight of their gazes on me. Wondering who I am, wondering how I managed to land Venice's most eligible bachelor. The men are curious and leering, and the women's gazes stab me with envy.

"Ugh," I say under my breath. "I really don't like being the center of attention."

"And you wonder why I don't attend these things," he replies. He lifts his hand, and a waiter materializes in front of us, bearing a tray with flutes of champagne. Antonio retrieves two and

The Thief

hands me one with a grin. "Drink up, cara mia. The last time I was here, a very trendy caterer served us droplets of meat jelly topped with vegetable foam. Fifteen courses, and I was still hungry at the end."

My eyes widen. "You're joking."

"I wish."

He lays his palm on my lower back, a subtle gesture of claiming. We wind through the crowds, making our way to our table.

Felix Mayer intercepts us. "Lucia," he says, kissing my cheeks like long-lost friends. "How good it is to see you." He sticks his hand out to Antonio. "Mr. Moretti, I'm Dr. Felix Mayer, the assistant curator in charge of acquisitions."

Antonio's smile doesn't reach his eyes. He looks at Felix's outstretched hand for a fraction of a second too long and then shakes it. "I've heard a lot about you."

Felix is too tone-deaf to hear the warning in that sentence. "Only good things, I hope." He doesn't wait for us to respond before barreling on. "I've been following your acquisitions for a long time, Mr. Moretti. I'm a great admirer of yours. You're planning to set up a museum, I hear? If you're ever looking for someone to work with you—"

"I'll ask Lucia," Antonio interjects. "Obviously." He nods curtly to Felix and puts his arm around my waist. "Please excuse us."

Call me petty, but I can't help snickering once Felix is out of earshot. "That was delightful," I giggle. "Did you see Felix's face when you rebuffed him? He was crushed. What was that about, by the way? A museum?"

"I own a lot of art," he says. His lips twitch. "Most of it is lawfully acquired. People automatically assume I want to set up a private museum."

I glance at him. "Do you?"

He smiles down at me. "Are you interested in the director role, Lucia?"

My mouth falls open. "Is this a job offer?"

"If you want it to be." His voice lowers and turns seductive. "Only if it didn't interfere with us. I can hire a dozen people for my museum, but. . ."

"But?" I forget to breathe.

His eyes are warm. "There's only one person I want at my side."

"Oh," I say faintly. Antonio's looking at me, waiting for me to respond, and I don't know what to say. After spending years protecting myself from feeling anything at all, Antonio's become so important to me in a few short weeks that I can't contemplate life without him.

And now, with the museum. . . He's given me the perfect opening to tell him about the Uffizi, but I keep silent. I'm afraid to rock the boat.

Because every moment we spend together is special. The heated debates over dinner, the evenings spent arguing about what we'll watch on TV, our banter about the true owner of the Titian—I love it all. I didn't realize how big the void inside me was until Antonio filled it.

I can't find the words to explain how much he means to me. So I squeeze his hand and hope he knows how much I love him.

And that he'll forgive me when he finds out the secret I'm keeping from him.

The evening starts with a formal dinner. A string quartet plays Vivaldi while we eat a five-course meal. The food isn't as bad as Antonio predicted, but it's also not particularly filling. The wine, on the other hand, is excellent. I'm quite tipsy by the time I'm done. "Let's get pizza when this is over," I whisper to Antonio under cover of the music.

He laughs at me.

After dinner, Dr. Garzolo takes the guests on a private tour. He showcases some of the museum's most prized possessions, highlights recent acquisitions, and finishes in the Illuminated Manuscripts exhibit. While the other guests are oohing and aahing over the richly colored illustrations, Antonio murmurs into my ear. "I'm extremely fond of this exhibit. And for the record, you're a much better tour guide than Dr. Garzolo."

The tour is followed by a live auction and dancing. By then, I'm tired of being gawked at and ready to go home. "Want to get out of here?" I ask Antonio.

"God, yes. I thought you'd never ask. Still want pizza?"

"Yes, please."

He gives me a fond look and turns to his bodyguard. "Carlo, do you know a place round here that's open late?"

"There's a pizzeria one street over, padrino. I've eaten there. It's good."

"Perfect. Lead the way."

The pizzeria is mostly empty. Carlo ducks in to check the premises while Simon stays with us. Once the place is clear, we enter. We're about to sit down to eat when the door chimes ring, and a man walks in.

It's the same man I saw at the airport. The one that was staring at me.

I don't believe in coincidences. "Antonio." Something in my voice must alert him because he's already turning around. "Marco," he says, his voice turning icy.

Everything seems to happen in slow motion.

Marco raises his hand. He's holding a gun. Oh my god, he's holding a gun—where did that come from? Carlo and Simon hurl themselves at him, but his finger is already on the trigger, the muzzle aimed straight at me.

Me?

Then Antonio is in front of me, blocking the bullet with his body.

He falls back, stumbles against a chair, and crashes to the ground.

And his blood—his bright red blood—spreads all over my golden gown.

ANTONIO

Chapter Thirty

A sharp pain fills me, and blood pours from a wound in my left shoulder. I flex my hand experimentally and am hit with another wave of pain. But I can move my arm, thank fuck. I'm not nauseous or sweating, and I can breathe.

I got lucky.

Had the bullet hit a major organ, things would look pretty grim. But it's just a graze. There's a ridiculous amount of blood, but really, the most embarrassing thing is me tripping over a chair and landing on my butt on the ground.

Marco was the shooter.

My subconscious process that, and my body goes cold. The former padrino's nephew has every reason to hate me. I'm the one that banished him from Venice. I'm the one that changed his life in one swift, brutal stroke, tearing him from his home and his family.

But he aimed at Lucia. Why? Is it because he blames her for the consequences of his own screw-up?

Or is it because he realized it would wreck me if she was hurt?

And if Marco—dull, uncurious, plodding Marco—has figured that out, what of my other enemies?

Leo warned me about this possibility. "The only reason she's a target is that she's connected to you," he said. "Things would be easier if you broke it off with her."

The Thief

But I didn't listen. In my hubris, in my greed, I thought I could protect her.

Lucia is crouched next to me, her face pale, her eyes horrified. "It's fine," I mutter thickly. "Just a scratch." Carlo is kneeling on the other side of me, applying pressure to the wound and screaming something into his phone. Lost in my own fog, I didn't even see him approach me. The room swims in and out of view, and I shake my head, trying to clear it. "It's fine," I repeat, gritting my teeth against the pain. "Nothing to worry about."

My stomach is churning, and I feel on the verge of passing out. Shock, probably. My body's reaction is annoying. The bullet barely hit me—there's no reason for theatrics.

At my side, Lucia looks distressed. Tears swim in her eyes and spill down her cheeks. She hates blood, I remember. Hates hospitals. She's probably not too fond of guns either—when her mother died, her father shot his brains out. She wasn't the one who discovered the body—thank fuck for small mercies—but she had to identify him.

She's the woman I love, and I'm putting her in harm's way and re-traumatizing her.

Good job, Antonio. Excellent work.

"Lucia," I start. "I. . ." My voice trails off. What is there to say? This is my life. All I have to offer her are blood and tears.

"Don't talk," she whispers. "It's okay. Simon's called for an ambulance."

"I don't want. . ." I grope for her hand. She's so warm. So alive.

And if she's to stay that way, *I need to let her go.*

With superhuman effort, I force myself to my feet. "It's nothing," I say. "Just a scratch." Dante pushes his way into the restaurant, and I nod to him. "Good, you're here. It was Marco."

"We have him in custody," Dante replies. "Antonio, sit down. I've got this."

"Are you telling me what to do?" I ask, my voice

turning to ice. "Because the last time I checked, I'm still the padrino." I'm aware I'm acting irrationally—Dante is loyal to a fault. He would never stab me in the back. But pain is a wild animal clawing my insides, and I'm lashing out.

I turn to Lucia. "You need to go."

"Antonio." Her voice is soft. Hurt but trying to keep it from showing. Her face is streaked with tears, and her beautiful gown, the gown she'd been so thrilled about, is marred with my blood. "You got shot. Please sit until the medics get here."

"Don't tell me what to do," I snap. Cold and vicious, that's what I have to be. "You're ready to faint at the sight of my blood. What use are you here? I don't need your tears and your sniveling, and I certainly don't need your advice. Dante, get her out of here."

Dante goes still. "Padrino, I—"

But I'm not looking at my second-in-command. I only have eyes for Lucia.

Shock slaps her face. She takes a step back and

then another. She's backing away from me, her expression horrified.

Good, I think, twisting the knife deeper into the wound. *She's finally seeing me for the bastard that I am.*

My mother abandoned me. Her relatives—my so-called family—wanted nothing to do with me. And now I have to make Lucia leave me too.

And it hurts—it hurts like a bitch—but it's the right thing to do. She's in danger because of me, and it's finally time for me to do what I should have done right from the start.

"Antonio," she pleads, a hand stretching toward me. She trembles, and with every fiber of my being, I want to put my arms around her, cradling her against my body and begging for forgiveness for risking her life. "Please. . ."

I turn away.

She doesn't react, not for a long moment. And then, finally, she leaves. I hear the door close.

Her absence opens a void inside my heart. A

raw, raging void of pain. "Follow her," I tell Carlo. "Make sure she gets home safely."

Dante stares at me, comprehension starting to dawn in his eyes. "Is that why—"

But the pizzeria is growing fuzzy. Gray dots swim at the edge of my vision, clouding my sight. The void expands to take control over me. My knees buckle, and I collapse.

And then I feel nothing.

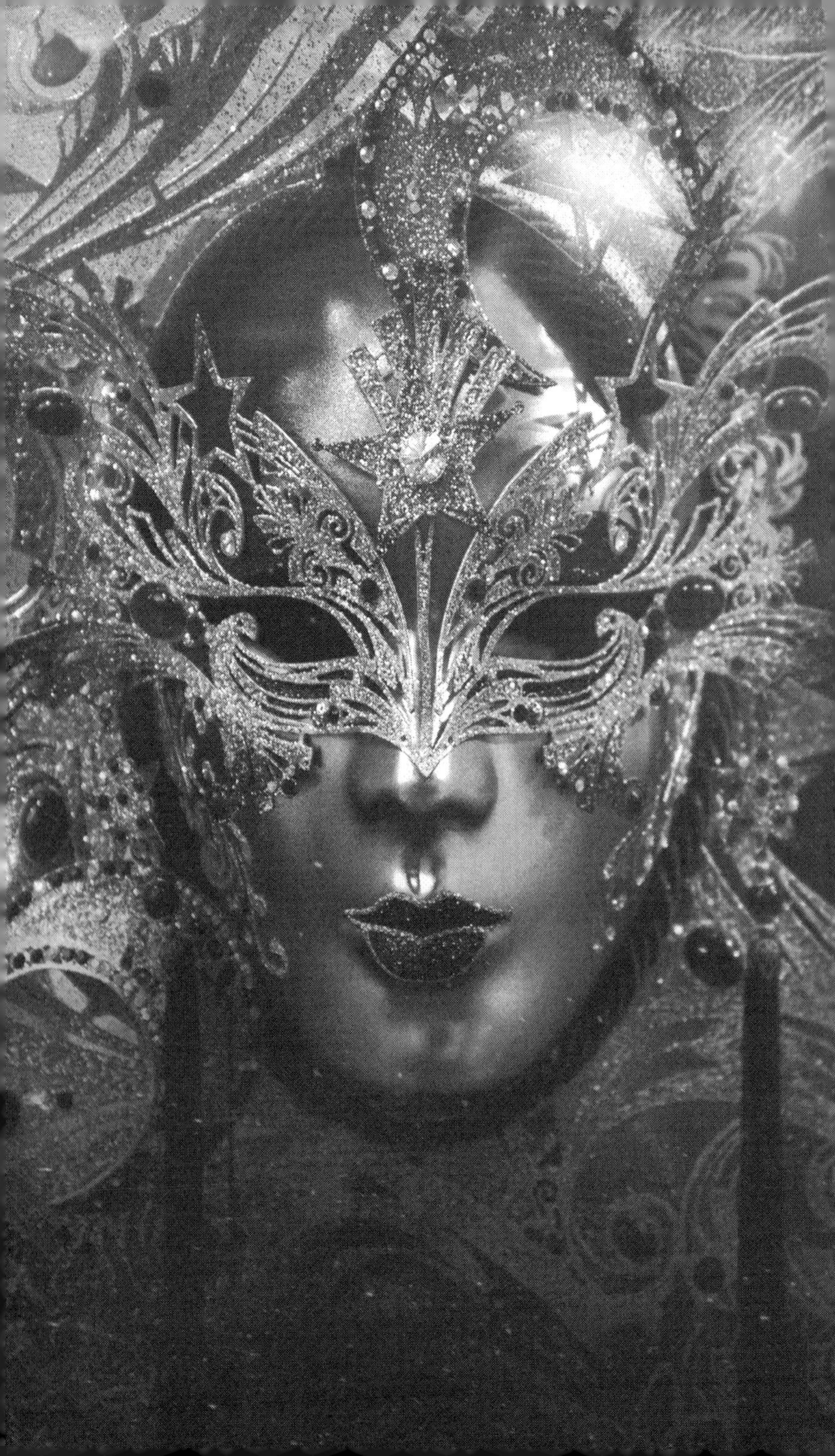

LUCIA

Chapter Thirty-One

A man aimed a gun at me, Antonio threw himself in harm's way, and now he's bleeding, hurt, and injured.

He put himself between me and a bullet.

My head spins. My vision is blurry through the tears falling freely down my cheeks.

He ordered me to leave.

He told me he didn't need my tears and my sniveling.

Words are a weapon, and he stabbed me with his.

He knows I'm afraid of blood. He knows hospitals freak me out because I told him. Against my better judgment, I demolished my walls for him and stripped off my armor. But when it really mattered, he yanked up his shields.

I gave him the power to hurt me, *and he used it.*

I can't stop shivering. Icy chills glide through my veins, a reaction caused by the brisk night air. But the real cold comes from within.

I should have known better. Falling in love is a fool's game, and *I'm the biggest sucker in Venice.*

I stumble home. It's late, and the streets are mostly empty. The few people I encounter gape at me, arrested by my blood-stained dress, but I'm oblivious to their stares.

Back home, I stand under the shower for a long time, but the shivers don't subside. I wrap myself up in a quilt and make a cup of hot tea, but warmth remains elusive.

Everything in my apartment reminds me of Antonio. Every item of furniture, every inch of carpet. Framed photos of my parents hang on the wall—I never would have made it to the storage unit without his support. A side table holds a vase overflowing with calla lilies. He bought them for me last week. The blooms are bright yellow, cheerful dots of sunshine in the winter gloom. "They remind me of you," he said as he handed them to me.

There's a half-finished bottle of Barolo on the counter. We opened it on Thursday and would have finished it tomorrow. That's not going to happen now.

It's over.

I open my cupboards, searching for something to fill the hollowness inside me. My trembling hands settle on a bottle of vodka. I find a glass and pour myself a liberal shot. The smell of the liquor takes me back to that night so long ago, the night I met Antonio Moretti.

I close my eyes and remember the heat of his body, the delicate touch of his fingers on my bruised skin. The way he growled, 'Who did this to you?' The warmth of the jacket he draped around my shoulders. His intoxicating scent of leather mixed with sandalwood and smoke.

It's all over now.

My stomach heaves, and I retch. I can gulp down the alcohol, and it would give me temporary oblivion, but I know from experience that I can't drown my pain in a bottle. In the morning, I'll still be empty. Broken. *Shattered.*

I have to get out of here.

I pour the vodka down the drain and head out of my apartment. I don't know where I'm going. All I know is that I can't stay where I am. There are too many memories here, and each one pours raw acid onto my broken heart.

It's long after midnight. The earlier drizzle has intensified, and rain falls in cold sheets. I put up my hood, but the persistent water soaks through the fabric and runs in icy rivulets down my neck. I walk and walk, uncaring about the weather, my destination, or anything.

But my feet know the way because I end up at the pier where I met Antonio ten years ago.

The last time I was here, the air was salty with an undertone of vomit and urine. The docks were a patchwork of planks, paint peeling and wood splintered, cracked from years of salt and sun. Rust and decay hung like a thick miasma over the area.

Not any longer.

The shadows have been replaced by streetlights. The crumbling warehouses of my past are gone, and bars, art galleries, vinotecas, artisanal cheese stores, and clothing boutiques fill the space they left behind. A couple of the bars are still open, laughing revelers inside filled with holiday cheer.

I pass a building under construction. The sign explains that a community center will open next spring, but that isn't what catches my eye. It's the logo of the company in charge of the project. A stylized M.

Moretti Construction.

This is Antonio's doing. He took something

broken and wrecked and brought it back to life. He's a good person who cares deeply about his city and his people. Valentina has never said a bad word about him. Enzo, who is a cop, and by all accounts, an honest, upstanding one, would walk through fire for him. Claudia and Miriam sing his praises to the stars.

If he's such a good person, why did he push you away?

He is the king of Venice, a ruthless one, but underneath that ruthlessness is a core of goodness. I've seen it in action over and over again.

His cruel, hurtful words ring in my ears. *You're ready to faint at the sight of my blood. What use are you here?*

I showed him my weaknesses, *and he judged me for them.*

Antonio's never once judged me.

Not when I was weaving through the docks, clutching a bottle of vodka, so drunk I couldn't see straight.

Not when I poured out my grief to him, raging in the darkness against the secrets my parents hid and how they abandoned me.

Not when he found out about my art-stealing proclivities. He could have ordered Valentina to stop working with me, but he didn't.

He's always been there for me. Always accepted me the way I am. What changed? Why did he send me away?

Nothing makes sense anymore.

A cynical part of me whispers, *Aren't you glad you applied to the Uffizi? Aren't you glad you have a safety net?*

But if this is the safety net, I'd rather keep falling.

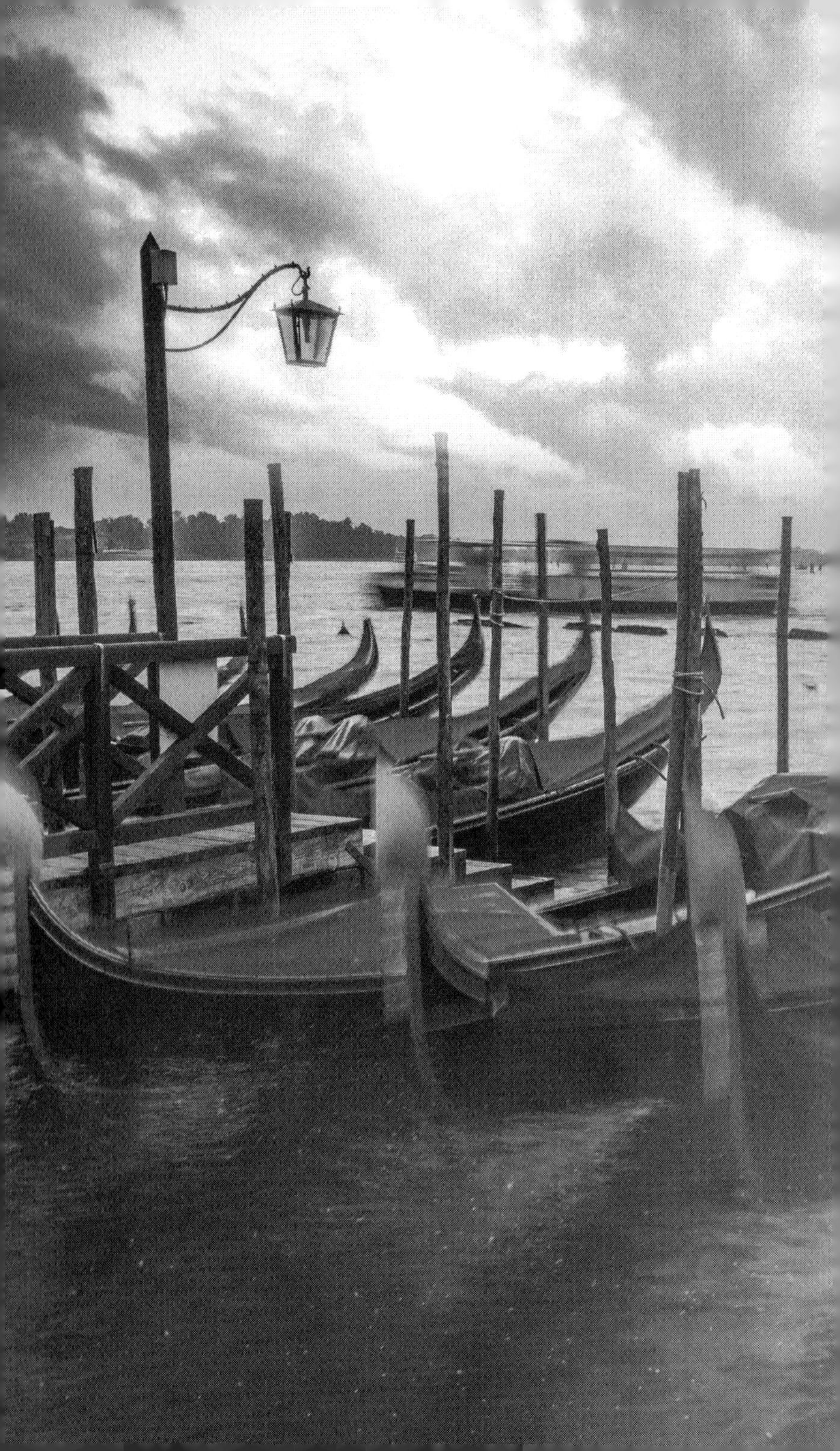

ANTONIO

Chapter Thirty-Two

I open my eyes, and fluorescent light sears my retinas. Machines beep shrill warnings. Heads bend over me, their voices a low, panicked murmur.

I'm in a hospital. It should worry me, but I feel detached. Disconnected from what's occurring around me. I'm untethered. Like a boat adrift on troubled water or a kite caught in a storm, tossed here and there by gusts of wind, I drift through the grim years of my life.

I touch down in my first foster home. I didn't

think I had any memories of that place, but the thick, cloying aroma of the rose-tinted prayer candles fills my nose. And the bawling. So much crying. My ears remember.

I went to my second foster home when I was two. Then another and another. I've lost track of how many there were. When I was six, I ended up with Alia Radulescu. Alia had blonde hair and a kind smile, and the first time I laid eyes on her, I thought she was an angel. I was determined to stay.

Except Alia's partner, Peter, believed in harsh discipline, the kind enforced with liberal beatings with a belt. And Alia was too cowed to protest.

The day after my tenth birthday, I fought back. I was out of her home six weeks after that.

I'd been there four years—long enough to think of Alia as my mother. I'd hoped she would fight for me, but she didn't.

No one ever did.

Lucia would have fought for you if you hadn't sent her away.

The Thief

Dante's voice intrudes into my memories. "He was fine," he says, sounding hard and desperate. "The bullet grazed him, nothing more. Now he's collapsed. What the fuck is going on?"

"It's a bone chip," the doctor replies, her voice clipped. "Fragments of the bone have caused damage to the surrounding blood vessels. Our imaging scan shows that it's lodged in Signor Moretti's pulmonary artery, restricting blood flow to his lungs, which are at risk of collapsing. We need to operate immediately."

Dante clenches his hands into fists. "Risks?" he barks.

"Major surgery is always risky," she replies. "Anesthesia, infection, anything is possible. But Signor Moretti is young. Is there a wife?"

"A girlfriend," Dante says. "Lucia. I'll get her."

She won't come, I try to say, though words don't leave my mouth. She has no reason to. Not after the way I hurt her.

The beeping intensifies. "His vitals are dropping!"

someone yells. "We need to prep him now."

Dante shoulders himself into the crowd around me. "Padrino," he says. "Antonio. Fight, goddamn it."

I might die.

The last image in my mind is Lucia. I shouldn't have pushed her away. I should have told her how much I love her.

But it's too late.

I wish she were here.

Next to me, her soft hand linked with mine.

I wish. . .

LUCIA

Chapter Thirty-Three

Dante and Valentina are in my apartment when I get back. One look at their faces and my heart stops cold. Something has gone badly wrong. "What happened?" I whisper through nerveless lips.

"Antonio collapsed," Dante replies soberly. "A bone chip from his shoulder blocked a blood vessel. He's in surgery right now."

I stare at them in shock, my brain refusing to

process those words. It can't be. Just a few hours ago, I was in the middle of a fairy tale. We were at a ball, dancing and joking about the food. Being gawked at by my coworkers. Talking about a museum Antonio was planning to set up. Making plans for the future.

"It's serious, Lucia," Valentina says gently.

My brain finally starts working again. "Which hospital?" I demand. "What are we waiting for? Let's go."

"Not yet." Dante puts his body between me and the door. He glances at Valentina, and something in her expression makes him continue. "I need to know what your intentions are."

"What the hell?"

"Antonio is more than my padrino," he replies. "He's my friend. He's my family. And you don't stick around. When the going gets tough, you run away. Right now, you're interviewing for a job in Florence."

I gape at him in shock and then glance at

Valentina, who looks uncomfortable. "I didn't snoop through your email," she says. "I would never invade your privacy that way. You had your cover letter open on your laptop screen. It was an accident."

She sounds miserable. "I don't think you're snooping," I assure her. "I trust you."

Dante's not done. "It's not just Florence. After your parents died, you didn't talk to Valentina *for two years*. You missed Angelica's birth. You missed..."

Guilt lacerates my insides. Had I kept in touch with Valentina, I would have recognized the signs of an abusive relationship. I could have helped. I don't know how, but I would have done something.

"I missed everything." I don't address my reply to Dante. I appreciate his concern, but he's not my best friend. Valentina is, and it's to her that I need to say these words. "I'm so sorry I wasn't there when you needed me. But I promise you things will change. I promise you—"

"They already have." Valentina's eyes are suspiciously bright. "The fault isn't yours alone. I could have called you too. But I was ashamed of the situation I was in, so ashamed that I hid the truth from everyone." She draws in a deep breath. "But that's not important now, and neither is the Uffizi. What's important is Antonio."

Antonio.

Who is in a hospital, fighting for his life.

Yes, he told me to leave.

No, I don't understand why.

But I know that I was broken, and Antonio healed me. My heart was a withered husk, and he brought it back to life. I kept pushing him away because I was a hurt, wounded animal, but he never left. He was my rock.

I might not know exactly why he pushed me away tonight, but I'm going to do what Antonio would do. I'm not leaving so easily.

His mother didn't fight for him.

His uncle turned his back on him.

The Thief

I'm not going to join them. *Fuck that*. I'm going to fight for Antonio Moretti. Because I love him and because he deserves it.

"He's your friend, and you care for him." I face Dante squarely. "You deserve to know that I'm not running away. I'm not going to leave." I take another step forward. "But the man I love is in surgery *right now*, and you're preventing me from being at his side." My voice turns hard, and what he sees in my face makes him move. "So, tell me what hospital he's in, and get the hell out of my way."

The wait. . . the less said about the wait, the better. It's agonizing.

But I'm not alone.

Enzo is here. Tatiana, too, huddled in a corner of the hospital waiting room, looking young and very vulnerable. Valentina is at home with

Angelica, but Dante is here, eyes grim and shoulders tense. Antonio's lieutenants, Joao and Tomas, arrive at some point during that long night. Agnese brings freshly baked bread and containers of warming soup.

Right after Agnese's arrival, I call Rocco Cacciola's work phone. He doesn't answer—it's four in the morning—but I leave a message. "I'm sorry to do this, but I need to withdraw my application."

I expect to feel a twinge of regret—it really is a great job—but I feel nothing but relief. Deep down inside, I didn't want to leave Venice again. This is my home again, and my family and friends are here.

There will be other jobs. There's only one Antonio.

The only person who's missing is Leo. "He blames himself for what happened," Dante replies when I rouse myself enough to ask. "He's questioning Marco. Uncovering the plot, putting a team together to take Verratti out."

Enzo lifts his head. "That won't be necessary," he says, his voice weary. "Verratti is in custody. The DIA took him in an hour ago."

Dante shakes his head. "This is a hydra. You can cut off one head, but it's not enough. We need to dismantle the organization."

And the violence will persist.

Yesterday, I might have had doubts about whether this was a life I wanted to choose. Today, I know better. Sometimes, you have to meet violence with violence. Sometimes, you have to do things—hard and dangerous things—to protect the people you care about.

And yesterday, I might have done what Dante accused me of—run away when things got difficult. Today, I've been given a fresh perspective. Life is short, and nothing is guaranteed to us.

I love Antonio. I want to spend my life with him. I'm going to seize the time we have with both hands and refuse to let go.

Six agonizing hours later, the surgeon who operated on Antonio comes into the waiting room. She looks around at the crowded room, and her face turns pale. I think it just occurred to her that she was operating on Venice's most dangerous man.

I'm on my feet immediately. "The surgery?"

She focuses on me. "Everything went well," she says. "We found some additional bone chips, which made the surgery more complicated than expected. But, like I said, everything went well. Signor Moretti is in post-op recovery." She appears to count the people in the waiting room. "He's sleeping off the effects of the anesthetic. I can allow one person in to see him for five minutes. Who will it be?"

"Lucia," Enzo says firmly. Tatiana nods in agreement. "It's got to be Lucia."

Thirty-six hours later, Antonio is transferred to the general ICU. Two days after that, he's moved into a regular hospital room, albeit a very fancy one in a private wing.

It's finally time for us to talk. I perch on the side of his bed and lace my fingers in his. "I figured out why you sent me away."

He stiffens. "You did?"

"It wasn't hard. As soon as I got over my hurt feelings, it became obvious. You freaked out because I could have been shot." I brush a kiss over his forehead. "You're not as inscrutable as you think you are."

"I almost got you killed." He sounds agonized. "Lucia, I can't—"

"But that's just it. You didn't get me killed. Instead, you dived in front of a bullet for me. You're the one who got shot, not me."

"I can't put you in danger." He doesn't pull away from me, though. "Life with me isn't safe."

"Bossy of you," I tell him lightly. "Presumptuous,

too, thinking you can make these decisions for me." I squeeze his hand gently. Any moment now, a nurse will come into the room and throw me out, so I need to hurry up. "Remember how I hate hospitals? How I get sick at the sight of blood? And yet I'm still here. Not fainting. You didn't think I'd be here, did you?"

"I was clearly wrong."

I look around with exaggerated shock. "Where are witnesses when I need them?" I ask. "It's not every day that Antonio Moretti admits he's wrong."

His lips twitch. "Brat." He draws in a breath. "Lucia, nothing's changed. I can't promise safety."

He's still trying to push me away. But I saw the shock in his eyes when he woke up and saw me in his hospital room. Shock and *relief*. And it's the memory of how that relief turned into fierce joy that gives me the courage to stay. To fight for us.

"The thing is, I love you." I meet his eyes. "You can send me away, and I'm still going to love you. I can leave Venice and move to, I don't know,

Siberia or something, and I'll still love you."

"Or Florence?" he asks wryly.

I sit up in shock. "You knew? Why didn't you ask me about it?"

"I figured you'd tell me when you were ready." He shrugs. "It didn't seem that important. Florence is only a couple of hours away, and I own a private plane."

"I pulled out of the process. I don't want to be in Florence." I squeeze his hand again. "I want to be right here."

"Lucia, I—"

"I don't want safety," I continue. "Safety is an illusion. My parents covered me in protective bubble wrap, and my heart still broke. I just want you."

His eyes are both hungry and haunted. A conflict rages inside him. "You should leave me," he grinds out, his grip on my hand tightening. "It's the smart thing to do."

"Never going to happen." I give him a tremulous

smile. "This is the part where you realize you're stuck with me."

He stares at me for a long time. I see the exact moment he stops fighting it because his eyes flare with possessive fire. He opens his arms, and I move in closer and lean into the warmth of his body. "I'm never stuck with you," he says. He smiles at me and moves my hand over his heart. "Stuck implies an absence of choice. I love you, Lucia. There's no one else for me, little thief. I *choose* to spend my life with you."

Warmth spreads through me. He holds me in his arms, and I feel like I've finally come home. Of course, I can't resist one last quip. "I still think you should return the Titian to the museum."

He gives me a wicked smile. "It's sitting in your closet, cara mia. You're the one who's refusing to return it to the Palazzo Ducale. I wonder why. After all, the Bassano you stole from Powell is already back in Turin."

I feel myself blush. "I've been busy."

His lips twitch. "Of course. Well, it's a pity you stole it from me. If you hadn't, I would have given it to you as a wedding present. I'll have to think of something else now."

My mouth falls open. Is this a—

"You should see your expression." Antonio laughs softly at my reaction. "This isn't the actual proposal, by the way. I'll be damned if I'm going to ask the woman I love to marry me dressed in a hospital gown." He brushes a kiss across my lips. "Consider it a preview."

"If this is the preview," I manage, "I'm going to love the main event."

My heart overflows with joy, and I hug Antonio as tightly as I dare. No more safety nets—I don't need them. I'm finally ready for a leap of faith. We're going to live happily ever after.

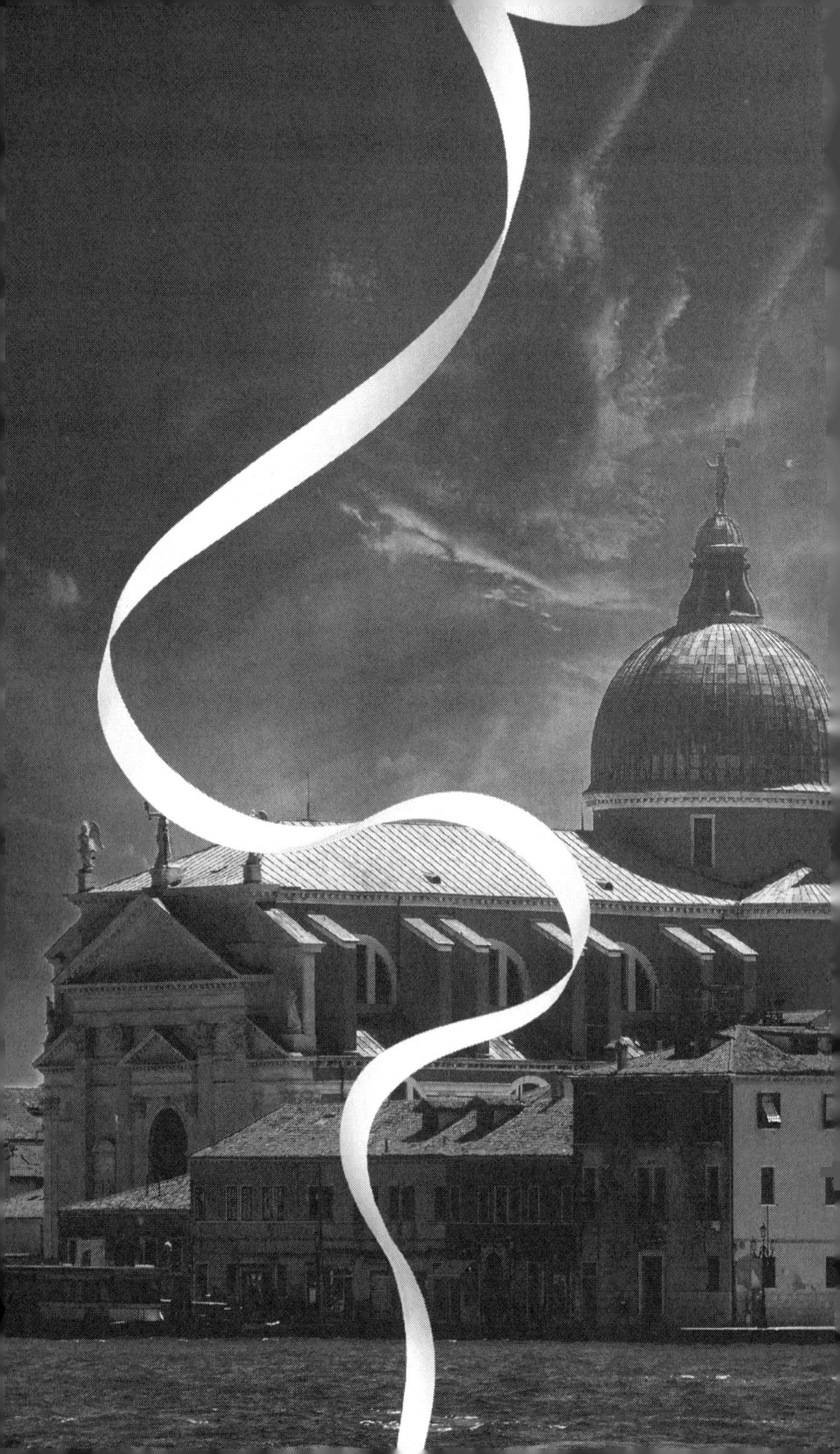

EPILOGUE
LUCIA

Antonio gets discharged on Christmas Eve. The proposal—the real one, as Antonio insists on calling it—happens on Christmas Day. We're lying in bed together after the low-key festivities when he retrieves a small box from his bedside table and flips it open.

"This is it," he says. "The real deal. Remember, you already said yes." He holds the ring out to me. "Yes?"

I stare at my engagement ring in shock. A central oval ruby is surrounded by diamonds and encased in filigree. It looks like an antique, but the design simultaneously feels timeless. The stone catches the light and glows like fire.

Like the bracelet he gave me, it perfectly matches my mother's pendant.

How?

I prop myself on an elbow. "How long have you had this?"

He gives me an enigmatic smile.

"Antonio," I say, my voice rising in pitch. "Seriously, how long?" He said he commissioned the bracelet the day he met me. He didn't commission the ring at the same time, did he? I can't decide if that would be the most romantic gesture ever or serious stalker-like behavior.

A little from column A, a little from column B.

"I can't tell you all my secrets," he says with a grin but relents. "Do you know the story of your mother's pendant?"

I bite back my smile and fake ignorance. "What story? My father gave it to her as a wedding present."

He grimaces. "Fuck. Now I'm going to destroy your illusions."

He looks guilty, and I can't cause him any stress. His doctors will kill me if he ends up back in the hospital. "As tempting as it is to see you squirm, I already know he stole it for her."

He leans back on the pillow. "You had me worried," he says. "When I don't feel like a truck ran me over, I'm going to make you pay for that, *cara mia.*" The words are a delicious promise, and a shiver of anticipation runs through me at the way his voice roughens.

But not now. Sadly, the doctors have vetoed sex for a few more weeks.

"My dad stole the pendant. It was supposed to be fenced, but my mom fell in love with it, so he gave it to her instead." I smile wistfully. "I always thought that was the most romantic thing ever."

My parents loved each other with a fierceness that I am finally beginning to understand. Those agonizing hours in the hospital, waiting to find out whether Antonio would be fine, taught me something. I don't think I'd ever make the same choice my father did, but I finally understand it. Losing the person you love is a terrible thing, and grief isn't rational. It's a wild and desperate beast clawing at your heart.

"Interesting how you find some grand larceny romantic, but when I steal a painting from a museum, it's all *don't do this, Antonio,* and *it belongs to the Palazzo Ducale, Antonio.*"

I roll my eyes and pretend to throw a pillow at him. "Stop whining," I tell him. "It's a terrible look on you."

He flashes me a glance that promises retribution.

I can't wait.

He wraps his arm around my waist and tugs me closer. "Back to the ring," he says. "Your father stole the pendant from the Duke of Aosta. I asked around, and it was, I gather, a crime of opportunity."

"I didn't know that. They didn't talk much about their work."

"No doubt they were trying to discourage you from following in their path."

"Pity that didn't work out," I quip. "And now I'm marrying another thief. They're probably rolling over in their graves." That's a lie. Antonio would have charmed the pants off my parents. My mother would have made all her favorite dishes for him, and my father would have insisted the two of them hang out in his study and smoke cigars. His highest form of praise, reserved only for the people he genuinely liked.

"Anyway, the pendant was part of a set, and there was a matching ring." He slides it on my finger. "This one."

I stare at my left hand. The king of Venice is in bed next to me, and I'm wearing his ring.

It still feels a little unreal.

I think it always will.

"Did you steal it?"

"I was tempted," he admits with a small laugh. "It would be very poetic. But it's too recognizable a piece of jewelry, and unlike the pendant, you can't keep it hidden." His eyes flash with possessive fire. "I don't want you to keep it hidden. I want the world to see it. I bought it in an auction last month." He kisses my hand. "If you don't like it, we can shop for a different—"

"Don't you dare. I love it."

We get married two weeks later. It's a small, intimate ceremony, and only the people most important to us are invited. Enzo and Tatiana are there, of course, as are Dante, Valentina, Joao, Tomas, and Leonardo. Antonio invites Agnese and Liam, the manager at Casanova. "He's a hard bargainer," he fake-grumbles. "I sold Casanova to him for too little money. Can't believe I'm inviting the bastard to my wedding as well."

Agnese is delighted to be invited but somewhat less so that we won't let her cook. "No, we just want you to enjoy the wedding," I insist. "As our guest." She reluctantly agrees though I'm pretty sure some of my luster has dimmed in her eyes. Agnese loves to cook for her people.

Valentina is my maid of honor, and Angelica is the flower girl. I also invite Alvisa Zanotti, Claudia and Miriam, and Rosa, who also designs my wedding dress. "Two weeks," she bitches at me through a mouthful of pins during my first fitting. "What is the hurry? Are you pregnant?"

Valentina chokes on her glass of champagne, looking like she's on the verge of breaking out into giggles. "Are you?" she asks when she's done coughing. "And you never said anything."

I glare at both of them. "I am not, thank you. But we want a small wedding, and I don't see any reason to wait. Now, stop monopolizing the champagne and pour me a glass."

We don't want to wait, that part is true. But that's not the only reason. I want to get married in winter. Ten years ago, my parents died this time of the year, and I want to replace that memory with a happier one. It doesn't mean I'm going to forget about their deaths, and it certainly doesn't mean I don't still miss them every day.

But it's a reminder that life holds both sweetness and bitterness. Both joy and sadness and it's this duality that makes us human.

It's the same reason we're getting married at Il Redentore. Antonio and I aren't religious, but this is the church he was abandoned in as a baby. Every time he walks past it now, that won't be his only memory.

Fuck the past. Fuck those demons. We're going to make our own future, and it's going to be glorious.

The night before our wedding, I'm in bed with Antonio. I know it's tradition that I spend this night without him, but I don't see the point of it. "I have a present for you," he says. His gaze meets

The Thief

mine, and a smile touches his lips. "Wife."

"Husband." I try the word out experimentally, and a possessive surge runs through me. Yes. My husband. *Mine.* "Another present? Antonio, we've discussed this."

"No, *you've* discussed this." He offers me a small rectangular box. "Open it."

I frown at him. "If it's more jewelry, I'm going to. . ." I open the lid, and my voice trails away. "This is a key," I say, confused. "A key to what?"

"To a museum. Well, right now, it's an empty space on the floor above the new community center. But I'm hoping you'll shape it into a museum, one that feels accessible to everyone."

A museum located near the dock we met, one accessible to street kids like him. I stare at him in shock. "You want me to set up your museum?"

"Why do you look so surprised? I already told you I wanted you to do it. Unless you feel you're not up to the challenge." He gives me a wicked smile. "Of course, some of my collection has been. . . ahem, dubiously acquired, so you'll have to figure out how to return those to their original owners." He glances at the painting in my closet. "Starting with the Titian, no doubt."

I contemplate the Venetian masterpiece. "Won't you miss it?"

"I thought I would. But—"

"But?"

"But I prefer the painting you bought at the market, the one with the flowers," he says with a sunny smile. "It reminds me of you."

"You said that already. As I recall, you also called me energetic in that same conversation. Once the Titian goes back, you can't change your mind."

"I don't care, cara mia," he says. "I have more important things on my mind." He cages me in with his body and palms my breast, pinching my nipple. "Now, show me how energetic you can be."

The Thief

The wedding is beautiful. The church is lovely. Valentina and Rosa oversee the decor and do an amazing job. The altar is adorned with fragrant white roses and lilies, interspersed with tall candles. Garlands of greenery wind around the marble columns, and small arrangements of roses dot the pews. After a week of overcast skies, the sun comes out, streaming through the windows and filling the church with light.

Angelica walks down the aisle, wearing a cream silk dress with a lace overlay and a tiara in her hair, looking every inch like a fairy-tale princess.

Then the music swells, and it's time to marry the man I love.

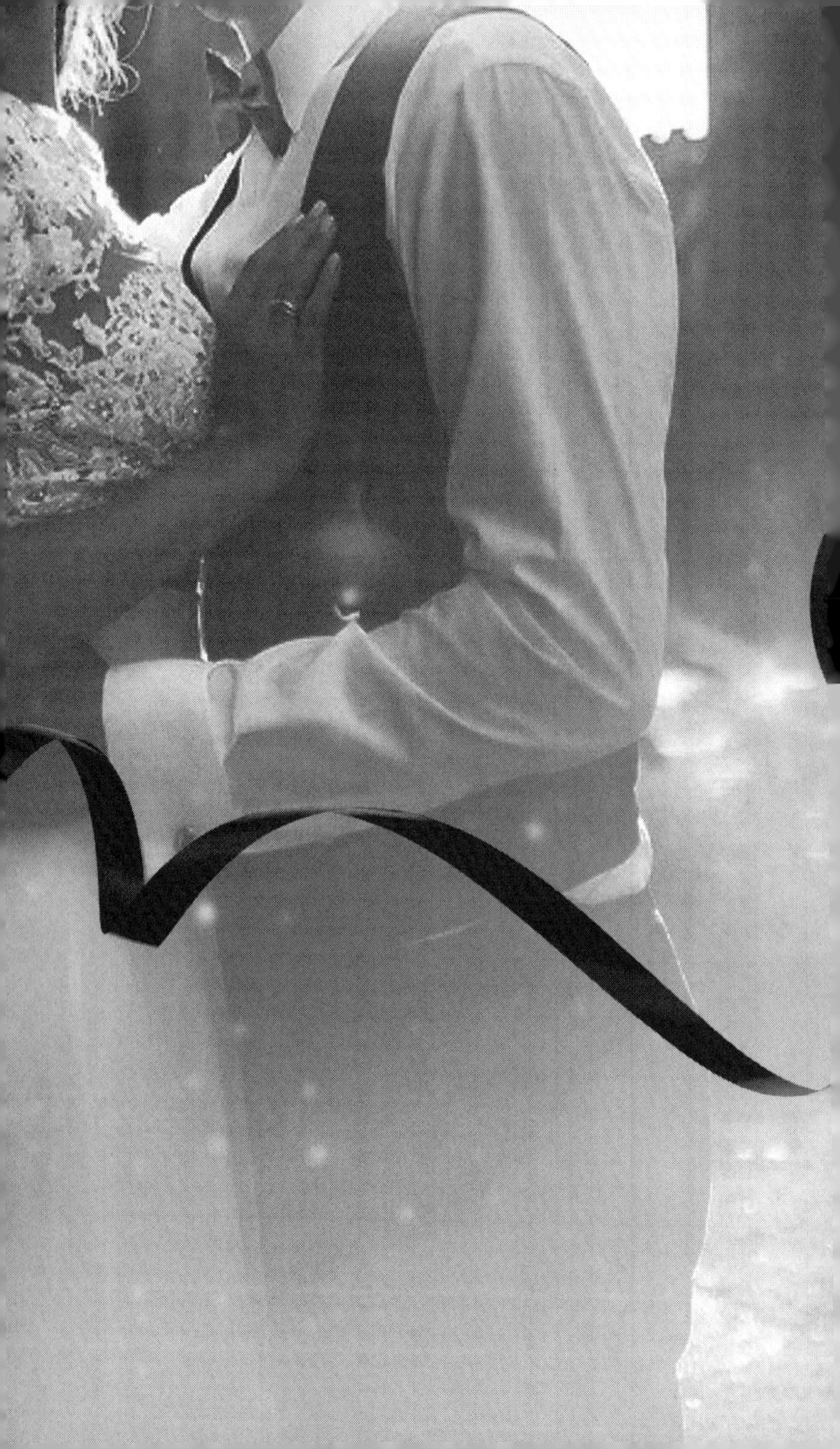

EPILOGUE
ANTONIO

Lucia is a vision in ivory silk. She glides to me, her hair falling around her shoulder in soft waves, her green eyes luminous and soft. Behind her, the doors to the church are flung open, and Venice gleams in the backdrop, a golden jewel sparkling in a sea of sapphire. Today though, I don't have eyes for my city, just for my beautiful, *beautiful* thief.

My bride.

Mine.

She glides toward me, each step drawing her closer. And I find I can't stand still; I can't wait. So I go to her, ignoring the priest's raised eyebrow. "My little thief," I murmur, cupping her cheek.

She's actually doing this.

She's choosing me.

She lifts her eyes up to mine. "Antonio," she whispers. "What are you doing?"

"Marrying you."

A flash of pertness peeks through. "What are we waiting for, then? Let's go do that."

That's my Lucia. I lift her hand to my lips, then we walk, hand in hand, to the somewhat scandalized priest.

Last night, in bed, we made a bet. "You're going to cry," I predicted. "You might pretend otherwise, but I know you, tesoro. You'll be tearing up when you say your vows."

But it turns out I'm wrong.

In the church where I was abandoned as a baby, surrounded by the people I consider my family, I look into the jewel-green eyes of the woman I love and promise to stay at her side in sickness and health. I promise to love, honor, and cherish her for the rest of my life. And when she repeats the same promises, her hand in mine, it's not Lucia who tears up. It's me.

And shockingly, I'm okay with it.

"Okay, this is ridiculous." I glare at the two offending members of my organization. Dante and Valentina have always had a tumultuous relationship, but somehow, things have escalated to the point of utter chaos. I assumed that they would sleep with each other during the Verratti affair and get some of that sexual tension resolved, but no. They've been sniping at each other with increasing venom over the last four weeks.

"It's the day after my wedding," I continue. "I'm leaving for my honeymoon in *three hours*. And instead of eating a lazy breakfast with Lucia, I find myself here." My withering gaze falls on Dante and then Valentina. "Dealing with your petty squabbling."

Joao grimaces in sympathy until I focus on him but quickly forces his expression back to neutral.

"This latest fuck-up at Pascale." I glance down at Tomas' report. "Would either of you like to explain what went wrong?"

"I told Dante—" Valentina starts.

"Valentina wouldn't listen—" Dante interrupts.

"Enough," I snap. "This is not a fucking playground, and the two of you aren't cranky toddlers." I stare at them in frustration. All I want to do is leave for my honeymoon with the knowledge that my organization will still be here when I get back. But that's not guaranteed with Valentina and Dante in their current moods.

Time for drastic action. I don't like to throw my weight around, but if there was ever a need for it, it's now.

"I'm tired of this," I say, leaning forward and

fixing my gaze on them. "It's obvious there's some sexual tension between you."

"Sexual tension?" Valentina goes red. "Between Dante and me? With all due respect, Padrino, not even if he was the last man in the city."

"You wish," Dante sneers.

"I'm delighted to hear you say that." I smile evilly. "Because you work together. Dante, you're Valentina's superior. If we had an HR department, they'd be freaking out about workplace harassment."

Guilt flashes on Valentina's face. "He's not—"

"I'm not done." I sink some steel into my voice. "Your personal issues are disrupting team morale. So, I forbid it."

Dante's head snaps up. "What?"

"The two of you claim you're not interested in each other, so this shouldn't be a problem. Just so we're clear, there are to be no dates. No cozy, intimate glasses of wine after Angelica has gone to bed. No sneaking around and no sex." Tomas is studiously reading something on his phone, and

Leo is trying not to laugh at Dante and Valentina's consternation. "I forbid it all."

Lucia is drinking a cup of coffee when I get back. "What was the big emergency?" she asks.

I fill her in, and she starts to giggle. "Oh, you are *evil*," she says. "If there's anything that'll make the two of them—two of the most stubborn people I know—see sense and realize they're perfect for each other, it's you telling them no. Making it forbidden fruit." She cocks her head to one side. "Did you plan this?"

"Of course. After insisting they hated each other, they could hardly protest my edict. You should have seen their faces."

"So conniving." She kisses me. "I love you. By the way, not that I'm complaining or anything, but we leave for our honeymoon in *two hours*. Are you going to tell me where we're going?"

The Thief

I bite back my smile. Turns out Lucia *hates* surprises. I offered to plan the honeymoon and told her to take two weeks off and pack warm, and ever since, she's been trying to figure out what I have in store. It's driving her crazy.

"Sure." I hand her a manila envelope.

She frowns. "What's in this? It can't be a plane ticket; nobody does that anymore."

"I could tell you," I reply dryly. "Or, and this is just a suggestion, you could open it."

She rolls her eyes at me. "Everyone's a comedian," she grumbles. She extracts the contents of the envelope and looks at them with a puzzled frown. "Okay, this is some kind of blueprint, a couple of sheets of numbers, another blueprint... What exactly am I looking at?"

"A heist." What else could the two of us do on our honeymoon? *Apart from sex, of course.* And trust me, we'll be doing plenty of that. But when we're not in bed... We are thieves, after all. "For our honeymoon, I thought we could fly to England

and rob Arthur Kincaid. What do you think, cara mia? All thirty-seven stolen paintings in one fell swoop?"

She stares at me, shocked, and then laughs. "Best. Idea. Ever." She shakes her head, her eyes dancing with mirth. "You're insane, do you know that? Yes, absolutely."

Thank you for reading

The Thief.

More Antonio & Lucia?!

Want to see Antonio & Lucia pull off the heist? I've written a bonus scene exclusively for my newsletter subscribers. Sign up to read it at http://taracrescent.com/bonus-the-thief/

Want more Venice mafia?

The next book in the series, **The Broker,** features **Dante & Valentina.** Preorder this rivals-to-lovers+forbidden love+stuck together mafia romance today!

About Tara Crescent

Tara Crescent writes steamy contemporary romances for readers who like hot, dominant heroes and strong, sassy heroines.

When she's not writing, she can be found curled up on a couch with a good book, often with a cat on her lap.

She lives in Toronto.

Tara also writes sci-fi romance as Lili Zander. Check her books out at http://www.lilizander.com

Find Tara on:
www.taracrescent.com
tara@taracrescent.com

Also by Tara Crescent

Contemporary Romance

The Drake Family Series

Temporary Wife (A Billionaire Fake Marriage Romance)

Fake Fiance (A Billionaire Second Chance Romance)

Spicy Holiday Treats

Running Into You

Waiting For You

Hard Wood

Hard Wood

Not You Again

Standalone Books

MAX: A Friends to Lovers Romance

MÉNAGE ROMANCE

Club Ménage

Menage in Manhattan

The Dirty series

The Cocky series

Dirty X6

Printed in Great Britain
by Amazon